THE BARON AND THE LADY CHEMIST

The Grantham Girls
Book Two

By Alissa Baxter

ARE YOU SIGNED UP FOR DRAGONBLADE'S BLOG?

You'll get the latest news and information on exclusive giveaways, exclusive excerpts, coming releases, sales, free books, cover reveals and more.

Check out our complete list of authors, too!

No spam, no junk. That's a promise!

Sign Up Here

www.dragonbladepublishing.com

Dearest Reader;

Thank you for your support of a small press. At Dragonblade Publishing, we strive to bring you the highest quality Historical Romance from some of the best authors in the business. Without your support, there is no 'us', so we sincerely hope you adore these stories and find some new favorite authors along the way.

Happy Reading!

CEO, Dragonblade Publishing

Additional Dragonblade books by Author Alissa Baxter

The Grantham Girls Series
The Duke and the Lady Gardener (Book 1)
The Baron and the Lady Chemist (Book 2)

CHAPTER ONE

"MERCIFUL HEAVENS!" DOROTHEA Grantham gazed in horror at her blazing hemline. Somehow the glass phial containing the phosphorus had burst, dropping onto the edge of her gown, setting it alight.

The air was too hot. Phosphorous was dangerous to work with when the temperature reached 86 degrees Fahrenheit. How foolish of her to forget that. She froze for only a moment, and then, with acrid smoke billowing around her, she raced to the wooden door and flung it open.

As Thea dashed outside, something hard and warm stopped her dead. She staggered backward, tilting her head to meet the gaze of a brown-haired, blue-eyed gentleman dressed in buckskin breeches and a wool hunt coat.

He glanced at her burning skirts and, in one swift motion, pulled her down onto the ground and began to stamp it out. But the fire kept springing back to life.

"Get some dirt to smother it." She gasped. "It's a phosphorous fire."

The gentleman grunted before plunging his gloved hands into the nearby vegetable patch and tossing some soil onto her skirts. Then, pressing down hard with his boots, he eventually doused the flames.

"Thank you." She released a shaky breath. "I'm in your debt."

A scowl descended upon his brow. "What the blazes were you doing in there?"

"Starting a blaze?" Her lips curved into a weak smile as she rose to her feet. He extended his hand, and she grasped it as she rose to her full height. Although she was quite tall for a lady, he still towered above her.

She removed her hand from his clasp as she gazed up at him. The sun caught the gold in his hair and lent subtle warmth to his skin, bathing him in its shimmering light. She blinked and adjusted her spectacles before lowering her lids once more. It was as if she had just woken from a dream, and the vestiges of her imagination were still at play. Handsome golden gentlemen did not usually appear in the middle of the English countryside, after all.

A voice hailed them, and Thea turned to see her brother-in-law, the Duke of Stanford, walking in their direction. He drew to a halt and studied her singed skirts with raised brows. "Good afternoon, Thea. One of your experiments go awry?"

"I'm afraid so." She sighed. "This gentleman very kindly assisted me in dousing the flames after my hem caught alight."

"I'm relieved you came to no harm." A quizzical expression crossed Stanford's face. "Although, your aunt will no doubt ban you from using this outbuilding for any future experiments once she sees the state of your gown."

"I know." Thea released her breath in a puff of frustration but refrained from further speech in front of the unknown gentleman.

Stanford spoke again: "May I present my friend, Lord Castleroy, to you, Thea? He is our guest at Durbridge. He's come to view the improvements we've made to the estate. Castleroy, my sister-in-law, Miss Grantham."

"Lord Castleroy." Thea inclined her head and dipped into a curtsey as her rescuer bowed. Her sister, Alexandra, had mentioned that one of Stanford's old schoolfriends would be staying at Durbridge Hall this week to learn more about the agricultural improvements the duke had instituted on the estate.

He was a baron, she had said, and was considered a most eligible young man.

How dreadfully awkward that she had encountered him in such an embarrassing manner—although she could not regret that he had passed by at such an opportune time.

Lord Castleroy's eyes narrowed. "Are you sure that you've come to no physical harm, Miss Grantham?"

"Oh, yes! Quite sure, my lord. The only harm is to my pride. I am not usually so careless."

"You perform such experiments routinely here, ma'am?" The note of surprise in his voice was unmistakable.

"Um. Upon occasion." She cleared her throat. Even though both Grandmama and Aunt Eliza had recently lectured her at length about the inadvisability of expounding on her scientific interests in the presence of gentlemen, particularly eligible gentlemen, she felt he deserved some kind of explanation after rescuing her. "I have my laboratory in the stillroom at Grantham Place, but sometimes a little more space is required for experiments in the domestic sphere."

"Ah. I see. Are you familiarizing yourself with the experiments in *Conversations on Chemistry*, by any chance? My younger sister is most interested in that text as it clearly explains scientific principles to young ladies."

"It is indeed an excellent book." Thea beamed at him before turning abruptly to Stanford. "I must return home now; otherwise, I will be late."

"Yes, indeed." The duke met his friend's gaze. "My sisters-in-law, Miss Grantham and Miss Abigail, have accepted an invitation to dine with us at The Hall this evening along with their aunt."

Lord Castleroy bowed in Thea's direction. "I look forward to furthering our acquaintance, Miss Grantham," he murmured.

Thea gave him a distracted nod before turning on her heel and hurrying away.

The building at the edge of the vegetable patch bordering Grantham Place was the perfect place to perform her experiments and was only a short walk from home. Her aunt Eliza had reluctantly allowed her to work there alone, but once her older relative learned that Thea had encountered a single gentleman there, she might change her mind. Particularly as that single gentleman now knew of her interest in chemistry.

Was there some way Thea could avoid telling her aunt about the unfortunate encounter? She wrinkled her forehead. Lord Castleroy would probably mention he had already been introduced to Thea when they arrived at Durbridge Hall. She came to a sudden halt. Unless she contrived to communicate her wish to keep their meeting a secret. She started walking again, her shoulders drooping slightly. How awful that this unexpected encounter could put a halt to the most exciting work she had ever undertaken.

Thea donned an ivory muslin evening gown upon her return to Grantham Place, barely paying any attention to her maid's careful ministrations as she helped her dress. When they arrived at Durbridge Hall, Aunt Eliza exclaimed with such enthusiasm over Alexandra's new evening gown that the older lady quite missed the moment when Lord Castleroy exchanged greetings with her two nieces in the drawing room before dinner.

After Stanford had presented his guest to Abigail, she conversed with Lord Castleroy for a few minutes before leaving him alone with Thea. He looked down at her, a frown in his eyes. "You've suffered no lingering ill effects from your mishap, Miss Grantham? Is your breathing easy? Those fumes may have adversely affected your lungs."

"I am very well, thank you." She stole a sidelong glance at her aunt, still in conversation with Alexandra on the other side of the room. "I . . . I would appreciate it if you did not mention our encounter to my aunt, my lord. She is of an anxious disposition, and I am concerned she may not allow me to continue my experiments if she knew what happened."

He remained silent for quite some time. Eventually, he raised his brows. "Perhaps you shouldn't continue your experiments,

Miss Grantham, if you are in the habit of placing yourself in harm's way."

His words came like a blow, and she took a step back. "I am not in the habit of placing myself in dangerous situations, my lord. Nevertheless, there is an element of risk involved in all chemical experiments. I accept that." She pulled her golden shawl more tightly around her, huddling a little in its soft, silken folds.

Lord Castleroy looked as if he were about to respond, but then his gaze rested on her shawl. "Is that imported silk?" he asked abruptly.

She blinked. "I beg your pardon?"

"Your shawl . . . I have never seen anything quite like it. That silk is surely not from an English mill?"

"I assure you, my lord, that I am not dealing in smuggled silk." Her voice was stiff.

"I did not mean to imply that you were, Miss Grantham. However, many ladies are happy to turn a blind eye to the source of the silk items they buy."

"I am not one of them."

He bowed, but the skeptical look in his eyes made it evident that he did not believe her.

Turning away, Thea made her way to Alexandra, who had just moved away from her aunt and Abigail.

"Thea, dearest, you look charming in that shawl," her sister said with a warm smile. "Is it one of your designs?"

Thea nodded and then jerked her head in the direction of Lord Castleroy. "Your guest believes that I am wearing smuggled silk."

"Oh dear, does he? Did you set him to rights?"

"I informed him that I do not deal in smuggled goods."

"You told Lord Castleroy that you made the shawl yourself?"

"No, I didn't. Grandmama advised me not to advertise the fact that I design my own haberdashery. She is concerned I will be viewed as an oddity in London if it's known that I stain silk cloths using my chemistry experiments."

Alexandra sighed. "She may well be right. Unfortunately, Society is full of traps for the unwary. Indeed, I am amazed I survived my first Season without any serious social solecisms."

"You did not merely survive it, Alex. You became the toast of the Town."

"That was only because my beloved husband wanted to play a trick on the *ton* by forcing them to accept me and my unconventional ways." She glanced across at the duke, a slight smile playing about her lips.

"I doubt I will be accepted as warmly, though, when I make my come out as I don't have your beauty." Thea's tone was matter of fact. She had never envied her two sisters, who were like two peas in a pod, with their thick copper tresses, creamy skin, and sapphire-blue eyes. Thea and her brother John were more similar in looks, sharing the same shade of pale red hair without a natural curl in sight. And although Thea's eyes were as blue as her sisters' and brother's, they were hidden behind the spectacles perched on top of her lamentably unremarkable nose.

Alexandra frowned. "You cannot say that, Thea."

"But it's the truth. You and Abigail are the image of Mama, while John and I favor Papa in our features."

Alexandra linked arms with Thea. "Which makes you all the more lovable, dearest."

They remained silent for quite some time until Thea finally whispered, "I don't remember her face anymore. When I try to picture it in my mind, it's just a blank."

Her sister pressed her hand. "I know. It is the same for me. Another loss."

Thea released her breath slowly. At least her sister understood. It had begun to haunt her that her beloved mother's face had faded from her memory after her death a number of years ago. And although Alexandra and Abigail shared Mama's features and looked exactly as she had at their age, according to Grandmama, Thea did not look at her sisters and see Mama. Mere features did not make up a person, after all. Instead, the spirit behind the features brought a face to life.

"Have you heard from John lately?" Alexandra asked. "He is so wrapped up in newly-wedded bliss that he has become a very poor correspondent. And Emily is not much better. I haven't received a letter from her in weeks!"

"I received a letter from him yesterday. He and Emily have decided to extend their stay in Brighton until the end of the month. He is enjoying the sea air far too much to leave any earlier—he says it does wonders for his health."

Their brother had suffered from a bronchial complaint his whole life, which sea air appeared to improve. Upon his marriage to Emily Hadley a few months before, he had taken her to Brighton for their wedding trip, leaving Thea and Abigail in the care of Aunt Eliza. Grandmama had also stayed with them at Grantham Place for a while. However, she could never abide the countryside for long and had returned to the Metropolis a few weeks ago, promising to return for Thea before the Season started, so she could introduce her granddaughter to London Society before the rest of the *ton* descended on the Town.

"A gentle introduction to Society will suit you best, my love," she had said with her kind smile. "And I trust you will cause me less anxiety than your sister did, young lady!"

"Oh, I am as docile as a lamb, Grandmama. I shan't cause you any trouble at all," Thea had assured her.

"Hm. Well, it is often the docile ones one needs to watch, as your dear grandpapa was wont to say."

The memory of her grandmother's words rang in her ears as Thea looked across the room and met Lord Castleroy's eyes. Although the man could never be described as docile, he was definitely someone she needed to watch. A word in her aunt's ear, and he could wreck her scientific plans for the rest of the summer.

She couldn't allow that to happen.

CHAPTER TWO

T O HER GREAT dismay, Thea was seated next to Lord Castleroy at dinner. She suppressed a grimace and stole a sidelong look at him as she took her place. But then she drew a calming breath. Perhaps this was a blessing in disguise—an opportunity to request his silence once again.

But with such a small party—only six people sitting down at table—the conversation was general, and no opportunity presented itself for private discourse. Thea was on tenterhooks the whole meal that Lord Castleroy might mention their earlier encounter. However, he refrained from saying anything. When Alexandra indicated it was time to leave the gentlemen to their port after the dessert course was served, Thea sprang to her feet, earning a reproving frown from her aunt, who sat on her other side.

As Thea prepared to follow Alexandra out of the room, she nearly knocked her wine glass over when Lord Castleroy murmured, "I am not in the habit of telling tales, Miss Grantham."

She met his impassive gaze for one fraught moment and then, without a word, followed her female relatives through the door, listening with one ear to her aunt's exclamations about Lord Castleroy as they made their way back to the drawing room.

"Such a charming gentleman, to be sure," Aunt Eliza said

with a sigh. "He is a baron, I believe?"

At Alexandra's nod, she continued, "I vaguely remember seeing his mother in Town some years ago. A quiet lady." Her forehead wrinkled as she sat on a scroll-end sofa and settled back against the gold-striped satin cushions. "Wasn't there some scandal attached to her marriage to old Lord Castleroy?"

"I wouldn't know, aunt." Her eldest niece's tone was repressive as she took the chair opposite her, but their relative paid no heed to Alexandra as the wheels of her mind began to spin.

Aunt Eliza had a vast knowledge of the important personages of the *beau monde*, gleaned no doubt from her endless stream of correspondence with friends who resided in London. "Now, let me think . . . Lady Castleroy . . ." Her eyes narrowed as she stared into the middle distance. "She was always attired in the finest of garments, but it did not stand her in good stead as her family was connected with trade, and she was never at ease in high Society. She eventually retired from the London scene. I believe her health was poor, and I read a notice of her death in a newspaper some years ago . . ."

Abigail released a sigh. "So Lord Castleroy is an orphan like us. Poor gentleman."

"One does not refer to a grown man as an orphan, Abigail." Aunt Eliza's tone was dampening.

Her younger sister raised her shoulders but did not respond, and Aunt Eliza carried inexorably on. "Even though I cannot like the antecedents of his mother, Lord Castleroy is still an excellent catch. I am sure your Grandmama will encourage you to pursue the connection, Thea."

"*I* should pursue the connection?"

"Well, of course! Abigail is too young. And you are next in line to be married, after all."

"I may well be next in line, but that does not mean I shall marry in the near future."

"And why not?" The older lady straightened her spine.

"I have no need to rush into marriage for financial reasons, so

I am in no hurry to tie myself down." Thea tapped the edge of her glasses. "Besides, you've told me countless times that my spectacles make me look far too bookish. I doubt I will attract many suitable prospects."

"You must contrive to remove them while at parties, my dear."

"But then I will trip over my feet and make a spectacle of myself—in quite a different sense of the word, of course."

Abigail smothered a giggle, and Alexandra made a choking sound which she repressed by placing a hand to her mouth just as Stanford and Lord Castleroy entered the drawing room.

"With such charming company awaiting us, we decided not to linger over our port." Stanford's smile encompassed the whole party, but the light in his eyes as they rested on Alexandra was so devoted that Thea caught her breath. *He loves her so much.* A strange pang assailed her heart, and she frowned. No doubt the odd feeling was due to indigestion. The sauce served with the goose at dinner this evening *had* been very rich.

As her brother-in-law advanced into the room, Aunt Eliza beckoned Lord Castleroy, who stood at the door. He moved to the armchair at a right angle to the sofa where her aunt sat.

"Do sit down, my lord." She waved at the gilt and ebonized piece of furniture. "I was just informing my nieces that I was once acquainted with your dear, departed mother."

"Indeed?" His tone was not forthcoming.

"Oh, yes! Such a charming lady. I remember her sartorial taste was quite excellent. She was almost a leader of fashion."

The baron did not respond as he took his seat. But, undeterred by his silence, Aunt Eliza carried on: "You have a younger sister, I believe?"

"Yes. Anne is at Castleroy at present with our cousin, Mrs. Worrell, who will accompany her to London next year for the Season."

Abigail pressed her hands together. "Oh, your sister will be in Town when Thea is presented, my lord!"

He turned his head to meet Thea's gaze. "Your grandmother is to bring you out, Miss Grantham?"

"Yes. I depart for London early next year."

He leaned back in his chair and smiled at Alexandra. "Anne will not know anyone when she arrives in Town, but Her Grace has kindly offered to take her under her wing when she and Stanford arrive for the Season."

"I look forward to making your sister's acquaintance, my lord," Thea murmured.

"I am sure she will be pleased to meet you, particularly as you share a mutual interest."

"Ah, yes." Her gaze slid away. "You mentioned she had read *Conversations on Chemistry*."

Abigail's lips curved into a smile. "How lovely for Thea that she will be able to discuss her interest in chemical science with another young lady."

"Yes. Although Anne merely reads about the experiments."

Thea met the baron's inscrutable gaze and blushed, but before she could respond, her aunt made a tut-tutting sound. "Really, Dorothea. I do hope you haven't been expounding about chemistry with his lordship. It is not a topic of interest to most people."

"Oh, I find it interesting enough, madam." He turned sideways in his chair, leaning his arm along its back as he studied Thea. "In fact, I have been thinking how the hot weather we have been experiencing this summer could prove to be somewhat hazardous to unwary chemists."

Thea's lips fixed into a faint smile. "I was thinking the same thing today, my lord."

"I am pleased you are aware of the danger, Miss Grantham." He turned back to Aunt Eliza. "Do you go to London next year for the Season, ma'am?"

"Oh, no, my lord. I shall remain at Grantham Place with Abigail. Although, I will travel to London for Thea's coming out ball, of course. It is to be at Stanford House."

The conversation moved on to other matters, but Thea remained silent, her brows knit together in a frown. Lord Castleroy's warning was wholly unnecessary. As if she did not know phosphorous was a highly flammable substance that could spontaneously ignite in hot air. The problem was that the warm summer temperatures they were experiencing this year were highly unusual. And the shed where she performed her chemical science experiments had poor ventilation, raising the room's temperature significantly.

It rankled that the baron believed her to be such an amateur. But he did not know that she had an excellent knowledge of chemistry, so she couldn't, in all fairness, hold his warning against him. He probably thought he was being a responsible citizen, preventing the start of dangerous fires.

"Dorothea!" Her aunt's sharp voice made her jump.

"Yes, aunt?"

"You are woolgathering." Her relative inclined her head in the baron's direction. "Lord Castleroy has just addressed you."

"Oh!" Thea turned to him. "Forgive me, my lord." She raised her brows in polite inquiry.

"Did you hear anything we've been discussing?" His voice was amused.

Her aunt waggled her brows in warning, but Thea merely sighed. It was of no use pretending she had been following the conversation. "I am afraid not, Lord Castleroy."

He bent his head. "A penny for your thoughts?"

"Oh, they wouldn't be of any interest to you, my lord. They are somewhat weighty."

"A pound then?"

Her lips flickered into a smile. "I don't deserve any recompense for displaying such incivility."

Stanford chuckled. "I am sure Lord Castleroy will forgive you, Thea. Dreaminess is not such a crime, after all. We were discussing the possibility of you and Abigail traveling to Bath for a couple of months. I have a house there as my mother used to take the waters quite frequently."

Alexandra nodded at the baron. "Lord Castleroy would like his sister, Miss Pellier, to grow accustomed to mixing in Society before her come-out next year. He is thinking of sending her to Bath for the next few months. She could spend some time there with you and Abby. And it would also do you good to go about in Society a little before your presentation, Thea."

"Oh! I . . . er . . ." Thea's throat constricted. This wasn't at all how she had planned to spend the summer.

"I don't think Thea wants to leave her stillroom so soon after being reunited with it," Abigail said eventually.

She shot her younger sister a grateful glance. "I *have* been enjoying my work."

"Work?" The note of surprise in Lord Castleroy's voice was unmistakable.

"Not actual *work*." Aunt Eliza gave a nervous titter. "My niece merely enjoys spending time in the stillroom, don't you, dear?" She cleared her throat. "For many centuries, it was considered quite unexceptionable for the Lady of the House to preside over her stillroom. It is only in more recent times that this custom has fallen away."

"The headmistress of the seminary we attended did not allow us to pursue our interest in natural philosophy," Abigail said in an aside to Lord Castleroy. "Poor Thea was desperate to return home to her experiments."

"Experiments of a domestic nature, you understand," Aunt Eliza interjected. "It is admirable for a lady to retain the skills of the ladies of old, do you not agree, my lord?"

"Indeed." Lord Castleroy studied Thea with keen eyes. "The last thing I want to suggest is that you be dragged away from your home against your will, Miss Grantham." He paused for a moment. "But you could pursue your chemistry pursuits in Bath if you were so inclined. Have you heard of Dr. Wilkinson's lectures in the Kingston Lecture Room?"

Thea sat up straighter in her chair. "I believe he opened a

Chemical Institution in Bath, but we were not allowed to attend any of his lectures while we were at school."

"I have attended one of Dr. Wilkinson's courses. He has made a study of the properties of the Bath waters and teaches his pupils similarly to analyze soils and mineral waters. His instruction is given on Tuesday and Thursday afternoons. It would be a pity if you were to miss out on such an opportunity." He leaned forward slightly. "I am sure my sister would like to attend the lectures. A couple of years ago, I took her to Robert Bakewell's course of lectures in the Kingston Lecture Room. A family ticket was available, allowing admittance to a gentleman and a female family member."

Thea tilted her head. "Will you escort your sister to the Chemical Institution as well, my lord, when you travel to Bath?"

"I will."

"What a kind brother you are!"

"I shall also procure a ticket for you if you choose to join us." His mouth twisted into a wry smile. "My kindness extends to understanding that my sister will not be happy in Bath with only me and our cousin for company. I'll be relieved if she can meet friends of her own age. She has lived a secluded life since our mother died, and I hope to remedy that."

"As I said, my lord, you are very kind."

The conversation became more general as Abigail questioned Stanford about his house in Bath, and Aunt Eliza turned to speak to Alexandra.

"I hope you will forgive me," Lord Castleroy said in a low voice.

She blinked. "Pardon me?"

"I did not mean to imply you were dealing in smuggled silk."

"Oh. Oh yes." She drew her brows together. "Do many ladies procure imported silk illicitly?"

"More than you would suspect. Usually, the contraband items are kept under the counter, even in respectable shops." He tapped his fingers on the side of his chair, frowning slightly. "If you do not mind my asking, Miss Grantham, where did you acquire that shawl?"

Thea swallowed hard. "Um . . ." What could she say? She couldn't reveal her secret hobby to him—Aunt Eliza would have hysterics. "My brother bought it from a mercer in Bath, my lord, but I don't know his name." That much was true. She had never bothered to ask John the name of the mercer who supplied him with the white silk cloths she used to make her shawls. Of course, the plain fabric bore no resemblance to the finished products she created.

But Lord Castleroy didn't need to know that.

CHAPTER THREE

MISS GRANTHAM HAD a secret. James had no idea what it was, but she was hiding something. Her cheeks were faintly flushed, and she failed to meet his eyes. Although Miss Grantham had denied obtaining the shawl illegally, members of the upper classes frequently smuggled silk into the country for their friends and family members. Perhaps that was how she had acquired it.

But how ever she had come by that silk shawl, it wasn't a locally-made item—that shade of glittering gold could only have been imported from foreign shores. And the raised decorative work on the hem was extraordinary—a fine, intricate floral pattern embroidered with silver thread.

If only he could examine the fabric more closely with his quizzing glass. But that was not possible. His interest in the silk industry was not something he advertised. Time to steer the conversation into less turbulent channels. "Would you tell me about the experiment you were conducting earlier today, ma'am?"

If anything, the young lady appeared even more uncomfortable. She shifted in her chair and gripped her gloved hands together. "Er, well . . ." She shot a look at her aunt before saying in a lowered voice, "I would rather not speak about it, my lord. My maid has promised to repair the hem of my gown and I would like to avoid telling Aunt Eliza I set fire to it."

He bowed. "As you wish."

"I am most grateful to you for coming to my assistance."

"It is my pleasure. Although I hope you will refrain from further experimentation with such a dangerous substance."

She pulled her shawl more tightly around her arms. "Never fear. I have learned my lesson."

He narrowed his eyes. "Playing with fire can be tempting sometimes."

"Perhaps for naughty children, my lord. But I am very sensible."

"Are you indeed?"

A slow tide of color stained her cheeks as she met his gaze. "Er . . . did you have a good journey to Durbridge Hall, my lord?"

"I did, thank you."

"I am very pleased to hear it."

He leaned back in his chair as she proceeded to ask him about the length of his proposed stay. Miss Grantham spoke quickly as if by hurrying the conversation along, she could retreat from dangerous ground.

His lips curved into a faint smile. She was adorable.

THEA SIGHED WITH relief when her aunt asked for their carriage to be brought around. Maintaining a civil conversation with Lord Castleroy was exhausting. He had an odd look in his eyes as if she amused him. Which she probably did. She was chattering on like a fool merely because he'd made a comment that could be construed as flirtatious. The man flustered her. His steady gaze revealed nothing of his own emotions yet somehow could rouse her own.

When the butler announced their carriage, she rose to her feet with alacrity, bidding Alexandra and Stanford farewell with a bright smile. It faded from her lips, however, as Lord Castleroy stood and bowed. He murmured something polite to Aunt Eliza and Abigail before turning back to Thea when they moved away. "Good night, Miss Grantham. I believe you will slumber well after your busy day."

"Thank you, my lord. I am sure I shall."

"I hope to see you again in Bath, if not before."

"Er . . . yes." She glanced at her aunt and sisters. "Although, it is not yet decided."

"That is why I expressed a hope of seeing you, not a certainty."

"I suppose we shall go." She released a sigh. "Once Aunt Eliza decides in favor of a scheme, she rarely changes her mind."

"Then I bid you *au revoir*, Miss Grantham, as opposed to *adieu*." A warmth kindled in his eyes, not unlike the fire that had sparked to life earlier in the shed. *Spontaneous combustion*. That was the official scientific term. That the process could happen again right in front of her eyes was concerning indeed.

But this time, she was determined not to catch fire.

She turned abruptly away and stood beside Aunt Eliza and Abigail, avoiding looking in his direction as they took their leave. She would have to be on her guard with Lord Castleroy. He was a completely unknown element, and his presence caused her to feel most unsettled.

Unfortunately, it was unlikely that she would be able to avoid him in Bath. As a protective brother, he would be bound to accompany his sister around town. Thea would probably bump into him at every corner, and if he acquired the promised tickets for the lecture courses and the Chemical Institution, she would spend many hours at his side in a far more intimate setting. She went first hot and then cold at the thought and suppressed a shiver. What an odd reaction she had to him. She needed to pull herself together.

On the way back to Grantham Place, Aunt Eliza chattered away nineteen to the dozen about their upcoming visit. "I must say, my dears, that it is excessively generous of Stanford to offer you his house in Bath. It is in the Royal Crescent—a most desirable address. We will be able to visit the Pump Room and all the most modish shops and attend the concerts and assemblies. Oh!" She clasped her elder niece's arm. "What a splendid introduction it will be for you, dearest, into Polite Society! I am excessively glad Lord Castleroy suggested the idea."

"I thought it was Alexandra's idea."

"That is what comes from not paying attention, Dorothea." She tapped her on the arm. "It was his lordship's plan. He said he was troubled about his younger sister, who has retreated very much into herself after their mother's demise. She has a governess, of course, and her cousin to keep her company, but not nearly enough time with girls her own age. Lord Castleroy is concerned that she will not be at ease in London Society when she makes her come out, so he thought of bringing her to Bath. Then he asked Stanford if you and Abigail would be visiting the town in the next few months, and so the idea was born."

"Oh." Thea frowned. How neatly he had manipulated the situation.

"I have heard that Dr. Wilkinson offers lectures in astronomy as well as other branches of experimental philosophy, which I will hopefully be able to attend," Abigail said. "I think this is an excellent turn of events."

"I suppose so." Thea released a breath. "But I have so been enjoying my chemistry work."

"How many shawls have you made thus far?" her sister inquired.

"Six."

"Well, this is an excellent opportunity for you to finish them. You can embroider to your heart's content while we are in Bath."

"Indeed. I tend to get ahead of myself with the staining process, but the embroidery is just as important."

"And you are so good at it, Thea. I wish I had your nimble fingers."

"Your skill at embroidery is an accomplishment for which you can be commended," Aunt Eliza intoned. "Indeed, I believe it is your saving grace, Dorothea. Your sisters have not applied themselves to this skill as much as I would have wished. But you have a natural talent for it."

"Thank you, aunt. I am glad I have a saving grace."

"It is a vast relief to me, I must say. Although, I hope you will refrain from informing any visitors that you stained the shawls yourself. The fabric is very eye-catching, and it might invite questions from curious ladies." She sniffed. "Your grandmama told me that it would be best not to draw attention to your interest in chemistry, and I could not agree with her more. Nothing will be more detrimental to your chances of securing a favorable match than this news getting about. You already look scholarly enough with those spectacles. No need to let the gentlemen know that you have an interest in such a peculiar subject."

Thea felt Abigail stiffen beside her. "Lord Castleroy did not appear to mind, aunt. Besides, it isn't an exclusively male subject. Books on chemistry have been written for the female audience, so Thea's interest in it is not unusual."

"Indeed, which was why I was careful to indicate to his lordship that Dorothea's experiments take place in a stillroom, a most feminine domain."

Thea shrugged. "Creating shawls and scarves is a pursuit of a purely domestic nature. I don't see what all the fuss is about."

"The fuss?" Her aunt's voice rose. "Imagine what his lordship would think if he learned you stain silk in an outbuilding of all places! I still cannot believe Stanford gave you permission to use that ramshackle structure on his estate for your experiments. One would have thought he would be more sensible."

"The duke is progressive in his thinking about female education."

"Well, it is a mistake. Mark my words. Once a young girl becomes educated, she starts to wish for all sorts of things at odds with the womanly sphere of life."

"But shawls epitomize womanly apparel, Aunt Eliza. Chemistry is leading me in the direction of femininity, not away from it."

Her older relative shuffled her skirts noisily but, for once, did not reply. As the carriage rumbled home in the darkness, Thea smiled faintly. It wasn't often she managed to stun her aunt into offended silence. She would enjoy the peace while it lasted.

CHAPTER FOUR

THE GRANTHAM LADIES left for Bath the next week. Thea accepted the decision with equanimity, if not joy. As she had mentioned to Abigail, she tended to get so carried away with her staining work that she neglected to finish the garments. She was always putting off the needlework for another day, such was her excitement at furthering her chemical experiments. Now that she needed to stop her investigations, she would take the opportunity to create the intricately embroidered hems that set off the shawls so beautifully.

When the coach clattered to a stop at Stanford's house in the Royal Crescent, Thea descended from the conveyance with mixed feelings. Bath held no happy memories for her. She and Abigail had been sent to the town a couple of years ago to finish their education. Before that, they had shared John's lessons as he had been instructed at home instead of attending Eton and Cambridge due to his poor health. Their father had hired a succession of tutors to teach John, and from a very young age, Thea and her sisters had studied alongside him.

They had excelled at their lessons, acquiring knowledge in the traditionally male-dominated fields of learning, including Latin, mathematics, and classical studies. However, when Thea began showing an interest in her father's chemistry experiments and Abigail became fascinated with John's astronomical studies, Aunt

Eliza grew alarmed and wrote to their grandmother, Lady Longmore, insisting that she intervene in her granddaughters' education.

Having already failed to curb Alexandra's passion for horticultural science, Aunt Eliza intimated that a strict schoolmistress might have better success in shaping the interests of her younger two nieces. Although Grandmama had responded that cultivating the mind of young girls was important, she was concerned that her younger granddaughters might, like Alexandra, neglect the all-important accomplishments required of a young lady in Society.

Consequently, Thea and Abigail had been packed off to a seminary in Bath, where they had been trained in the essential feminine arts of drawing, dancing, playing the pianoforte, and needlework. But Thea had missed her home and family dreadfully and hadn't spared a backward glance for the school when John had arrived earlier that year to take her and Abigail home. But now they were back in the resort town, and she wasn't quite sure how she felt about it. On the one hand, she was no longer a young girl with no say in how she spent her days; on the other, she would be required to spend a great deal of time with Aunt Eliza, with whom she had never shared a harmony of mind.

Her aunt had a narrow view of the world and how women fit into it. She was single-minded about her nieces marrying well and spent an inordinate amount of time plotting and planning for their presentations. She had a memory for details of the most commonplace kind, but she became mired in the brushwork, unable or unwilling to see the larger canvas upon which they were painted.

Thea's gaze encompassed the grand sweep of houses in the Crescent, with their colossal Ionic columns and fixed fenestration. The sweeping, curved façade of Bath stone was both elegant and graceful, giving the impression of a majestic palace-like structure. All in all, this was a far more comfortable place to live than the rather cramped quarters of the seminary, and Thea felt her spirits rise as Aunt Eliza led the way into the house.

The butler, Chadwick, greeted them with a deferential bow and showed them into a parlor with a white marble fireplace, an exquisitely carved rosewood chaise longue, and Prussian blue paper hangings. Two splendid gilt mirrors hung on the walls, one above the fireplace and the other directly opposite it.

Thea wandered over to the sash windows and gazed outside. The Royal Crescent was an excellent example of *rus in urbe* with its splendid views of the parkland opposite, giving a sense of the country in the city. The impression of space and calm acted as a balm on her spirit, and she drew in a deep, quieting breath. Perhaps her time in Bath would be enjoyable after all.

Her aunt poured the tea she had ordered on their arrival, and after Thea had partaken of a cup of the refreshing brew, she followed a footman upstairs to her bedchamber. As she entered the room, her lips parted in delight. How pretty the matching blue chintz curtains and bed hangings were!

Thea kicked off her slippers and lay down on the delicately carved mahogany bed, gazing up at the canopy. The silk counterpane was smooth beneath her touch and brought to mind the work she planned to do while she was in Bath. She had packed all her stained-silk shawls and scarves in her trunk and would begin embroidering them as soon as possible. Fortunately, it was considered perfectly acceptable for a lady to work on her stitching whenever a spare moment presented itself, which would give her ample time to finish her shawls.

As long as no one looked at them too closely. Thea sat up against the pillows, frowning a little. Lord Castleroy's interest in her work was surprising. The man did not appear to be a dandy, overly concerned about sartorial matters, yet he had asked her several probing questions the other night. Perhaps he had merely been making conversation, but there was something curious about the way he had studied her shawl.

Why was he so interested?

JAMES CALLED ON the Grantham ladies the day after they arrived in Bath. Anne accompanied him on the visit, and although his sister appeared shy at first, Miss Grantham and Miss Abigail welcomed her warmly, setting her at ease. The girls' chaperone and aunt, Mrs. Grantham, was engaged in conversation with another morning caller, so James took the chair beside Miss Grantham while Anne sat beside Abigail on a sofa near the window, their heads drawing instantly together in earnest conversation.

A sense of relief permeated him as he observed his sister. She had lived an isolated existence these past few years as he had been largely absent from Castleroy, dividing his time between London and Macclesfield as he sought to assist his grandfather with the troubles besetting his business.

Now, however, it was time to establish Anne in Society. He had set aside the next few months to squire her around to social events. Hopefully, her stay in Bath would bolster her confidence. Although she was no milk-and-water miss, Anne had an aversion to putting herself forward in any way. She could easily fade into the background if her first introduction to the *ton* was at a London ball, with all the pressure that entailed.

He glanced at Miss Grantham, who had been working on her embroidery when he entered the room. The edge of the material she had hastily shoved into a basket was still visible, and he studied the corner of the fine silver cloth with raised brows. The lady appeared to have acquired yet another item of imported silk since their last encounter.

When he met her eyes, she blushed. Was it guilt that caused that flare of color in her cheeks? He leaned back in his chair. "You are a keen embroiderer, ma'am?"

"Indeed. I always have my sewing basket with me."

"Pray don't stop your stitching on my account."

"It is rather delicate work, which requires a great deal of concentration. I need to give it my full attention, so I would rather not work on it now."

His lips twitched. "I am flattered you wish to give me your full attention."

Her cheeks flooded with even more color. "I did not mean . . . that is . . ." She released her breath in a puff as she folded her hands together. "After our last encounter, my aunt read me a lecture about falling into reveries at inopportune times. I am doing my best to remedy this bad habit."

"Ah. Then we must find an interesting topic of conversation to make it easier for you to stay focused." He smiled. "What would you like to discuss?"

She gave a tiny shake of her head. "No, no, my lord. The point is that I need to become more at ease with general social chit-chat. I must avoid the topics of conversation I truly wish to discuss as they are of no interest to other people, particularly gentlemen."

"This is according to your aunt?"

She inclined her head.

"Perhaps the gentleman to whom you speak should be the judge of that? I, for one, find it refreshing that you have such an unusual hobby. When did you become interested in chemistry?"

"My father was a horticulturist as well as a chemist. I used to observe his experiments in his laboratory."

"In the garden building where you had your accident?"

"Oh, no! Papa built a laboratory at Grantham Place. And he set up a smaller one for me in the stillroom as I was always under his feet as a young girl."

James drew his brows together. "For what purpose is the outbuilding used, then?"

"John took over Papa's laboratory for his scientific experiments. So Stanford permitted me to use it when I came home from school as I need more space than the stillroom provides."

"For your phosphorous experiments."

"Yes."

He narrowed his eyes. "I know something of chemistry. What experiment were you performing?"

She shifted in her seat, not meeting his gaze. "I discovered that phosphorous is soluble in ether, so I dissolved a small quantity of phosphorous in that fluid. A straightforward experiment. Where are you resident in Bath, sir?"

Evidently, she did not wish to elaborate on the subject—a pity. Miss Grantham's experiments were much more interesting than topics of an inconsequential nature, which he would be forced to endure for the next while. He could only imagine the dreariness of everyday conversation as he escorted his sister around town. Before the sennight was over, he would be impatient to return to Castleroy to implement some of the agricultural improvements he had seen at Durbridge Hall.

He leaned back in his chair. "We've taken a house in Laura Place."

"How lovely to be so close to Sydney Gardens."

"Yes. A compensation."

She opened her eyes wide. "You don't like Bath, my lord?"

"It is not a matter of not liking it. But I am not used to idling my time away."

Miss Abigail rose to her feet at that moment and moved in their direction. "Dearest, I wish to show Miss Pellier your scarf. The needlework pattern is from *Ackermann's Repository*, is it not? Perhaps you could lend the design plate to Miss Pellier once you have finished using it. I am convinced it will be a suitable pattern for the hem of a handkerchief, which is what Miss Pellier is seeking a pattern for."

Miss Grantham appeared to be rooted to her seat. She frowned, but Miss Abigail's attention was on the fabric Miss Grantham had secreted in the sewing basket earlier, and she did not notice the daggers flashing from her sister's eyes.

The length of lustrous silver silk Miss Abigail withdrew from its hiding place made James blink with its brilliance. His lips tightened at the stricken look on Miss Grantham's face, and he bent his head. His suspicions were correct. The silken cloth must have been illegally obtained. And the young lady sitting across from him was fully aware of this fact. His ribs tightened in disappointment, but then, after a moment, the tension eased. Perhaps Miss Grantham did not understand the potentially grave consequences of her actions. He hoped so as he had no wish to court a young lady with an avaricious streak in her nature.

CHAPTER FIVE

LORD CASTLEROY'S DISAPPROVAL emanated from his being like the rays of heat from a fire. Thea repressed a sigh. What could she say? Her scarf looked nothing like the silk items English manufacturers produced, and his lordship, no doubt, believed the worst of her once more.

"Do you know anything about the British silk industry, Miss Grantham?" he asked gravely.

"I know very little. But I imagine you plan to enlighten me?"

"If you will permit me to do so, I shall."

She inclined her head. "Please continue."

He remained silent for a long moment before saying slowly, "The demand for foreign silks is an enormous threat to the producers in this country, which is why the importation of these silks is prohibited in England. Unfortunately, many gentlewomen give no thought to indulging their desire for such things." He adjusted the cuff of his sleeve. "They may not realize their support of smuggled silk harms the livelihoods of poor, hard-working English families."

"It is indeed reprehensible, my lord. But I can assure you, as I did on the first day we met, that I do not deal in smuggled silk."

He looked up. "I am sure you don't, Miss Grantham. However, buying silks from shopkeepers or mercers one suspects might be involved in illegal trading should be avoided. It is important to ask about the provenance of the items you purchase. However, I suspect your brother did not realize he was purchasing illicit silk when he bought those items for you. I see you embroider the hems yourself?"

She hesitated a moment before nodding. Anything to get him off the subject of illicit silk. "Yes."

"The raised decorative work on the shawl you wore the other evening is extraordinary. You are to be complimented on your skill, Miss Grantham."

"Thank you."

"A word of warning, though." His mouth twisted wryly. "Specialist French silks used for intricate decoration are also frequently smuggled into the country. Revenue officers regularly seize materials such as bundles of threads and embroideries from tailors and mercers. I suspect the silver silk thread you used was imported from foreign shores."

Her eyelids fluttered down. "Oh! Oh, dear."

"Indeed. But I'm sounding alarmingly like a Customs official, which is not at all my intention on a morning call."

He glanced at his sister at that moment, and when she met his eyes, she rose to her feet. The visit of ceremony was over. Mrs. Carlton, who had been conversing with Aunt Eliza, stood as well, and Aunt Eliza rang the bell amongst a flurry of farewells.

When William, the footman, entered the room to attend to the visitors, Thea curtseyed in response to Lord Castleroy's bow. Thank goodness morning visitors never stayed beyond twenty minutes—she had been spared the necessity of elaborating on her embroidery work.

When the callers left the room, Aunt Eliza resumed her seat. "How delightful to see Lord Castleroy again. Miss Pellier seems a charming young woman, although she is quite a dab of a girl, isn't she? More like a small brown sparrow than a swan, which is surprising when her brother is such a fine figure of a man." She frowned a little. "It is a pity Mrs. Carlton monopolized my attention to the extent that I was unable to say more than two words to them." She turned to her younger niece. "I saw you showed Miss Pellier Thea's embroidery, Abigail?"

"Miss Pellier is a keen needlewoman. She was much taken with Thea's work."

"I will lend her my pattern design if she would like to use it," Thea said, sitting down.

"I am sure she would," Abigail responded. "Perhaps you could give it to her later this week if you have finished with it? I suggested a walk in Sydney Gardens as she tells me she plans to take the air there every morning."

"What an excellent idea!" Aunt Eliza tapped her chin with a finger. "You must both strive to cultivate the friendship as it is his lordship's particular wish." She swung her narrowed gaze around to Thea. "I expect I will hear wedding bells chiming soon, my love. Lord Castleroy appears to be taking an interest in you. He paid you marked attention today."

Thea nibbled her bottom lip. In actual fact, the baron had paid her *shawl* marked attention, not her. But her aunt would never believe that. How many gentlemen took an interest in female haberdashery? So peculiar. She shook her head. "I believe his lordship is merely concerned with making social connections for his sister, aunt."

"Well! The fact that he considers you and Abigail suitable friends for Miss Pellier is significant, my love. No doubt this is due to your connection to Stanford, but it is a connection you should make full use of. When you are looking for a husband, you need to avail yourself of every advantage. And a duke in the family is an advantage indeed!"

Thea grimaced. "Set a duke to catch a baron, aunt?"

"Really, Dorothea! There is no need to be vulgar." Aunt Eliza shuffled her skirts. "I am merely looking out for your best interests seeing as how you seem to possess no feminine wiles at all. You are far too matter of fact and frank. A little allure would go a long way in your dealings with gentlemen. You need not be so . . . so . . . prosaic about everything."

"I have never been any good at dissembling."

"I am not asking you to *dissemble*, Dorothea. I am merely asking you to *assemble* a few social graces." She laughed at her little joke.

"Yes, aunt." Thea's voice was wooden.

"Excellent. I know you are a good girl at heart. You just need a little push sometimes in the right direction."

"Perhaps that has been the problem all along," she mused. "I frequently lose my way."

"None of us is perfect, my love. And it might even work to your advantage, not knowing your left from your right. It should bring out a gentleman's protective instincts."

"Another saving grace . . ." Thea murmured.

"What?" Her aunt's brows drew together.

"Are we going to the Pump Room tomorrow morning?" Abigail asked hastily.

Aunt Eliza turned her attention to her other niece. "Yes, my love. We must visit the Pump Room every morning. It is an excellent opportunity to see and be seen. And I trust drinking the waters will improve my failing health." Her voice faltered. "I haven't been in prime form for quite some time, so taking the waters will be the very thing to set me to rights."

When they arrived at the Pump Room the following day, Thea looked around with interest at the spacious saloon, which terminated at each end in a semi-circular recess. A small orchestra played in a music gallery, and well-dressed people promenaded about or stood in small groups drinking water out of yellow-looking tumblers.

The pump was located in a window embrasure at the back of the room. Aunt Eliza immediately headed for the alcove, leaving Thea and Abigail trailing behind her. However, as their aunt hastened on ahead, blinded temporarily to her chaperoning duties as the lure of better health hovered irresistibly before her, Lord Castleroy and Miss Pellier approached them.

"Good morning, Miss Grantham, Miss Abigail," Lord Castleroy bowed. "May I procure you each a glass of water?"

Miss Pellier wrinkled her small nose. "I am afraid I abandoned my glass. It has a metallic taste which I couldn't enjoy."

"Perhaps I shall try it another morning then," Thea said. "I am not feeling particularly brave today."

"Come, Miss Grantham." A smile lit Lord Castleroy's eyes. "You are one of the bravest ladies I know."

A tide of warmth rushed to Thea's cheeks as she met his steady gaze. However, the ability to form coherent speech appeared to have left her, and she nearly kissed Abigail when her sister filled the lengthening silence by saying in her light voice, "I should like to taste the waters, my lord."

"Very well, Miss Abigail. If you would wait here."

As Lord Castleroy moved away, Miss Pellier smiled at Abigail. "I hope you like it more than I did."

Her sister shook her head. "I probably won't, as I detest drinking warm water. But I am far too curious not to try it. Miss Mason used to tell me that curiosity is my besetting sin."

"Miss Mason?"

"She was the headmistress of the seminary we attended here in Bath."

"Did you enjoy being sent away to school?" Miss Pellier glanced from Abigail to Thea.

Abigail lifted a slim shoulder. "Miss Mason's lessons focused exclusively on feminine accomplishments, so we found it a trifle dull. But you cannot forbid anyone from studying the stars, thank heavens, so I was a little better off than Thea."

Miss Pellier's eyes were full of sympathy. "I hope you will tell me more about your interest in astronomy, Miss Abigail, as I do not know much about that subject." She turned to Thea as Lord Castleroy returned with Abigail's promised glass of water. "I believe we share an interest in chemistry, Miss Grantham."

"Indeed. Lord Castleroy mentioned that you have read *Conversations on Chemistry*."

"I have. Although, I am still grappling with the more complex aspects of the text. The chapter about the chemical agencies of electricity is particularly interesting." She tilted her head in a slightly bird-like pose. "I hope to attend Dr. Wilkinson's lectures on electricity and galvanism while I am in Bath. I was wondering if you would care to accompany me."

"I should like that, Miss Pellier. Thank you."

Lord Castleroy directed his attention to Thea. "I attended a series of Dr. Wilkinson's lectures on galvanism a couple of years ago and can highly recommend them. Indeed, I met the author of *Frankenstein* there."

Thea opened her eyes wide. "I read *Frankenstein* earlier this year, although my aunt would be horrified if she found out. What is the author's name? I have been wondering who he is."

"The author is a *she*, Miss Grantham—a Mrs. Shelley. I met her at the Kingston Lecture Rooms, where Dr. Wilkinson proposed that the dead could be reanimated by electricity. Mrs. Shelley informed me then that she was writing a novel on the subject."

"How fascinating," Thea said. "I wonder if she read the chapter in *Conversations on Chemistry* about the connections between electricity and chemistry. It describes Professor Galvani's experiments on muscular irritability, in which he laid a piece of metal on the nerve of a frog that had only just died." She furrowed her brow. "The limb that contained the nerve rested upon another piece of metal, and the limb moved suddenly when the two pieces of metal touched or were joined by a conductor."

Miss Pellier paled. "How eerie that a chemistry experiment could have inspired a book about a monster."

"Have you read the novel, Miss Pellier?" Thea pushed her glasses up.

The other girl shook her head. "I haven't. My governess would not allow me to. But my brother told me about the story. And I see now how it connects to the hypothesis of electricity— that there are two kinds of electricity, positive and negative, which are attracted to one another." She gave a slow nod. "It is impossible to deny electricity's influence on chemical combinations. Indeed, in Mrs. Fulhame's *Essay on Combustion*, she writes about the ability of electricity to facilitate both the reduction and calcination of metals, just as heat does."

"Oh, have you read Mrs. Fulhame's essay, Miss Pellier?" Abigail said eagerly. "My sister is a keen student of her experiments."

Thea stilled at her sister's words. The last thing she wanted was to draw attention to this particular subject. So, meeting Abigail's gaze, she gave a tiny shake of her head. Her sister's eyes momentarily widened before she nodded.

Grateful for her sister's quick-wittedness, Thea turned to Miss Pellier and said calmly, "I have always found it interesting that only the opposite electric fluids attract each other. To quote the author of *Conversations on Chemistry*, 'electricities seem to me to be a kind of chemical spirit, which animates the particles of bodies, and draws them together.'"

"It sounds oddly like courtship," Lord Castleroy murmured.

The corners of his mouth twitched, and a betraying flush rose once more in Thea's cheeks. She bit her bottom lip. How she hated her pale complexion! It gave away her feelings time and time again. Lord Castleroy must be in no doubt by now that his comments disconcerted her. Provoking man. She drew in a calming breath. "Although in chemistry particles of the most dissimilar nature have the greatest tendency to combine, in real life, too much difference repels people rather than draws them together."

"I am in full agreement," he said. "Which is why establishing common ground is a crucial part of the process."

"The process, my lord?" She folded her arms as she met his calm gaze. "You make courtship sound like a scientific experiment."

The smile which had tugged at his lips now spread to his eyes. "It has distinct similarities, I would say. Is it not always embarked upon with the hope of a good conclusion?"

His gaze held hers, mesmerizing her, and it was only when Miss Pellier gave a small cough that Thea lowered her eyes in confusion.

Lord Castleroy was far too unsettling.

CHAPTER SIX

AGAINST HER EXPECTATIONS, Thea found herself rather enjoying her time in Bath. She accompanied Miss Pellier and Lord Castleroy to the Chemical Institution every Tuesday and Thursday afternoon between 1 p.m. and 3 p.m. The available laboratory was well-equipped with a range of apparatus that Thea, Miss Pellier, and the other students were permitted to use. As Miss Pellier had never dabbled in practical experimentation before, she eagerly seized the opportunity to do so now. And although Thea joined in the lessons with enthusiasm, she missed her own laboratory and the work she had left behind.

Thea, Abigail, and Miss Pellier also attended Dr. Wilkinson's lectures on Experimental Philosophy on Wednesdays and Fridays. Their interest in the subject was so profound that Aunt Eliza voiced her concern that her nieces were focusing too much on education as opposed to entertainment. "I cannot understand why you girls are interested in learning about natural philosophy when you should be out and about enjoying yourselves like normal young ladies. I only allow it because Lord Castleroy is your escort." She gave Thea an arch look. "Indeed, I believe he is on the verge of making you an offer, Dorothea."

She shook her head. "You are mistaken, Aunt. Lord Castleroy acts merely as his sister's escort."

Aunt Eliza's eyes narrowed. "I have seen a great deal more of the world than you have, my dear, and I am convinced he is about to propose. I confess I am as surprised as you are—he could have his choice of young ladies in the kingdom—but perhaps he has chosen you to be his bride as you get along so well with his sister."

Abigail stared. "What a very odd reason to marry someone!"

"No, indeed." Aunt Eliza's voice was complacent as she folded her hands in her lap. "A young lady's London presentation is a great deal of work, and Miss Pellier's cousin is not quite up to the task, is she? Mrs. Worrell seems to be a very timid, shy sort of woman with no sense of fashion or style."

"And you believe I would do any better?" Thea's tone was dry.

"Oh, dear me, no, child! You must be awake upon every suit in London to navigate the social waters smoothly. And you most definitely are not. But the Duchess of Stanford is your sister, after all, so your social path is already paved." She narrowed her eyes as she contemplated her niece. "And although you are no beauty, Dorothea, you have inherited your grandmother's sense of fashion and style. You have an excellent eye for color, you know. Far better than Alexandra or Abigail."

"I am utterly cast down, aunt." Abigail shook her head mournfully.

The older lady turned her head. "You needn't be, my dear. You have me to guide your way. I was merely pointing out dear Dorothea's—"

"Saving grace?" Thea interjected.

"Yes, indeed." Her aunt stared. "You have an uncanny way of reading my mind sometimes, Dorothea. It is most discomposing." She glanced at the mahogany clock on the wall and, with a shake of her head, rose to her feet. "I must speak to Chadwick about dinner."

When Aunt Eliza left the room, Thea looked across at her sister. "My Three Graces should hopefully save me from too much social censure in London."

Abigail sighed. "Aunt Eliza never means to be unkind. But, oh! Her lack of tact is abysmal—telling me I have no eye for color." She wrinkled her brow. "I wonder what my saving grace is?"

"You don't need one, my love. You are beautiful." Thea's expression was wry. "I only need a saving grace because I am plain."

"You are not plain! How can you say that?"

"Because it is true." She picked up her embroidery.

"No, it isn't. I know Aunt Eliza says your spectacles make you look plain, but you have a charming countenance." Abigail tilted her head to one side as she studied her sister. "And you have something that Alexandra and I lack, which we both *wish* we had."

Thea raised her brows. "What would that be?"

"A certain serenity. You are so peaceful to be around. Calming, you know."

"Oh!" Thea knit her brows together. "Well, I often feel quite the opposite, you know."

"Yes, of course. But you have the ability to present a calm face to the world in spite of any agitation." She paused for a moment. "It appears Lord Castleroy appreciates your excellent qualities too. Miss Pellier told me yesterday that she believes her brother dances attendance on her so frequently because he hopes to see you every day. And the best way to accomplish that, of course, is to accompany her all around Bath. He could easily allow his sister to go out with only Mrs. Worrell for company, but he is always with them."

Thea set her embroidery to one side. "Miss Pellier must be mistaken, Abby."

"Indeed, she is not. I believe he wishes to offer for you."

"Because he is looking for a wife to chaperone his sister next year?"

"Of course not! Aunt Eliza has some very odd notions." Abigail smiled. "No, I believe it is because he is developing a *tendre* for you."

Thea stared meditatively ahead. "I wonder."

While it was true Lord Castleroy appeared to enjoy her company, and his manner was flirtatious at times, Thea had noticed in recent days that he had begun asking her far more pointed questions about the exact nature of the scientific experiments she conducted at Grantham Place. He interspersed his questions quite naturally into their discussions, but Thea, very much on her guard about her chemistry work, noted his tendency to bring the conversation back to it. Did he perhaps suspect she stained her silk scarves herself?

Abigail had let slip that very first morning in the Pump Room that Thea was a student of Mrs. Fulhame's experiments. And, if Lord Castleroy had read *An Essay on Combustion, with a View to a New Art of Dyeing and Painting* by that lady, he could very well have guessed the nature of Thea's work, especially as he had studied her gold and silver shawls with such a keen eye.

However, Thea had promised her grandmother she would not make too much of her interest in chemistry to any gentlemen she met. Guilt swamped her suddenly when she recalled the scandalous manner in which Lord Castleroy had first discovered her knowledge of the subject. However, if he believed her understanding to be limited to the schoolgirl experiments described in *Conversations on Chemistry*, Grandmama could not be too concerned. Besides, Lord Castleroy had suggested his sister attend the lectures at the Chemical Institution with Thea, so he, like Stanford, must be progressive in his ideas about female education.

When Lady Longmore had brought Alexandra home from London a few months ago to escape the trouble she had fallen into in London, she had informed Thea that it would not do for her to set herself apart during her first London Season. "I am not saying that you must never discuss your interest in chemistry, Dorothea. Indeed, it has become quite fashionable for ladies to learn about chemistry, and they attend lectures at the Royal

Institution," the older lady had said. "But at the start of the Season, it is best that your studies do not define you as I am well aware your interest extends well beyond what a typical young lady might be expected to know."

"Did Alexandra not mention her scholarly interests at all when she went to London?" Thea had asked, drawing her brows together.

"Unfortunately, she did." Her grandmother had frowned. "When your sister first arrived in Town, she corrected a gentleman on his inaccurate account of plants used in India as a source of medicine. According to Lady Jersey, some Society matrons were quick to pounce on this as a reason to discredit her as they believed her to be not only bookish but a trifle too bold. However, Stanford stepped in in the end and saved the day by launching Alexandra into high fashion."

"And I cannot expect Stanford to rescue me in a similar fashion," Thea had said flatly.

"Precisely, my love. Although you are his sister-in-law, which gives you a certain amount of credit, it will not do to cultivate a reputation for being an oddity."

"Very well."

Grandmama had patted her knee. "I am glad you see the sense of what I say."

As she recalled their conversation now, Thea wondered what Lord Castleroy would make of her interest in staining silk. He appeared to be very well informed about the workings of the silk industry, although it was unclear how he had come by this knowledge. But, as an intelligent gentleman with an excellent grasp of the sciences and current affairs, no doubt he knew a great deal about any number of topics. Even chemistry. She sighed as she rose from her chair and wandered over to the window to gaze outside. The baron's appreciation of this experimental branch of natural philosophy rivaled her own, and she'd had to bite her lip on numerous occasions to prevent herself from launching into deeper discussions with him which would reveal her superior understanding of the subject. Instead, she limited herself to the topics discussed in *Conversations on Chemistry*.

But it was most frustrating to have to keep her opinions hidden away in this manner. Just this week, she had been about to enter into a debate with Lord Castleroy about Mrs. Fulhame's antiphlogistic hypotheses after a particularly interesting lecture at the Chemical Institution. However, she had recalled her grandmother's warning just in time and hastily changed the subject.

Lord Castleroy had studied her quizzically when she'd stopped mid-sentence, and she had a nasty suspicion that he knew she was deliberately expurgating her conversation. But what else was she meant to do? She had promised Grandmama not to appear too much out of the common way. And, although she doubted Lord Castleroy was a gossip who would spread the word of her unusual preoccupation with chemistry throughout the *ton*, one could never be too careful. He had already extinguished one blaze she had created due to her chemistry experiments. There was no need to start another.

Thankfully, Miss Pellier's knowledge of chemistry was quite limited because her governess knew nothing about the subject. Miss Pellier was eager to learn, however, and Thea was happy to fulfill the role of fellow student and mask her own expertise. She wished for more, though—so much more. And unfortunately, it was Miss Pellier's brother who could provide the forbidden fruit of conversation she hungered for. But it was out of her reach, at least for now. How frustrating it all was.

She looked across at Abigail, whose brow was furrowed as she attempted to stitch a sampler. Her sister was convinced that Lord Castleroy intended to offer for her. But, although Thea could not deny that Lord Castleroy had directed his attentions to her, she had an odd feeling that he was not being entirely open in his dealings with her.

Lord Castleroy had a secret. Thea had no idea what it was, but he was hiding something.

CHAPTER SEVEN

"So, if Lord Castleroy proposes, will you accept his offer?"

Abigail's voice dragged Thea out of her ruminations. She blinked a few times before walking back to her chair. "I haven't even considered it."

"Surely you must have given some thought as to whether you'd like to marry him or not? You appear to enjoy his company, after all." Abigail tilted her head, her eyes twinkling. "Aren't you falling just a little bit in love with him, Thea? He's very handsome."

"All I want at present is to concentrate on my chemistry experiments. I won't be able to do that if I marry Lord Castleroy. The wife of a peer of the realm has any number of responsibilities that I do not seek."

"I suppose that's true." Abigail nibbled on her lower lip, and then her face cleared. "But he is only a baron, after all, not a duke, so the duties won't be as onerous as the ones Alexandra has taken on. And his lordship seems quite open to the idea of young ladies learning about chemical science. Otherwise, he wouldn't take you and Miss Pellier to the Chemical Institution."

"That would all come to an end if I married him, Abby. Lord Castleroy would expect me to take on other more mundane duties if he proposed matrimony to me."

"But if you fall in love with him, you may *wish* to take on those duties."

Thea shrugged. "I seek a quiet life. We are fortunate that our portions liberate us from having to marry for financial security. And John has indicated that he is happy for us both to continue living at Grantham Place for as long as we wish. Within a few years, I shall be in control of my inheritance, and then I will be able to decide my future. Maybe then I shall consider marriage."

"If you fall in love, that is."

"Love should not come into it. Such an important decision should not be clouded by sentiment."

A frown descended on Abigail's brow. "But don't you wish for a grand passion, dearest?"

Thea gave a decided shake of her head. "Not at all. When I work in my laboratory, I am in a state of pure contentment. *That* is my grand passion." Her lips twisted ruefully. "I know it sounds odd, but I see my work as a combination of scientific experimentation and artistic creation. Nothing gives me greater joy than being able to make my shawls. I would be miserable without my work, and no man deserves a wife who is unhappy and frustrated with the ties of wedlock."

Abigail gazed at her. "But you will be so lonely if you never fall in love and have a family."

Thea released a slow breath. "Papa became a mere shadow of himself after Mama died. That is what his grand passion did to him. It was his scientific work that finally brought him a measure of happiness again, not us."

A shadow of pain crossed Abigail's face. "Theirs was a true love match."

"And it ultimately ruined Papa's life. If you rely on human relationships for fulfillment, you are placing yourself in a position to be blown about by the whims of fate. At any moment, that love could be snatched from you, leaving you alone and desolate. It is far better to rely on other things, such as creative or productive work, for personal happiness."

"Have you told Grandmama you don't plan to marry?"

"No, as I *may* marry for companionship. A scientific gentleman who shares my interests might suit me very well."

"As long as he doesn't ignite a grand passion within your breast."

Thea lifted her shoulders. "Truth be told, I don't think I am capable of such feeling."

"You only think that, Thea, because you haven't fallen in love yet. Look how happy Alexandra is with Stanford. I long for that sort of love." Her voice was wistful.

"Well, I don't. Being blown hither and thither by high emotion is not something I aspire to."

"Hmm. Well, Cupid's arrows are not always predictable, you know."

Later that day, her sister's words came to Thea's mind when she and Abigail went for a walk with Lord Castleroy and Miss Pellier at Sydney Gardens. They strolled along the well-graveled paths, which wound through groves of luxuriant flowering plants, before coming to an ornate cast-iron footbridge spanning the width of the Kennet and Avon Canal. Thea stopped halfway along the bridge to gaze down at the calm expanse of water below, meandering between stone embankments with well-grown trees hanging overhead.

The baron came to a halt beside her. "A picturesque scene, is it not?"

"It is indeed." She continued to gaze at the water, not looking at him.

"Miss Grantham."

She turned to face him. "Yes, my lord?"

"I am making up a party for the Grand Gala night here on Wednesday for the Prince Regent's birthday. There is to be a concert and fireworks."

"It sounds delightful."

"Your aunt accepted my invitation to join my party earlier when you went upstairs to fetch your hat."

"Oh." Noticing the distinct lack of enthusiasm in her own

voice, she quickly added, "Thank you, Lord Castleroy. I have heard excellent things about the Gala fêtes in Sydney Gardens."

"I trust you will enjoy the evening." He studied her for a moment. "You seem a little preoccupied today. Is anything the matter?"

"Oh, no." She cleared her throat. "It is only that I have a slight headache. The fresh air will cure it in a trice, I'm sure."

Thea began to walk again to catch up with Abigail and Miss Pellier, who were already on the other side of the bridge.

"I must thank you and Miss Abigail for your kindness to my sister," Lord Castleroy said, pacing beside her. "She has come completely out of her shell since her arrival in Bath and is enjoying her visit immensely."

"I am so pleased to hear that, my lord. It must be hard for Miss Pellier, having no sisters. I don't know what I would have done without Alexandra and Abigail."

"You all seem very close."

"We are. And the bond grew even stronger after our mother died."

"Stanford told me about that," he said quietly. "A tragedy indeed."

"Yes." Her voice was strained, and she cleared her throat again to dislodge a sudden constriction.

They joined Abigail and Miss Pellier then, and the conversation turned to the upcoming Gala night. Although Abigail was not yet officially out, Aunt Eliza had told Lord Castleroy that she would allow her youngest niece to attend the fête if they did not stay out too late. Abigail was delighted at the prospect and chattered about the upcoming treat all the way home.

Aunt Eliza had ordered some new evening gowns for her nieces from a fashionable dressmaker in Bath, and the dresses, to their relief, arrived the night before the evening of the Gala in Sydney Gardens. Thea's maid, Lewis, helped her to don the lovely white gauze round dress with its short full sleeves, ending in a row of white satin points. The hem of the skirt was trimmed with braids of white and Calamine blue satin, and a single fall of blond lace adorned the tiny bodice. As Lewis adjusted Thea's headdress, a toque of moderate height composed of British net and blue satin ornamented around the crown with rolls of white satin and a bird of paradise plume, Thea blinked at her image in the mirror. She did not look like herself at all.

Lewis clasped a pearl necklace around Thea's neck, which matched the delicate earrings she had placed in her ears. White Levantine slippers, kid gloves, and her silver scarf, which her maid had laid on her bed, completed the fashionable ensemble. However, Thea hesitated before throwing the fine silk garment around her shoulders. What if Lord Castleroy commented on it again? It was the same scarf he had seen the day he and Miss Pellier had paid that introductory morning call.

However, it was doubtful that he would make any remarks. It would be impolite to hark back to the subject of smuggled silk, especially as Thea had informed him most clearly that her brother had acquired the shawls for her. If Lord Castleroy wished to discuss their provenance, logically he should approach John about it.

It was rather odd that he had voiced his opinions about smuggling in the first place. It wasn't a topic commonly discussed within the walls of a lady's drawing room. But, perhaps as a member of the House of Lords, he took a particular interest in Britain's protectionist policy in regard to the silk industry. John had told her that all foreign wrought silks had been outlawed and that this legislation was won during the last century due to petitions from English silk manufacturers.

Thea had only brought her questions to her brother when she had wanted to find out why he had struggled to find the gold braiding she needed to trim her shawls on his last trip to Bath. John had told her that the specialist French silks she had spotted some of their neighbors wearing, which she had asked him to procure for her, must have been obtained illicitly. It was then that Thea had devised the idea of staining white silk thread to make the gold lace herself. She hadn't realized at the time, however, that it could place her in such a suspicious light.

Thea sighed as she left her bedchamber and went downstairs to join her aunt and Abigail. in the drawing room. Stepping across the threshold, she adjusted the position of the scarf, a crease between her brows. Life was becoming rather complicated.

They met the Castleroy party at the Sydney Hotel and entered the illuminated pleasure gardens via that building. Thea glanced back at the orchestra installed in the semi-circular balcony on the first floor of the hotel and the two rows of boxes marching down either side of the columned structure. No doubt that was where they would eat their supper later.

She took a deep breath of the pure summer air as she strolled along the well-graveled principal walk beside her aunt. Lord Castleroy, Abigail, Mrs. Worrell, and Miss Pellier were slightly ahead, but Thea had fallen back a little to accommodate Aunt Eliza's slower pace. The gradual incline made the older lady puff, but when they finally reached the semi-circular stone pavilion supported by pillars at the top of the gardens, she acknowledged it had been worth the walk. "The lights are charming indeed," Aunt Eliza said as she lowered herself onto a seat. "And how different it looks at night! I would not have believed I could be dazzled at my age, but I am."

The variegated lamps in the pavilion lit up the building spectacularly, and Thea blinked at its brilliance. "How lovely this is." She turned to Lord Castleroy, who had come to stand beside her. "There must be thousands of lamps in these gardens."

"I believe there are over 15,000," he said. "It rivals London's Vauxhall Gardens in its splendor."

They left the pavilion a short while later and walked around the gardens, passing through lit-up arches and along paths leading to botanical grottoes and secluded alcoves. Lord Castleroy eventually directed them to the supper box he had hired for their party, where strains from the nearby orchestra wafted magically in the night air.

Thea glanced around happily as Lord Castleroy seated her inside, and once her supper was set before her, she partook of the light meal with an appetite sharpened by exercise. She was chatting to Miss Pellier about an upcoming concert the other girl wished to attend the following week when Miss Pellier inclined her head in Aunt Eliza's direction. "Please ask Mrs. Grantham if you will be able to join us, Miss Grantham. It would be lovely if you and Miss Abigail could accompany us."

Thea turned to her aunt, who was seated beside her, but before she could say anything, from across the table, Lord Castleroy said with a smile, "Miss Abigail and I have been discussing an excursion to Wells, Miss Grantham, as your sister wishes to visit the Gothic cathedral. I have access to a friend's landau and would be pleased to arrange the expedition if you like the idea."

Thea stared up at him, at a complete loss for words. Eventually, she murmured. "I am afraid . . . that is . . ."

"My sister does not enjoy traveling in landaus, my lord," Abigail said after an awkward pause.

Lord Castleroy raised his brows. "But it is the perfect vehicle for viewing the surrounding countryside."

Thea recovered the use of her voice. "I imagine it will be a lovely outing, my lord. But as the landau only seats four passengers, I will be pleased to give up my seat to my aunt, who told me just the other day that she would like to visit the Bishop's Palace."

Aunt Eliza nodded. "Yes, indeed, my love. I would be delighted to accompany Abigail to Wells."

Lord Castleroy looked as if he were about to object, but then he collected himself and began making arrangements for the excursion with Aunt Eliza. After her aunt had spoken at great length about the upcoming outing, a sudden silence settled on their party. Thea glanced down at her feet before looking up and meeting the baron's thoughtful gaze. It was almost as if she could see the cogs turning in his head.

She sighed with relief when he eventually glanced down and withdrew his pocket watch. "We had better leave now if we wish to see the fireworks."

Thea rose to her feet with alacrity and left the box, walking beside her sister as they made their way to the rear of the Sydney Hotel. A throng of people had already gathered in the central space beneath the first-floor balcony.

Lord Castleroy came to a halt. "The display will take place here, I believe. Signor de Mortram and his son are in charge of it."

The show began shortly afterward, and Thea soon forgot the people milling about her as she gazed in fascination at the manifestation of the eruption of Mount Vesuvius in the night sky. Burning lava appeared to spew out from the mountain's crater. It was such a life-like representation of the historic event that had taken place in Pompeii all those centuries ago that Thea almost expected molten rock to start pouring down onto their heads.

Feeling someone's regard, she glanced to her side and met Lord Castleroy's eyes. And suddenly, something very much like a firework seemed to explode between them. A burning sensation spread through her body, and it was impossible to drag her gaze away from the magnetic pull of his eyes as they drew her closer, closer . . .

She suppressed a small gasp and eventually contrived to look upward once again. *What had just happened?* Somehow, the fire lit within her seemed to be outburning the rockets above. The fortress she had retreated to upon her safe, comfortable plateau was being threatened by a blue-eyed baron who seemed determined to extricate her from it, destroying the measure of peace she had found there this past year.

Thea was content to be alone on her high plain, not wishing to be disturbed by deep emotion. In some odd way, her wrung-out feelings had freed her to concentrate on other things, more stable things, than the transience of human relationships, which could falter—or die—at any point. Close links with other people only led to misery, despair, and pain.

She wanted none of it.

CHAPTER EIGHT

AUNT ELIZA HURRIED into the drawing room, where Thea and Abigail were working on their embroidery the day after the Gala evening. "My loves," she said with a beaming smile. "I have just received word that John and Emily will be coming to visit us before they return home from Brighton early next week." She glanced down at the letter in her hands. "They will only stay for a few nights as John needs to return to Grantham Place. But I am sure that will be ample time to catch up on all their news."

Thea set her embroidery frame aside. "That will be delightful, aunt. John mentioned in the letter I received from him last week that they were considering coming to Bath, but he wasn't sure then if they could manage it, so I did not say anything to avoid disappointing you. How lovely it will be to see them."

"Yes, indeed," Abigail said. "I can't wait to hear all about the changes which have been made to the Brighton Pavilion. I believe the architecture is a sight to behold."

Thea picked up her frame again. "Well, I want to find out more about the bathing machines. John mentioned that he bathes in the sea every day. He is convinced salt water and sea air are far more curative for ill health than drinking the Bath waters."

Aunt Eliza wrinkled her brow. "Never say that, Dorothea. The Bath waters are doing me the world of good, you know. My delicate constitution is much improved since I started taking them every morning. And I am determined that John should at least taste the waters while he is here. I believe he came to Bath with your dear mama when he was a young boy to drink the waters to improve his health, but he disliked the taste so much he refused to cooperate."

"Yes. I remember when Mama took John to Bath." A small smile played about Thea's mouth. "They returned before a week was up as John spat all the water out."

"Oh, dear!" Aunt Eliza's eyes widened. "Children can be so difficult at times. I had my own trouble managing all of you when I came to look after you. And only Alexandra could ever get John to take his medicine." She nodded at Thea. "But you also helped immensely, my dear, when you made those licorice lozenges and lemon drops to encourage him to take the more unpleasant-tasting remedies." Aunt Eliza shook her head as she sat down on the sofa. "I must say your papa was very lenient to allow you to work with boiling citric acid and sugar in the stillroom at such a young age."

"Oh, Papa wasn't concerned," Thea said. "He knew I was a careful worker. Besides, he kept an eye on what I was doing in his rather absent-minded fashion."

"But frequently he left you to work there unsupervised. A most odd arrangement. And look where it has led! Your experiments have advanced in complexity to an alarming degree."

"My early experiences in the stillroom gave me a very good grounding in chemistry, Aunt Eliza. It is only natural that my work has progressed beyond the elementary."

"Well, all I can say is that I am glad we have come to Bath and you have begun to experience the more conventional entertainments on offer for young ladies, which you seem to be enjoying, thank heaven!"

"Yes." Thea's expression was contemplative. "I've surprised myself at how much I have enjoyed our time here."

The older lady rustled her skirts. "Perhaps it has something to do with the charming company of our new friends. And one friend in particular . . ."

"Indeed." Thea fiddled with her spectacles as she frowned at her stitching. Her aunt was so persistent. "Abigail and I are most pleased to have become acquainted with Miss Pellier."

In honor of John and Emily's visit, Aunt Eliza arranged a special dinner for the day of their arrival, inviting some of their new acquaintances to dine with them in the Royal Crescent. "For I am sure John and Emily have had more than enough time on their own these past few weeks," she said to her nieces. "And it will be an excellent opportunity to introduce them to Lord Castleroy and Miss Pellier."

John and Emily arrived a couple of days later, and Thea rose swiftly to her feet when they entered the drawing room. John appeared to be a different person from the pale wraith who had returned from London a few months previously. The city air had not suited her brother's constitution, and his health had deteriorated while he was in the Metropolis, courting Emily. Now, however, he looked to be in prime form, and as Thea studied his much-loved face, she released the breath she had been holding. Always at the back of her mind was the possibility that John's life could be cut short by ill health. And she couldn't bear another loss.

Emily was also in blooming looks, the happiness radiating from her gentle face making her quite beautiful. Thea and Abigail led their new sister-in-law upstairs to her bedchamber, delighted to catch up on her news as they examined the new gowns Emily had purchased in Brighton.

Before she went downstairs that evening, Thea placed a Paisley shawl around her shoulders. This shawl had been made in Scotland and would not draw any unwanted attention from his lordship. However, when Thea walked into the drawing room a short while later, her heart sank into her kid-leather slippers when she saw that Emily was wearing the silk fichu she had given her as a wedding present.

Unfortunately, Grandmama had only warned Thea not to

speak of her chemistry work in public after John and Emily had already left Grantham Place on their wedding trip. Her sister-in-law would be unaware of Lady Longmore's directive. And Thea had been so eager to catch up with John and Emily today that she had not given much thought to the dinner party planned for this evening or the possibility that Emily might wear the item of clothing she had made for her.

Before she could warn her sister-in-law not to mention that Thea had created the item herself, Lord Castleroy, Mrs. Worrell, and Miss Pellier were announced. However, the conversation before dinner did not stray into any awkward subjects, and Thea breathed a sigh of relief when they sat down at table fifteen minutes later.

An old friend of Aunt Eliza's, Mrs. Gilbert, her husband, and their eighteen-year-old twin daughters had also been invited to dinner. Thea, seated between the two young ladies, was delighted to follow the rules of etiquette that dictated that it was impolite to talk behind one guest's back to another or to shout down the table. Lord Castleroy, as the highest-ranking male guest, was in the place of honor next to Aunt Eliza at the upper end of the table, so she was spared from having to speak to him.

When the ladies left the gentlemen to their wine a short while later, Thea hastened into the drawing room to warn Emily not to say anything to Lord Castleroy about her fichu. But unfortunately, her sister-in-law retreated upstairs immediately to repair a torn flounce in her gown, so Thea was unable to caution her. She considered following Emily up to her bedchamber, but Aunt Eliza requested Thea to play the pianoforte, so the opportunity was lost.

As Thea sat down in front of the fine musical instrument and ran her fingers over the keys, she drew in a deep breath. She was in a ridiculous panic about something that only had a small chance of coming to pass. How likely was it that Lord Castleroy would comment on the apparel of a lady he had never before met? Even if he noticed the fichu, he would never say anything to

Emily about it. Thea was silly to allow herself to become so agitated. As she started playing her favorite Mozart piece, she reflected that keeping her silk-staining a secret was not as easy as she had hoped it would be.

She would need to devise a proper plan to avoid answering questions about her unusual shawls in the future. Otherwise, she would be found out in no time at all. And Grandmama would be most unhappy if she laid herself open to such speculation in London.

Emily returned to the drawing room just before the gentlemen entered, and Thea continued to play until Aunt Eliza asked Abigail to take over.

Rising from her seat, Thea smiled at her sister before making her way across the room to Emily. Her sister-in-law was seated beside Miss Pellier on the sofa while John and Lord Castleroy sat opposite in two matching wingback chairs. Thea interspersed the odd comment into the conversation but was content to listen rather than speak as Emily and John gave their impressions of Brighton to the assembled company.

Thea had just allowed her shoulders to ease somewhat when Miss Pellier turned the subject and said quietly, "What a beautiful fichu you are wearing, Lady Grantham. I was admiring it from across the table at dinner. I have never seen that particular shade of purple. The gold shining through is so pretty and unusual."

Emily smiled as she touched the silk scarf tied around her neck. "Thank you, Miss Pellier. Dorothea gave this to me as a wedding present. It was a unique gift as she made it herself using her chemistry experiments."

"Indeed?" Miss Pellier glanced across at Thea. "How talented you are, Miss Grantham!" Her brow wrinkled suddenly. "Did you use one of Mrs. Fulhame's experiments to stain the silk by any chance? In her *Essay on Combustion*, she attempts to establish a new art of dyeing and painting using chemistry experiments."

Thea felt the color drain from her face as she gave a tiny nod. Then, slowly turning her head, she met Lord Castleroy's arrested gaze. Any hope that he may not have heard her sister-in-law's comment was extinguished. Swallowing hard, she turned back to Miss Pellier, who was studying Emily's fichu with renewed interest.

Her secret was out.

CHAPTER NINE

THEA WOKE UP with a feeling of dread in the pit of her stomach. The rest of the evening had passed in a haze. She had barely paid any attention to the after-dinner conversation in the drawing room. Lord Castleroy had not spoken to her about Emily's revelation, but she knew it would only be a matter of time before he broached the subject.

She sighed. Perhaps she was making too much of this. His lordship already knew that she had her own laboratory at Grantham Place. And it was the baron who had come up with the idea of taking Miss Pellier and Thea to the Chemical Institution. He was also a friend of Stanford, and if she asked Lord Castleroy not to reveal her secret to anyone when they arrived in London, she was sure he would keep it. As would his sister.

No, her sense of dread was more deep-seated than mere anxiety at not complying with her grandmother's instructions. Sitting up in bed, she drew her brows together. Why did she have such an unreasoning sense of panic? Over the last few weeks in Bath, she had sensed a certain intent in Lord Castleroy's demeanor which made her feel trapped. He was far too curious about her. And it wasn't only his interest in her silk shawls that put her on her guard; it was the fact that he observed her so keenly. He noticed her. And for someone accustomed to fading into the background in the company of her far more beautiful sisters, it was disconcerting to be the center of his attention in this way.

She did not like it at all. It made her feel vulnerable and exposed. And seen. She sighed as she fell back against her pillows again, staring straight ahead. It suited her to be the invisible sister, as it freed her to retreat into her own world, which was rich and interesting and far more rewarding than the general hurly-burly of human interactions.

And she sensed that Lord Castleroy knew this and that he was determined to draw her back into the real world, which she feared so very much. That was why she was eager to avoid him and to keep his knowledge of her as limited as possible. She had never been frightened that he would reveal her secret to Polite Society. Rather she was frightened that he would learn who she really was. And that was something she desperately wanted to keep hidden.

She entered the drawing room half an hour later and drew to a sudden halt. Miss Pellier and her cousin were there, which was odd as it was too early for morning callers. Mrs. Worrell spoke to Aunt Eliza while Miss Pellier was conversing with Abigail. Thea murmured a greeting to the two ladies, who looked up upon her entry into the room. They appeared somewhat agitated, and when Thea seated herself on a chair beside Miss Pellier, she discovered why.

"I was just informing your sister, Miss Grantham, that my brother received urgent notice this morning that our grandfather is unwell," Miss Pellier said. "We will be leaving Bath later today to travel to Macclesfield to see him."

"I am sorry to hear this, Miss Pellier. You must be very anxious."

"We are. My brother is making arrangements for the journey to Macclesfield as we speak. Once all our luggage has been packed, we shall leave Bath." She looked from Thea to Abigail. "I wanted to inform you in person rather than sending a note, as I am very grateful for your companionship these past few weeks. It has made my stay in Bath most enjoyable."

Thea smiled. "It has been delightful to make your acquaintance, Miss Pellier, and I wish you a safe journey. No doubt, we shall meet again in London for the Season."

"Indeed. James will be here shortly to bid you farewell." She hesitated. "Macclesfield is renowned for its silk, Miss Grantham. In view of your interest in staining silk, I wondered if I could bring you a bolt of white silk when I come up to London?"

Thea stared. "But that would cost you a fortune, Miss Pellier. I cannot accept such generosity."

"It wouldn't cost me anything at all." Miss Pellier lowered her eyes. "My grandfather owns a silk mill, you see."

"A silk mill?" Thea repeated.

"Yes. My brother is a part-owner of the mill and has already agreed to my request."

Thea vaguely remembered her aunt speaking about Lord Castleroy's mother's connection to trade. And suddenly, it all made sense. Lord Castleroy's unusual interest in silk stemmed from his maternal family's involvement in the silk industry. That was why he had so carefully examined her shawls and scarves and brought up the problem of smuggling. That was why he was so knowledgeable.

The door opened at that moment, and the baron entered the room. After bowing to Aunt Eliza, he crossed to the window where the younger ladies were seated.

Thea turned a concerned face to him. "I hope your grandfather makes a swift recovery, Lord Castleroy."

"Thank you, Miss Grantham. He has always been in the best of health, so the news came as a shock." He stared out the window for a long moment before turning around. "We wanted to bid you farewell before our departure."

"A sad day for us all," Abigail said. "I shall miss your sister's company, my lord. It has been delightful to attend Dr. Wilkinson's lectures with her."

Lord Castleroy smiled. "We shall all meet again in London, Miss Abigail."

"Yes." Her expression clouded with doubt. "Although, I will not be making my come-out next year, so I will only be in London for a brief visit when Aunt Eliza and I travel up with Thea in the coach."

"In that case, I trust your time in Town will overlap with ours." He turned his gaze to Thea. "When do you leave for the Capital, Miss Grantham?"

"I am not quite sure." Thea knit her brows. "Grandmama mentioned that she wanted me to come to London before the start of the Season to make some acquaintances."

"A good idea. London can be overwhelming on your first visit."

"Alexandra told me that as well."

Glancing at the clock on the wall, he frowned. "We must leave now."

Thea rose to her feet. "Farewell, Lord Castleroy."

She couldn't quite keep the relief out of her voice, and his face was rather grim as he bowed. "I look forward to renewing our acquaintanceship soon, Miss Grantham."

She gave a half-curtsey. "Yes, indeed, my lord."

The baron lowered his voice. "You give the impression of having received a last-minute reprieve, my dear."

Her mind whirling with chaotic thoughts, Thea remained silent. But as she met his questioning gaze, she swallowed hard. He was correct. Although she would never wish poor health on anyone, his grandfather's illness had given her a respite from the turmoil she experienced in his presence. Although Lord Castleroy was never antagonistic, he had the slight air of an inquisitor about him, summing her up, measuring her, trying to find out more about her. Something in the way he looked at her made Thea feel as if an inevitable day of reckoning awaited her, a time when she would no longer be allowed to graze peacefully on her plateau in isolation.

But for now, she would be left alone. Lord Castleroy was quitting Bath, and his unexpected departure gave her the opportunity to regroup and shore up her defenses against involvement. For that was the threat Lord Castleroy presented. An unmistakable current of awareness ran between them, which made indifference impossible. She would be lying to herself if she denied it. But just because she was attracted to him did not mean that she wanted to deepen her acquaintanceship with him. He was far too disturbing to her peace of mind, a state of mind she had fought so hard to establish this past year.

Catching her trembling lip between her teeth, she met his searching eyes. If she acknowledged she was relieved he was leaving, she would be venturing onto very uncertain ground indeed. So, in a rather prim voice, she said, "I wish you a safe journey, Lord Castleroy."

"As I said once before, Miss Grantham, I bid you *au revoir* rather than *adieu*."

Au revoir. "Until we see each other again." The words held a promise, which matched the light in his eyes, those blue eyes that seemed intent on discovering all her secrets. She cleared her throat, reminded of the one big secret he had recently learned. "My lord, I hope I can rely on your discretion regarding my chemistry work. My grandmother does not wish for it to become known amongst the *ton* that I stain silk, which is why I have not mentioned it to you before. I trust you will keep this knowledge to yourself."

"Of course, Miss Grantham. I can keep your secrets."

Her eyelids fluttered. His words sounded so *intimate*, which was precisely the opposite of the feeling she wished to generate between them. Therefore, in a somewhat repressive voice, she muttered, "Thank you, sir."

His mouth twitched a little at the corners as he bowed again. "Your servant, ma'am."

Thea turned away then to bid Miss Pellier and Mrs. Worrell farewell, and when William arrived to show them out of the drawing room, she sank onto the sofa, staring straight ahead. Their departure would leave a significant gap in their lives in

Bath.

Thea's aunt must have been thinking the same thing as she said, in a slightly anxious tone. "Well, my dears. What unexpected—and unwelcome—news. Bath will not be the same without Lord Castleroy and Miss Pellier. Indeed, I am quite cast down as I'd hoped . . ." Her gaze rested on Thea briefly before she smoothed her skirts. "Well, these things happen, I expect."

Emily and John walked into the room then, and Aunt Eliza related the news to them. "Perhaps it isn't such bad timing, aunt, as Emily will need a helping hand managing the household when we return home," John said. "Would you consider returning to Grantham Place with us? Emily would like it very much as she has been a trifle apprehensive about taking on her new role." His gaze encompassed them all.

Aunt Eliza puffed up with importance. "Yes, indeed. It will be a daunting task for you, Emily, to be sure. I shall be delighted to guide your way."

Thea rose to her feet again. Soon she would return to her laboratory, her scientific work, and a peaceful existence, precisely what she had hoped for. The fact that this quiet way of life seemed somewhat hollow all of a sudden was completely beside the point. Of course, it was natural to feel slightly flat as their time in Bath came to an end.

You've never felt this way before.

The errant thought echoed uncomfortably in her mind before she dismissed it with a lift of her chin. Grantham Place was exactly where she wanted to be.

CHAPTER TEN

Five months later

THEA STARED OUT of the carriage window as the conveyance clattered into London on a chilly, wet January morning. Their coachman, Biddle, kept the horses moving along at a steady pace through the wet, cobbled streets, and soon they entered what appeared to be the more genteel part of Town. From the warmth of the carriage, where Thea sat with Abigail and Aunt Eliza, she sympathized with the poor city dwellers, hurrying along with their heads bent low against an icy wind.

Hopefully, London would look more inviting when the sun was shining.

The rain had stopped when their coach finally drew up in front of Longmore House in Berkeley Square. Thea stepped down from the carriage with a sigh of relief after her aunt and Abigail. Her body was stiff after the long journey from Grantham Place, and she desperately needed to stretch her legs. As she walked to the house, Thea glimpsed some dripping wet shrubs and plane trees in the garden in the center of the Square, enclosed by an iron balustrade, and then the door opened, and Leighton, her grandmother's stately butler, welcomed them.

A footman led them upstairs to their respective bedchambers. Thea breathed in the comforting scent of burning coals and fresh flowers when she entered her allocated room, elegantly decorated in shades of blue and cream. Leaving her maid to unpack her trunks, she decided to lie down on the inviting-looking bed for just a moment and was startled when Wilson woke her up sometime later with the news that Lady Longmore awaited her in the drawing room.

Wilson quickly helped Thea into a fresh gown, and after checking her appearance in the mirror, she hastened downstairs.

Her grandmother, a stylish, handsome lady with elegantly dressed white hair, was seated alone in the well-appointed drawing room on a rosewood chaise longue in front of the fire. Dusky pink chintz curtains, which extended right down to the floor, were already drawn against the miserable weather, giving the apartment a snug feel. After kissing Grandmama on her cheek, Thea sank onto a mahogany saber-leg elbow chair and stretched her hands to the blaze.

"You had a good journey, my love?" Her grandmother's bright blue eyes were warm with interest. "I hoped we could have a chat before Abigail and your Aunt Eliza come down. They will be joining us later after they've rested awhile. Your poor sister looked dead on her feet when I saw her earlier and your aunt has never been a good traveler."

"Our journey was uneventful, but it was tiring. I was delighted to finally arrive."

"Yes, indeed. It is a long journey, and traveling is always fatiguing." She placed her head on one side as she considered her granddaughter. "You look very modish, my love. Is that one of the gowns your aunt ordered for you in Bath?"

Thea glanced down at her long-sleeved, sprigged muslin morning gown. "Yes, it is."

"Well, I am glad you have a few fashionable clothes, at least. When your sister arrived in London, we needed to buy her a whole new wardrobe as hers was woefully inadequate." She tapped her beringed fingers on the scrolled arm of the chaise longue as her eyes narrowed slightly. "I must have a look at your gowns, my love, and then we will go on a shopping expedition. It is quite a large undertaking for a modiste to fashion all the items of clothing a young lady requires in Town, which is why I wanted you to arrive well before the Season starts."

"I am particularly interested in the fabrics employed in dressmaking, Grandmama. Alexandra told me about the wide variety on display."

"Yes, indeed. You will stare when you see the warehouses." Her eyes brightened. "First, I shall take you to Grafton House. And I am sure you will enjoy visiting Harding, Howell & Co. in Pall Mall. It is quite a large place with four different departments, and they sell fur, fans, dress fabric, millinery, and all sorts of other necessities. And we must stop at G. Sutton, a silk manufacturer in Leicester Square. You have brought all your shawls to Town, my love?"

Thea inclined her head. "At least you won't need to buy me any items made of silk, Grandmama. I have designed a variety of silk shawls, scarves, and fichus to accompany my evening and ball gowns, and I have even fashioned my own reticules."

Her grandmother's eyes widened a little. "You are so talented, Dorothea. I look forward to seeing your creations. But, as I mentioned previously, please don't tell anyone that you made the items yourself."

"The only people who know about my silk-staining work are Lord Castleroy and his sister. Emily mentioned it to them when she paid us a visit in Bath. However, I asked Lord Castleroy and Miss Pellier to keep the knowledge to themselves."

"Ah, yes. Lord Castleroy." Her grandmother's gaze was steady. "Your aunt wrote to me about him and Miss Pellier. A charming girl, I believe."

"Yes. She is very interested in chemistry, and Lord Castleroy took us both to the Chemical Institution in Bath, which was wonderful."

"So your aunt said." She cleared her throat. "You must have been disappointed when they left Bath."

"Miss Pellier became a very good friend within a short time. Abigail and I were sorry to lose her companionship. However, we returned to Grantham Place shortly afterward, so . . ." She gave a small shrug.

"I believe Lord Castleroy arrived in Town last week with his sister and his cousin, so you will be reunited with your friend soon, my dear."

Thea smiled. "That will be lovely, Grandmama. Miss Pellier wrote to me about a fortnight ago to inform me that her grandfather was much recovered. She and Lord Castleroy were in Macclesfield for months after leaving Bath because he was taken very poorly."

"So I heard. Your aunt is an excellent correspondent, you know."

"Indeed." Aunt Eliza had no doubt written Grandmama a highly colorful account of Lord Castleroy's alleged interest in Thea. However, the older lady was treading with far more delicacy around the subject than Aunt Eliza, who had lamented for some time the unfortunate illness of the baron's grandparent at such a crucial time in their "courtship." In desperation, Thea finally managed to silence her aunt by informing her that she was in regular correspondence with the baron's sister.

Now that they were in London, Aunt Eliza would expect her and Lord Castleroy to become reacquainted. Thea, however, was not at all eager to meet him. She had been quite happy to retreat to Grantham Place, where she had attempted to banish the man from her mind by immersing herself in her work. And, although she hadn't entirely succeeded in doing so, she had at least regained her equilibrium which had become sadly shaken in Bath. Thea was once again in a state of calm serenity, and she did not relish the baron's blue eyes puncturing her armor once more like arrows shot from a tautly-strung bow.

Her grandmother spoke again. "I am glad you have a friend in London who shares your interests, Dorothea."

"Indeed. After Miss Pellier discovered that I stain silk to make my shawls, she promised to bring me a bolt of white silk from her grandfather's mill, which was very kind of her."

Her grandmother straightened her spine. "A bolt of silk, my love?"

"Yes. I did not wish to accept such an expensive gift, but Miss Pellier informed me in her last letter that it was old stock that had been left in the corner of the manager's office and wasn't available for sale anyway."

"Ah." Her grandmother regarded her in silence. "Does Miss Pellier speak freely about her grandfather's mill, dearest?"

"Oh, no! She did not mention it at all the whole time we were in Bath. It was only when Lord Castleroy received word that their grandfather was ill that she told me of it."

"Ah," she said again. "Well, it would probably be best to keep your silence on it, my love. I know that—very sadly for the deceased Lady Castleroy—her husband cut off all contact with his wife's family upon their marriage. Anything that smells of the shop in Polite Society can be ruinous to a lady's social career. Lord Castleroy must have made contact with his mother's family upon his father's death, but I am sure it is a delicate situation that he would not wish you to speak freely about."

Thea frowned. "I understand, Grandmama."

"Excellent, my love."

The door opened at that moment, and Abigail and Aunt Eliza entered the room. Thea was glad for the distraction as she pondered her grandmother's cautionary words. It was frustrating that so many rules and regulations governed what was acceptable for the *beau monde*. Miss Pellier's affection for her grandfather had shone through in her letters to Thea. How sad that speaking about him in polite circles would be frowned upon by so many.

Perhaps that was also why Lord Castleroy had not told her about his involvement in the silk industry. The worlds of trade and the *ton* did not mix, which made his lordship's position difficult, especially as his sister had stated that he was a part-owner of his grandfather's mill.

So many topics were not open for discussion, and Thea's head ached as she tried to keep a tally of them: the chemistry experiments she performed, her silk work, Lord Castleroy's involvement in the silk industry, his maternal relations. Her lips curved into a wry smile. How odd that silk was the common thread that bound all of these forbidden subjects together, weaving its way around them in a pattern of secrecy.

Lines from *Marmion* by Sir Walter Scott flashed into her mind: *O, what a tangled web we weave, / When first we practice to deceive!*

Thea sighed. Hopefully, her shawls would not draw too much attention in London as she did not relish the role of dissimulator. However, it seemed unlikely that the items she had made would attract any special notice in the Metropolis. John had informed her only the other day that imported silk was the order of the day in London, as members of the nobility and gentry were permitted to buy silk textiles on the Continent for their own particular use.

Besides, the adage that a man's home was his castle seemed to stand up well under the acts that prohibited foreign silks because goods in a gentleman's private residence were excluded from the legislation. Customs officers, therefore, did not have the power to search a returning traveler's house or lodgings or to prosecute individuals.

The shopkeepers, tailors, and other dealers who sold and distributed foreign goods were the real focus of the authorities in London—not ladies wearing silk to parties.

Thea really had nothing to fear.

CHAPTER ELEVEN

THEA GAZED IN wonder at the array of fabrics displayed in the warehouse her grandmother had brought her to. They had come here this morning to choose materials for the gowns Thea still needed. The shop was full of customers, yet her grandmother's consequence meant that they did not need to wait long for someone to attend to them.

After consulting with her granddaughter on her preferences, Lady Longmore discussed her requirements with the shopkeeper. Thea glanced around the interior with interest. The variety of people milling about rivaled the variety of fabrics. Thea eavesdropped for a moment on a grande dame at a nearby counter who was asking the assistant behind it a number of searching questions about the silks on display, while she watched a stylish young matron examining frills and furbelows with an air of helpless indecision. At another long counter, a young lady— hardly more than a girl—sighed over a delicately embroidered scarf, as a flirtatious young woman of about Thea's age raised sparkling eyes to the broad-shouldered male assistant serving behind it.

As Grandmama continued to engage with the linen-draper about the various gauzes, nets, trimmings, and other items her granddaughter required, Thea's gaze settled on the lovely colored muslins and silks the burly male assistant was presenting to the bold young woman.

The textiles were in a rainbow of shades—red, pink, yellow, orange, green, blue, and violet. Thea took a step closer, studying the materials more closely. None of the shades matched the magnificent metallic colors and vivid purples she managed to achieve with her chemistry experiments.

The bold young woman glanced down at the silks and said, with a flutter of her eyelashes, "I'm seeking a wrought silk scarf—" she lowered her voice, "—in the French style."

The shop assistant shook his head. "We don't stock French silk, madam."

The woman pouted a little but recovered her good humor when the assistant presented her with a "wedding ring shawl," made of Shetland lace so fine, he informed her, that it was possible to pull the material through a wedding ring.

The young woman exclaimed in delight before lowering her voice and saying something in a whisper, which caused the man's face to break into a broad grin.

Thea turned aside and took a step closer to her grandmother, who was concluding her discussion with the linen draper. As they left the shop together, Thea told her about the young woman's request for French silk.

The older lady sighed as she settled into their carriage. "Unfortunately, English silk producers cannot match the quality of their French counterparts, my love. The taste for foreign silks in London is well-established. I do not purchase contraband silk myself, but I know many ladies who do."

"It does not seem particularly patriotic," Thea said, leaning back against the squabs.

Her grandmother's lips curved wryly. "Even though there may be bitter acrimony for the French after the war, they still lead the way in fashion." Her smile widened. "Speaking of fashion, we have an appointment with Madame Bouchet tomorrow. Although you have a far better wardrobe than Alexandra had upon her arrival in Town, Dorothea, it is still inadequate for a London Season. You need a great many new gowns. Madame made the most beautiful gowns for Alexandra, effectively launching her into high fashion. I hope she will do the same for you."

"I doubt she will achieve similar success with me as a subject."

"Nonsense, Dorothea. You may not be beautiful, but you have a fine countenance and an excellent figure. You will do very well in Madame Bouchet's creations."

"But I wear spectacles, Grandmama."

Her grandmother raised her brows. "What of them, my love? They merely draw attention to your pretty eyes."

Thea smiled but made no reply. Her grandmother's bracing attitude was one of the things she liked most about her. Although she did think Grandmama was being overly optimistic about the effect of Thea's glasses on her overall appearance. No matter how one looked at it, the spectacles did give Thea something of the air of a schoolmistress.

Nevertheless, she accompanied her grandmother to Madame Bouchet's dress shop in Bruton Street the following day. The spacious apartment's Aubusson carpet, gilt armchairs, and gilded mirrors gave it the appearance of an elegant salon rather than a shop.

Madame Bouchet matched the modishness of her surroundings as she curtseyed low upon their entrance. She tilted her head to one side as she listened attentively to Lady Longmore, who nodded in Thea's direction. "This is my second granddaughter, madame. Her hair is not as bright as her sister's, as you see, and her skin is even fairer. This unusual coloring calls for fabrics in a unique palette of colors."

The modiste studied Thea through narrowed eyes. "*Oui*, madame. Grafton House delivered the materials you ordered this morning, and I am in full agreement. *Les couleurs d'automne* you have chosen will suit mademoiselle very well. It would be fatal to dress your granddaughter in the wrong shades. But in the right clothes . . ." She spread her hands wide.

"Thank you, madame. Alexandra looked beautiful in your designs, so I look forward to seeing what you can do for Dorothea."

The dressmaker's considering gaze came to rest on Thea's round dress of fine cambric muslin worn under a blue and white pelisse of striped tobine silk, trimmed all the way down the front with broad swansdown. On Thea's head was perched a Cambridge hat of blue satin, ornamented with a cream ribbon, while in her hands, she held an ornamented blue velvet reticule with a fancy clasp that she had fashioned herself.

Madame Bouchet gave a slow nod. "Mademoiselle Grantham dresses with decided *élégance*, madame. I can see that she wears her clothes rather than allows them to wear her, which can be very *weary*ing indeed in some young ladies!" Madame Bouchet gave a small smile at her pun. "Mademoiselle does not make the mistake of trying to conform to the vagaries of fashion, and it lends her a distinction of style which is very welcome in this age when all ladies look so very much alike."

Thea's measurements were taken, and then Madame Bouchet and Lady Longmore conferred over the current rage for extremely small bodices and very high waistlines. Madame studied Thea critically. "*Heureusement*, it is a style that will suit you, mademoiselle, as your bosom is not too large. Some young ladies wish for this design, but I cannot accommodate them as they will look a little like *une saucisse, vous savez*."

Madame Bouchet showed Thea a fashion print of an exquisite gown of white lace over a white satin slip. "This would be perfect for your coming out ball, mademoiselle," she murmured as Thea studied the print closely.

The hem of the skirt was decorated with white lace drapery interwoven with pearls, with roses in full bloom in a recurring pattern upon a rouleau of white satin. "How charming this is!" Thea exclaimed, smiling at her grandmother.

The older lady nodded her head slowly as she examined the

design. "Yes, indeed, my love. You will look beautiful in this."

Madame Bouchet showed her customers other prints of morning gowns, carriage dresses, riding habits, evening gowns, and day dresses. After Thea and Lady Longmore had chosen the most becoming costumes, they left Madame Bouchet's premises and went on to a milliner's shop in Conduit Street, where Thea tried on a variety of stylish hats. Studying the selection on display with a critical eye, Thea took her grandmother to one side and said in a low voice, "I would much rather trim my own hats, Grandmama. If we could purchase the required materials, I will do this at home."

Her grandmother studied her doubtfully. "Are you certain, my love?"

"Yes, indeed. I have brought my sewing basket to London with me, which has a long needle and a pair of long-shafted scissors. I would be delighted to work on this at home."

So, to the evident surprise of the proprietor, Miss Walker, Thea exited the milliner's shop with two unadorned straw hats, a plain satin bonnet, and a simple capote hat. She and Lady Longmore then went on to Bond Street, where Thea purchased a variety of ribbons, some artificial flowers, a length of net, a small quantity of lace, and some feathers and beads for the trimmings.

When they eventually climbed back into the carriage, Thea sighed happily as she leaned back in her seat. "I shall derive great pleasure from decorating these hats, Grandmama. Thank you so much for allowing me to do so."

Her grandmother's blue eyes crinkled at the corners. "I am sure you will do an excellent job, Dorothea, although I fear Miss Walker must think you quite Quakerish in your tastes!"

Thea laughed. "She did seem rather taken aback. She must think me something of a dowdy, I fear."

When they reached home, Thea showed Abigail and Aunt Eliza her purchases before hastening upstairs. She found her sewing basket and sat in an armchair near the window, making use of the fading afternoon light as she began decorating her satin bonnet. And, like the disappearing daylight, the state of nervous agitation she had labored under since her arrival in London began to fade as well.

Creative work always calmed her, and she released a breath as she set the bonnet to one side and rose to her feet. Walking over to the window, she gazed out at the oblong-shaped garden in the center of the Square, with its shrubs, pathways, and established plane trees.

Soon she would meet Lord Castleroy again. Although it had been many months since she had last encountered the baron, she could still see his face in her mind's eye, those searching blue eyes, the firm, uncompromising mouth, and the resolute chin hinting at determination and tenacity.

Lord Castleroy was no indolent gentleman. Indeed, he seemed to leash a certain power of being and strength of purpose in his economical movements. Perhaps the barely-contained force he exhibited, so at odds with the leisured demeanor of the true aristocrat, was due to his mother's blood flowing through his veins, the blood of generations of working men and women who had needed to fight to earn their living as their position in the world was not assured from birth.

Whatever it was that set him apart from other gentlemen, Thea sensed it and was alarmed by it because, on some instinctive level, she recognized this was not a man easily diverted from his purpose or put off by platitudes or politeness. When she met him again, would he still study her with that odd expression in his eyes as if he were trying to solve a particularly complicated puzzle? Or would she have faded from his thoughts in the months since he left Bath?

She hoped she had waned from them as she did not relish setting up her barriers once more in the face of his razor-sharp intelligence. That last-minute reprieve, as he had called it in Bath, had allowed her the time to rebuild her barricades. She was on her guard now, and nothing would distract her from her determination to keep those walls from tumbling down again.

CHAPTER TWELVE

JAMES PAID A morning call on the Grantham ladies after giving them a few days to settle into London. He had brought his sister and his cousin, Jane, to Town the previous week, taking up residence in his home in Grosvenor Square.

Anne had been patiently waiting to see the Grantham girls again, and as their carriage drew up in front of Longmore House, she tightened her grip on the bolt of silk she had brought with her. "It feels like an age since we were in Bath, James. I do hope they will be at home."

The manservant who opened the door confirmed the ladies were receiving morning callers and led them up the stairs to the drawing room on the first floor. As James advanced into the apartment, he bowed to Lady Longmore and Mrs. Grantham before turning to Miss Grantham and Miss Abigail, seated beside the window, their embroidery on their laps.

Miss Grantham sat as still as a mouse before rising slowly from her chair and joining in the general flurry of greetings. His cousin engaged Lady Longmore and Mrs. Grantham in conversation just as Anne pressed the bolt into Miss Grantham's hands. "This is the silk I promised you."

Miss Grantham ran a hand over the material as if it were the rarest of jewels. "Oh, thank you, Miss Pellier. You are far too generous, I fear."

"Will you not call me Anne? I feel like we are old friends already."

"Yes, of course . . . Anne. And please call me Thea. Only my aunt and Grandmama call me Dorothea. If anyone my age calls me by my full name, I feel that I am their black books."

Miss Grantham smiled as she sat down at an angle, fixing her gaze attentively on Anne, her head turned away from James. He repressed a sigh as he inquired about Miss Abigail's health. It was as he had suspected. Miss Grantham had sounded a retreat.

His unavoidable detainment in Macclesfield had disrupted his courtship, if he could even call it that. Miss Grantham had reluctantly allowed him into her world in Bath, but his departure had doused any smoldering embers of connection.

His mouth twisted wryly. How odd that he, of all people, should have fallen in love at first sight. But he had. Upon setting eyes on Thea, he had been lost. *Thea.* He liked the shortened version of her name. It suited her. Dorothea sounded starchy and proper, while Thea rolled off the tongue, smooth as silk.

Silk. The word was on his mind.

Thea smiled at Anne. "Would you like me to make you a shawl?"

His sister hesitated. "I did not give you the silk as a hint for a present, Thea."

Miss Abigail clasped her hands together. "Oh, you must let Thea make you a shawl, Anne! Her work is so beautiful."

"Well . . ." She leaned forward slightly in her chair. "If it isn't too much of an imposition, Thea, I should be delighted if you would make me one."

"Which color would you prefer?" Thea asked.

"I adored the purple fichu you gave Lady Grantham if it wouldn't be too much trouble to make me something like that?"

"Yes, of course." Thea glanced across at Lady Longmore. "Grandmama is permitting me to use the stillroom downstairs for my work. However, she has told me in the strictest terms that I mustn't get so caught up in my experiments that I forget the world exists." She pressed her lips together. "I tend to do that."

"Understandable, I expect." Anne tilted her head. "How long has it taken you to perfect your technique? Your shawls and scarves look so finished."

Thea drew her fine brows together. "I have performed a number of experiments over the years to produce the metallic materials Mrs. Fulhame describes in her essay. I started staining silk before I was sent away to school, you know. And since I left the seminary, I have attempted to combine the arts and chemistry in the hope that through trial and error, I will be able to refine an acceptable product."

"I would say it is more than acceptable," his sister said. "Your shawls are beautiful, and your embroidery quite exquisite."

"You will turn my head with these compliments." Thea smiled a little.

"I am perfectly sincere." Anne glanced across at James. "Indeed, my brother told me just the other day that he believed at first that your shawls were of French origin due to the fineness of the workmanship."

This particular comment directed Thea's attention to James. Although he would have preferred to bring the matter up himself, Anne's remark provided the opening he needed. "I have been thinking of your work, Miss Grantham, and should like to discuss it with you in more depth if possible."

She inclined her head. "I should be pleased to discuss it with you, my lord."

"Excellent." His brows drew together. "One thing—if you don't wish for it to become known that you create your own shawls, you will need to have a plausible excuse at hand to divert attention away from any unwanted questions."

"My brother informed me before I came to London that it is customary for members of the *ton* to wear foreign silk as travelers are allowed to bring these items into the country for personal use. So I doubt my shawls will draw too much notice as there are so many people wearing imported silk."

James leaned back in his chair, folding his arms. "I disagree. Your shawls are unique. You do not weave gold foil around a silk core as is done in the East. Instead, you stain the silk cloth using metallic salts. It has quite a different appearance and will provoke comment."

She wrinkled her brow. "My stained cloths do not look particularly burnished, though. In fact, the gold is quite a subtle shade."

He inclined his head. "My point exactly. I have read Mrs. Fulhame's essay, and she states that the metallic cloths achieved using chemistry methods are of a cooler shade of gold and ultimately more attractive than the garish gold attained with other methods. Your shawls stand out precisely because they have a restrained elegance."

"It appears you have made a careful study of Mrs. Fulhame's essay, my lord."

"I have." He met her gaze steadily. "Her work—and your interpretation of it—intrigues me."

"Oh!" As betraying color crept into her cheeks, James hid a smile. Thea blushed so easily.

"May I take you for a drive in my curricle in the Park tomorrow?" he said quietly.

"I . . ." She glanced at her sister before saying in a low voice, "Perhaps we could all meet in the Park for a walk instead? I know Abigail would love to join us for a breath of fresh air."

"Yes, of course. And I am sure Anne would like to come as well."

"I should like that very much," his sister said. "I haven't gone to the Park yet as the weather has been so poor. I hope it will be a fine day tomorrow."

Thea glanced out of the window. "It seems to be clearing up a bit. Unfortunately, January in London is not the most propitious of months for outdoor activities."

"Indoor entertainments are usually a safer proposition." He looked from Thea to her sister. "Would you and Miss Abigail care to attend a chemistry lecture at the Royal Institution on Friday? I am taking Anne there as the lectures are open to ladies and gentlemen."

"Oh, yes!" Thea sat up straighter in her chair as she glanced across at Lady Longmore. "That is if Grandmama allows it."

His gaze rested on Lady Longmore, still chatting to his cousin. "I am sure your grandmother will not object if I escort you there, Miss Grantham. I believe you and your sister would enjoy the demonstrations. They are very well done."

She nodded. "My father attended some of Humphry Davy's public lectures at the Institution many years ago. He told me that half of the audience was composed of women and girls with their notebooks and pencils in hand. I wonder if there is still such an interest in chemistry amongst women in London?"

"I believe a great number of ladies still attend the lectures. Sir Humphry has always supported feminine participation at the Royal Institution, and women are encouraged to subscribe to the lectures." He frowned a little. "However, there is an element of superficial scientific entertainment about the demonstrations, which some serious men of science reject. It is only fair to warn you of this, Miss Grantham."

Thea tilted her head to one side. "I do believe there is a place for both education and entertainment in chemical science. Sometimes the only way to make something accessible to novices is to dress it up as something more playful. I am a firm believer that entertainment can be educative as well."

"In some instances, the balance can shift in the other direction whereby some scholars neglect all entertainment in favor of their work."

Her gaze faltered. "I suppose that can become a problem as well."

"'All work and no play makes Jack a dull boy.'" His look was pointed.

She straightened her spine. "Are you calling me *dull*, my lord?"

"Not at all. I am merely hoping that you will have some time to play in London."

"Never fear." She folded her hands in her lap. "I am quite proficient at the pianoforte, you know, and dedicate many hours to practicing."

He chuckled. "I am sure that Lady Longmore is planning any number of entertainments for you in London."

Thea sighed. "Indeed. So many that they are bound to keep me away from the stillroom. Grandmama does not object to my interest in chemistry, but she does not wish for me to become too absorbed by it."

"And how do you feel about that?" A smile tugged at his lips. "I have the impression that your work is a happy refuge for you."

"Absorbing work is always satisfying, my lord." She cleared her throat. "I trust your grandfather is recovered?"

"He is, thank you, although he was ill for some time."

James met Anne's eyes then and rose to his feet. After they finalized the details of their excursion to Hyde Park the next day, he bid the ladies farewell and escorted his sister and cousin out of the drawing room.

A frown marred his brow as he left the house. Now that this visit of ceremony was over, he could start his campaign to win Thea's hand in marriage. A pity his attempt to spend some time alone with her tomorrow had been thwarted, but there would be other occasions when he could take her driving in the Park.

His time in Macclesfield had given birth to an idea he urgently needed to discuss with her. But she was very much on her guard with him. He had seen that at a glance. He needed to gain her confidence before speaking to her about his plan. He did not wish to act precipitately, but time was of the essence, and he would not be able to delay for much longer before broaching the matter with her.

It was a devil of a situation to be in.

CHAPTER THIRTEEN

T HEA DID NOT relish the idea of walking in Hyde Park with Lord Castleroy to the extent that she prayed for rain. But the weather did not oblige her and the next day dawned fine and clear. She sighed as she looked out of the drawing room window. Even the sun appeared to be under the baron's spell, appearing after an absence of many days to shine tauntingly on the Metropolis.

There would be no escape from his lordship today. Ordinarily, she would love to walk in the fresh air and get some exercise. But although she had hoped that Lord Castleroy's effect on her had waned with time, it seemed, instead, to have waxed to the point where she could no longer dismiss her attraction to him as a "bag o' moonshine" as her old nanny had been wont to say.

And the frightening thing was that he appeared equally attracted to her. If she were like other young ladies, she would joyfully respond to his overtures. But she did not seek involvement. In fact, it was the very last thing she wanted. She swallowed past the constriction in her throat. If only she could surmount the obstacle of her fearful frozen feelings. But they were like a mountain, blocking her path, preventing her from seeing the way forward.

Aunt Eliza and Grandmama had decided to walk in the Park as well, and Biddle drove them to their rendezvous at the appointed hour. It appeared that after the inclement weather of the past few weeks, the rest of fashionable Society had also decided to take the air, and the older ladies frequently stopped to exchange greetings with their friends and acquaintances, separating from the younger people, who moved on swiftly ahead of them.

Thea and Abigail walked beside Anne, who was engaged in telling them about her visit to Macclesfield, while Lord Castleroy and Mrs. Worrell followed slightly behind.

"I heard the strangest story about the origins of the silk industry in England while we were staying with Grandfather," Anne said as they came to a more secluded part of the Park. "Considering your interest in silk, Thea, I thought you might like to hear it."

"It sounds intriguing," Thea said. "Do tell."

"I would say it is more distressing." Anne gave a slight shiver. "Somehow, one perceives the silk industry to be a more genteel kind of business, but it is quite the opposite! My cousin, Jacob, told me about John and Thomas Lombe, two half-brothers, who established the silk industry in Britain in the 18th century."

"I believe my father mentioned the Lombe brothers to me once," Thea said. "They were very successful at mechanizing silk production, were they not?"

"Yes. Although, their methods of obtaining success were not the most scrupulous. The story goes that the Kingdom of Sardinia in Northern Italy was known to produce the finest silk in the whole of Europe. Thomas Lombe was determined to learn more about the Italians' silk-throwing machines, so he sent his brother to Italy to find out how they worked."

Thea came to a halt under the shade of a tree. "And did he?"

"The story is that he obtained work in a Piedmont silk shop through bribery." Anne stopped beside Thea, furrowing her brow. "He would stay behind after the workday ended to sketch the design of the machines they used there in secret before sending off the drawings. They were hidden in bales of silk and shipped to England. Lombe's spying eventually came to light, though, and he fled from Italy on an English ship and returned to London."

"So the Lombe brothers blatantly copied the Italian machines?" Abigail asked.

"They did. Silk-throwing machines were installed in the Derby mill after Thomas Lombe obtained a patent for the machinery. The mill became very successful and eventually led to the development of the silk industry in other parts of England. However, John Lombe died in 1722 at the age of 29. Legend has it that he was poisoned by an Italian woman he had known in Italy. She secured employment at the Derby mill on the instructions of the King of Sardinia, who, having heard of the mill's success, directed this female assassin to travel to England to kill Lombe. It is rumored that she administered slow poison to him and that he suffered for two or three years before dying an agonizing death."

"What a shocking story." Thea's gaze encompassed Lord Castleroy, who had also come to a halt under the sheltering arms of the oak.

"A fantastic tale indeed," he said. "Although Lombe's death at the hands of a female assassin was never proven due to a lack of evidence, I would not be surprised if it were true. The Sardinian government imposes the death penalty for thieves of technological ideas."

"And how rich that Thomas Lombe then applied for his own patent in England after copying the Italian machines!" Thea shook her head. "The audacity!"

"Indeed. However, if you are seeking justice in this . . . er . . . yarn, Miss Grantham, Italian silk is still more sought after than English silk in furniture, clothing, and haberdashery."

"*Yarn*, my lord?"

His eyes gleamed. "I'm afraid it was irresistible."

As they walked on, Lord Castleroy offered Thea his arm, and they drew slightly apart from the rest of the party as he stopped to point out some white flowers pushing through the soil.

"Snowdrops. Spring is on its way."

Thea studied the delicate blossoms of the plant, which had fought bravely through the cold, hard earth, before quoting in a soft voice:

"'Courageous snowdrop, blossoming in unrelenting ground,
A frozen teardrop, tenacity unbound,
Spring's initial flower, pure and sublime,
A snowflake awakened in England's icy clime.'"

She met his eyes and smiled tentatively. Hopefully, he wouldn't think her foolish for quoting poetry in this way.

A faint line appeared between Lord Castleroy's brows. "'The Awakening' by Mary Anne Taylor." He searched her face for a moment before saying, "You left out the preceding lines, my dear:

'Winter's barren cold is not forever,
A season of warmth will beckon us ever.
Seeds of friendship, once firmly planted,
Are never unfruitful, forlorn, or unwanted.'"

Thea took a tiny step back, unable to look away. She felt stripped of her defenses, and ironically, she had been the one to provide Lord Castleroy with the means of breaching them. *Seeds of friendship, once firmly planted, are never unfruitful, forlorn, or unwanted.* The words echoed in her mind with a quiet sense of inevitability, trapping her breath.

He tucked her hand into his arm once more, drawing her onward along the path to catch up with the others. As she walked in silence beside him, she grappled with the strangeness of the feeling within her. It was as if something had melted, like the snowflake in the poem that had turned into a flower. The warmth of Lord Castleroy's eyes had kindled a tentative hope in her heart. She did not care to examine it too closely, but it was reassuring to perceive that green shoot springing to life in what she had thought was a barren wilderness.

As if sensing her shift in mood, he slowed his pace before coming to a complete stop. Then, after studying her features for a moment, he held out his hand. "Friends, my dear?"

She drew in a breath at this moment of choice. For that was what it was. She could choose to shake his hand, or she could refrain. He wasn't forcing his friendship on her. Instead, he was offering it to her without coercion.

And that was what decided her in the end. "I should like that, my lord," she said, briefly clasping his hand.

As they continued along the path, Thea stole a glance up at his profile. "I am surprised you are so familiar with 'The Awakening' that you can recite from it."

"My mother was fond of everything Mary Anne Taylor wrote and frequently quoted from her works. And as she did not enjoy living in London, she found these verses from 'The Awakening' particularly comforting:

'Away from the city's empty soul and shimmer,
I hasten to the country where life is ever simpler.
Away from false friendship and empty, mindless measure,
I hasten to the meadow where Nature's hope is treasure.'"

Thea remained silent for a moment. "There is something particularly healing about being out in nature, is there not? All our anxieties and concerns fade to nothing. It places our lives in their proper perspective."

"Yes. Although, as in all things, a sense of balance is required. Nature can be a healing retreat, but it isn't wise to make any sphere of life a permanent refuge."

Thea studied the ground. Was he drawing a parallel with her chemistry work, her welcome escape from the world? Perhaps not. But when she glanced up at his strong profile, she knew, suddenly, that he had been doing exactly that. Lord Castleroy did not make idle statements.

What exactly had she committed herself to by accepting his offer of friendship?

CHAPTER FOURTEEN

THEA WALKED ALONG the paved gravel path in her grandmother's walled garden, tucked behind Longmore House. Barely sparing a glance for the geometric flower beds or the potted plants and urns ornamenting the pathway, she headed past a topiary and a sundial before stopping at a wrought iron garden bench in front of a tall hedge. Sinking onto the seat, she stared straight ahead at the rose trellis on the opposite wall.

Another fine day had dawned, and Thea was conscious of the promise of spring in the air. People were returning to London in ever-increasing numbers, and Grandmama had told her of the invitations she had already received for several evening parties. Soon, they would be inundated with social activities to the point that Thea would have very little time for anything else.

Fortunately, she had already begun staining Anne's silk fichu as she doubted she would be able to give it the attention it deserved later in the Season.

Thea always tried to follow Mrs. Fulhame's method as closely as possible and had combined sulfuric ether and a solution of gold in nitro muriatic acid in her grandmother's stillroom early this morning, which had formed the dyeing solution. After dipping a length of white silk in this, she'd hung it carefully within a tall glass cylinder she'd thankfully unearthed in the stillroom last week. She'd then mixed diluted sulfuric acid and iron filings in a glass bowl and placed the cylinder and silk over it. The sulfuric acid and iron filings would produce hydrogen gas that would wash over the silk as it exited the top of the glass cylinder. Over time, this exposure would create the brilliant purple color Anne had asked for with a spangle of gold on one end that would make it perfect for an eye-catching shawl. Then Thea would embroider the hem, and *voilà*! Anne would have her fichu.

Lord Castleroy came into her field of vision, and Thea rose slowly to her feet. What was he doing here? She had hastily donned her oldest gown when she woke this morning and wasn't in a state to receive visitors.

But the baron seemed not to notice her dowdy appearance as he bowed. "Miss Grantham, what a peaceful spot." He glanced around the secluded space before returning his attention to her. "Forgive me for disturbing you at such an hour, but I shan't keep you long as I do not like to leave my horses waiting. I am on my way to an early meeting. Would you care to join me for a drive in my curricle upon my return?"

The gardener, Gibbs, walked up to them, trundling a wheelbarrow along the path. He doffed his hat before disappearing behind the hedge into the kitchen garden. Only when he was out of sight did Thea respond. "I . . . I'm afraid, my lord, that I do not ride in curricles."

A frown descended on his brow. "Why not?"

She released her breath. Trust Lord Castleroy not to beat around the bush. "I simply don't care for it."

As she started walking back to the house, he fell in step beside her. "Is it only curricles and landaus you dislike, Miss Grantham, or every sort of open vehicle?"

She stopped. "Every sort."

"I see."

Thea stared straight ahead. "I have my reasons, my lord."

"Your mother died whilst traveling in an open carriage, did she not?"

She clenched and unclenched her hands before giving a jerky

nod.

Without a word, Lord Castleroy took her arm and led her back to the garden seat. She slumped onto it, quite unable to say anything for some time, as her companion sat quietly beside her.

Eventually, Thea released a shaky breath. "Forgive me, my lord. I don't speak of this. Ever."

"Perhaps talking about it might help?" he said gently.

She shook her head. "I don't see how. It just brings to the fore the memory of that terrible day. I can still see it so clearly."

When she failed to continue, he spoke again. "See what?"

"I witnessed the accident." Her tone was expressionless.

He reached over and held her hand. The unexpected touch prompted her to say in a halting voice, "I . . . I was out walking with my governess that morning. Abigail and Alexandra had chosen to stay at home, but I love nature rambles, and Miss Johnson had promised to take me to the woods to examine the wildflowers. The road from the house runs parallel to the woods, and I saw my mother driving alone in her gig." She swallowed. "A . . . a dog ran into the road, causing the horse to shy. The carriage overturned and Mama was thrown from her seat. We raced to help her, but it was too late. She died instantly."

Lord Castleroy now took both her hands in a comforting grip. "How old were you, my dear?"

"Twelve." The warmth of his hands seemed to infuse strength into her. "I couldn't speak for a month after the accident. I kept seeing what had happened. Over and over again." She released a shaky sigh. "I've never driven in an open carriage since."

Lord Castleroy studied her gravely. "A natural reaction to such a harrowing event."

She removed her hands from his grasp as Gibbs and his young assistant walked out from behind the hedge. One of the footmen, Andrew, stepped out of the house then, too, perhaps sent by Leighton.

The baron frowned. "I'm afraid I must leave now, Miss Grantham, as I am late for my appointment. May I visit you later?"

Thea swallowed past the knot in her throat. Why had she told him so much? She kept her gaze at the level of his chest as they both rose to their feet. "I won't be here this afternoon as I am going out with Grandmama and Aunt Eliza."

"Tomorrow then?"

She raised her eyes to his and, after an infinitesimal pause, gave a tiny nod. Then, placing her hand on his arm, she walked slowly back to the house. After Lord Castleroy had taken his leave, Thea went upstairs to her bedchamber and walked across to the window. She was just in time to see the baron giving his horses the office to start before he drove them out of the Square at a brisk trot.

Everyone in her family knew of her fear of driving in open carriages. And her grandmother was most concerned about how it would affect Thea's ability to participate fully in all the social activities in London. Only yesterday, Lady Longmore had shaken her head and said, "My love, is there any way you could contrive to overcome this fear? Gentlemen who wish to pursue an acquaintanceship with you will be calling to ask you to drive with them in the Park. Or you may be asked by a hostess to travel in an open carriage to a picnic. You will be perceived as having a very odd kick in your gallop if you turn down all these invitations."

Thea had grimaced. "But horses with an odd kick in their gallop are precisely the problem, Grandmama. The traffic in London is dreadful. All those carriages, carts, and coaches trying to navigate the narrow streets. Not to mention the wagons blocking the way and the hackney coachmen attempting to pass other vehicles on the pavement. No wonder the horses startle."

"Indeed, my love. But the traffic in London is an unfortunate part of life that one must learn to live with. Your refusal to go anywhere in an open carriage makes things very difficult for me, particularly as I was hoping to take you to the Park on fine days in my barouche. It would be an excellent opportunity to show off your new carriage dresses."

At her grandmother's unhappy expression, Thea had sighed. "I wish I could overcome my fear, Grandmama. I really do. I just don't know how to."

Now, as she thought of her grandmother's concerns, she realized how difficult it would be to enjoy her London Season if she didn't conquer her anxiety. But the thought of driving through the busy streets was utterly terrifying, and she didn't know how she could ever manage it.

When Lord Castleroy arrived to see Thea the next day, she was in the drawing room, reading a novel. Abigail was near the door with Aunt Eliza, who was helping her with her embroidery. The baron greeted them politely before making his way over to the window, where Thea sat.

"Miss Grantham. I trust that you are well?"

Evidently, this was no idle greeting. Thea's cheeks warmed at the baron's thorough appraisal as he sat down on the chair she indicated.

She placed her book to one side. "I am . . . better today. Thank you."

He continued to study her through slightly narrowed eyes. "If I may be of service in any way, you have only to ask. I hope you know that."

Thea pressed her lips together. "Thank you, Lord Castleroy. That is very kind of you." She hesitated. "As a matter of fact, I have been mulling over an idea, but I don't know if it would be possible to execute it. It . . . it's rather embarrassing."

He raised his brows but said nothing as he waited for her to continue.

She bit her lip. "I have been thinking . . . that is . . . Grandmama has pointed out how difficult it will be for me to refuse all invitations to drive in open carriages in London. At Grantham Place, my family was able to indulge my fear. But here . . ." She raised her shoulders. "I am very much afraid that I am making things hard for Grandmama, and I hate to disappoint her."

"I am sure Lady Longmore understands."

"She does, but I feel as if I am letting her down. Which is why—" she drew in a deep breath, "—I have decided that I need to try to conquer my fear. Would you be able to take me for a very short drive in your curricle, my lord?"

"Yes, of course." He studied her thoughtfully. "But if you feel overwhelmed at any point, you only have to say the word, and my groom will take the reins so I can escort you back to Longmore House."

"Thank you."

"For your first excursion, I think it would be best to drive around Berkeley Square," he said. "Then, if you become frightened, it will only be a short walk home."

"Did you drive your curricle here today?"

"I did."

She gripped her hands together in her lap. "Could we go out for a drive now?"

"You are quite sure you wish to do this?"

"I think it is better to attempt it now before I lose my nerve. I have been steeling myself all morning to ask you, you see."

He rose to his feet. "Very well."

"If you would wait a moment, Lord Castleroy, I will get my hat."

With a fleeting smile, Thea hastened from the room, determined to follow through with her plan before her courage failed.

CHAPTER FIFTEEN

J AMES ASSISTED THEA into his curricle before climbing up beside her and nodding at Peter, who held the horses. When his groom ascended to the seat behind them, James looked down at his companion. "Ready, Miss Grantham?"

Thea looked as pale as a ghost as she stared straight ahead. When she did not reply and merely raised anguished eyes to his, he frowned. "Perhaps we should leave this for another day."

She caught her breath. "No. No, I want to do this today. I'll never do it if I put it off." Her words came out in a staccato rhythm as if each syllable was an effort.

"I'll drive slowly."

She nodded as her eyelids fluttered closed, and James's jaw tightened as he set the curricle in motion. Her fear radiated to him, as tangible as the heat from a raging fire.

James had already taken his greys to Hyde Park that morning as they had been fidgety and in need of exercise. Fortunately, they were calmer now, and his matched pair stepped out calmly over the cobblestones.

Thea did not open her eyes as she swayed with the vehicle's motion. Then pressing her hands flat on the seat, she stilled, holding herself rigid.

"Must I stop?" he asked quietly.

She shook her head. "No."

"It may help if you open your eyes."

"You truly think so?"

"Yes. You will see there's nothing to fear." His voice was calm, without inflection.

As his team clip-clopped along the cobbled surface of the road, Thea fixed her gaze straight ahead. They were at the far end of the Square by now, and as he turned the corner, she gripped her seat again. But her fingers unclenched as the horses moved smoothly along, and she released her breath in a faint sigh.

James remained silent as he concentrated on his driving, determined nothing should disrupt their short journey. Although the Square was quiet, he kept an eye out for any hazards that might upset his spirited greys. If Thea contrived to maintain her composure during this first outing in an open carriage, she might well find the courage to be a passenger in such a vehicle again.

When he drew his equipage to a halt in front of Longmore House, James handed the reins to his groom before jumping to the ground to hand Thea down.

He studied her upturned face. "Now, that wasn't too bad, was it?"

"It was terrifying."

"But you soldiered through. That's what matters."

"Yes." Her voice was doubtful as she glanced away.

"I would be pleased to drive you around the Square again tomorrow." He tucked her hand into his arm and led her back to Longmore House. "In fact, it might be a good idea for me to do so every day until it becomes commonplace for you."

As they drew to a halt in front of the door, Thea frowned. "I doubt it will ever become commonplace, my lord. But it would help me immensely if you would be so kind as to take me out for short drives in your curricle until I feel more confident."

"Delighted to do so," he murmured as the door swung open.

He bowed then and took his leave before running lightly down the stairs. After he climbed into the driver's seat and retrieved the reins, he drew his brows together, staring straight ahead. He had intended to speak to Thea today about his plan, but her state of nervous tension had precluded any such discussion.

He would have to wait until she was in a better frame of mind before bringing up the matter.

As promised, Lord Castleroy came every morning to take Thea out in his curricle. At first, she was in a state of panic whenever he handed her up into the open vehicle. But she managed to control her anxiety to the point that she did not ask him once to set her down before he had completed his daily circuit of the Square.

It helped that his lordship arrived early in the morning before the majority of the residents were out and about. And his calmness was a boon as Thea found his presence infinitely reassuring. It wasn't that the baron was overly sympathetic in his manner. Rather, his matter-of-fact approach to the task at hand helped make the daily outing seem rather mundane, which in turn dampened her worry.

A fortnight after her first ride in his curricle, Lord Castleroy suggested a drive to Hyde Park. "It isn't too far away," he said. "And we shall go at an early hour to avoid the worst of the traffic."

They were seated in the drawing room with Lady Longmore, who nodded her head in encouragement. "I think that is an excellent idea," she said with a smile. "I cannot thank you enough, Lord Castleroy, for your kindness to my granddaughter. It is a vast relief to me that I will be able to take her out in the barouche when the Season starts."

"I am pleased to have been of assistance, ma'am. Although all the credit must go to Miss Grantham, you know." A slow smile spread across his face. "She is courageous to have faced such a debilitating fear."

"Indeed. I am very proud of her." She turned to look at Thea. "You have shown great fortitude to overcome this dread that has haunted you for so many years, my love. It was understandable, of course, but if you hadn't attempted to vanquish it, you would have been trapped in a cage of apprehension for the rest of your life which is the last thing your mama would have wished for you."

"I know," Thea said softly. "Mama always lived life to the full. She was like a star in the night sky guiding us all."

"Yes." Grandmama kept silent for a moment. Her eyes were suspiciously bright when she spoke again. "Our own particular star."

The next day, Lord Castleroy called to take Thea driving in the Park with him. She dressed with special care for the outing in one of the carriage costumes Madame Bouchet had created for her, a round dress of fine cambric with six flounces made from Indian muslin and a Tyrian purple velvet spencer trimmed around the bust with silk Brandenburgs. Wilson handed Thea a bonnet lined with white silk and decorated with a white ostrich feather, which she perched on her head at a jaunty angle before pulling on her Florence gloves and black satin slippers.

Thea drew a few deep breaths as she regarded herself critically in the mirror before going downstairs. Her cheeks were a little pale, but her new clothes instilled confidence in her. She defied anyone dressed in such a fine ensemble to succumb to an attack of nerves in the Park.

Lord Castleroy escorted her outside and helped her into his curricle. As he took the reins, the baron gave her an encouraging smile, but he did not speak as he set his horses in motion, for which Thea was supremely grateful. She wanted him to focus his full attention on his horses rather than concentrating on her. Indeed, she had never been so eager to be ignored.

Lord Castleroy directed his team out of the Square, and they drove the short distance to Hyde Park in complete silence. Thea stared straight ahead, looking neither to the left nor the right as she willed herself to remain calm. Her heart raced, and in spite of the coldness of the weather, small beads of perspiration broke out on her forehead.

Fortunately, the streets were not too busy at this hour, but when Lord Castleroy swerved to avoid a coal heaver, who swung around on the pavement, projecting his three-foot shovel into the road, Thea froze in terror.

However, his lordship deftly avoided the blunt instrument in their path, and Thea's pulse gradually slowed as they turned into the gates of the Park.

He glanced down at her then, his brows drawn together. "Are you all right, Miss Grantham?"

"Yes. I think so. Thank you."

The baron nodded as he directed his curricle along the carriage drive beside Rotten Row, where some grooms were exercising their employers' horses. He drove the length of the road before turning around and heading back. As they neared the gates, a lone gentleman on horseback touched the brim of his top hat and directed his horse in their direction. "Castleroy," he said, bowing.

Thea sensed her companion stiffen beside her, but Lord Castleroy sounded quite at ease when he responded to the man's greeting before turning to her and saying, "Miss Grantham, may I present Sir Percival Ponsonby to you? We were at school together at Eton. Ponsonby, Miss Grantham."

Sir Percival bowed from the saddle. He wore a green frock coat with long sleeves, reaching his knuckles, over a cream waistcoat trimmed in red that contrasted with the startling yellow of his kid gloves. His elaborate neckcloth was tied slightly to one side within a high-standing shirt collar. "Your servant, ma'am," he murmured as his strangely cold hazel eyes scrutinized her.

Thea shifted in her seat under the inspection and was relieved when he turned his head to speak to Lord Castleroy. After a somewhat desultory conversation, Sir Percival bowed once more before riding on.

Thea frowned a little as they left Hyde Park. The name "Ponsonby" had been extremely unwelcome to her ears.

After Lord Castleroy deposited her at home, Thea made her way upstairs to the small sitting room beside her grandmother's bedchamber, where the older lady wrote her letters.

Lady Longmore was engaged in this task when Thea entered the room, but she set her quill down immediately, her expression concerned. "How was your drive in the Park, my love?"

"I managed very well, Grandmama," Thea's brow creased. "It helped that Hyde Park was empty except for a few grooms engaged in exercising horses and one gentleman Lord Castleroy introduced to me as Sir Percival Ponsonby."

Her grandmother raised a hand to her cheek. "Oh no, my love. I had no idea Sir Percival was back in London again. He has been abroad recently and is the cousin of that wicked Edward Ponsonby."

"I wondered if there might be a connection." Thea sank onto the chaise longue beside her grandmother's writing table. "Do you think Sir Percival knows that his cousin tried to kidnap Alexandra?"

"I am sure he must. When Stanford banished Edward Ponsonby from England, the man went abroad to France. I am sure Mr. Ponsonby sought assistance from his cousin when he traveled there." Her forehead wrinkled. "What a pity he was introduced to you."

"Sir Percival did give me a rather odd look upon hearing my name."

"He is something of a dandy, my love, and takes great pride in his appearance. Rather an unpleasant man, I've always thought. However, I am sure he will steer clear of you if he knows about his cousin's shameless conduct."

"I hope so. I received the impression that Lord Castleroy has no real liking for him."

"Oh, there's bad blood between the Pelliers and the Ponsonbys, to be sure. Sir Percival's aunt was married to Lord

Castleroy's father, the fifth baron, but the marriage produced no children. After his first wife's death, the fifth baron married again and produced an heir. The Ponsonby family hoped to inherit some of the unentailed property on the Castleroy estate upon the baron's death, which they say was promised to his first wife's family, but everything was left to the sixth baron, Lord Castleroy."

"I see." Thea pressed her lips together. "It explains the coolness I sensed between them."

"Indeed. Sir Percival likes to bandy it about that Lord Castleroy's mother was of merchant stock and that Lord Castleroy, therefore, has tainted blood."

"What a horrid thing to say!"

"Indeed. A lot of people say horrid things in London, so it is best to be on your guard." Her grandmother glanced at the clock on the wall. "I must finish these letters, my love . . ."

Thea nodded and withdrew from the room, feeling rather chilled. Hopefully, she wouldn't encounter Sir Percival again. Something in his eyes had seemed positively malevolent. Suppressing a shiver, she hastened to her bedchamber.

CHAPTER SIXTEEN

INVITATIONS TO VARIOUS social entertainments started trickling into Longmore House just as Abigail and Aunt Eliza packed up and left London. After a tearful farewell, Thea watched her sister and aunt drive away in the coach. She had hoped that her grandmother might decide to present Abigail and Thea simultaneously as her sister was certainly old enough to make her formal debut in Society, having turned eighteen just the other day. However, Grandmama had informed them that she only wished to present one granddaughter at a time to give them the benefit of her full attention.

What had decided the matter was a letter Grandmama had received from her son, Lord Longmore, inviting Abigail to stay at Longmore Hall in Buckinghamshire. Their uncle needed a capable person to catalog and organize his astronomical observations. Naturally, he had thought of Abigail, who had been in the habit of keeping records of John's astronomical discoveries before she left to attend the seminary.

Abigail had been eager to accept the invitation, and after their return to Grantham Place, Uncle Longmore planned to send his coach to bring his niece to his country estate.

Thea's shoulders sagged as she stepped back into the house after seeing them off. Abigail was such a bright presence that the prospect of a London Season without her lively company was rendered somewhat dim. However, Thea straightened her spine as she walked up the stairs. There was no use in moping about something that couldn't be changed.

For her first evening party in London, Thea dressed in a white gown with puffed sleeves trimmed with pink rosettes and a neckline of white lace scallops. Thea's pearl earrings and her grandmother's matching necklace perfectly complemented the headdress of pearl cordons and white ostrich feathers that Thea had fashioned.

She studied the selection of shawls Wilson laid out on the bed. After much deliberation, Thea eventually chose the silver scarf she had worn to the Gala evening in Sydney Gardens. It was one of her favorites and finished her costume beautifully.

When Thea and Lady Longmore arrived at Lady Selby's home in Portman Square, Thea glanced around the large reception room, hoping Anne was there. Thea hadn't seen her friend in quite some time as Anne had been laid low with a nasty cold. Thea hoped she had recovered sufficiently to be in attendance this evening.

She had not seen Lord Castleroy in some days either, as he had been obliged to leave London the week before to attend to some urgent matter on one of his estates, so she was quite taken aback when he walked up to her and bowed. "Good evening, Miss Grantham. You look as charming as ever."

The blood rushed to her cheeks. "How do you do, Lord Castleroy? I thought you were still out of Town."

"I returned this morning to lend Anne my support at her first London party. My sister has always been disconcerted by large groups of people, preferring more intimate gatherings. However, the London Season precludes this to a large extent."

"Indeed. It is not quite the setting for those of us with more retiring natures."

He bent his head, studying her with an inquiring light in his eyes. "Your nature might be retiring, Miss Grantham, but your appearance is most definitely not. The elegance of your dress must always bring you attention."

"Oh!"

He smiled as he took her arm to move her out of the way of a large lady barreling toward Lady Longmore, who stood nearby in conversation with their hostess. "I have been wondering how you reconcile these two competing aspects of your character—dressing so fine while simultaneously wishing to retire into a corner in crowded places."

Thea adjusted her spectacles as the stout matron with her disconcertingly booming voice halted beside Lady Selby and began speaking to her, drowning out all the voices around her. "How do I reconcile them, my lord?"

"Indeed."

She gave his question careful consideration. "I think it has something to do with my appreciation of beauty. I see lovely clothes as works of art as I know how many hours have gone into their construction. I appreciate their workmanship and wear them almost as . . . well . . . a celebration." Her lips curved ruefully. "Or perhaps it is just that I love pretty things."

"Mm. Something else we have in common."

She shot him a suspicious look, and her color rose again at the unmistakable gleam in his blue eyes. The man put her out of all countenance. "Are you pleased to be back in London, my lord?" she said in a hurry.

"I am. I have no desire to fly from 'the city's empty soul and shimmer' at present." He drew her a little to one side, lowering his voice. "Probably because the friendships I am forming here are not false."

Anne and Mrs. Worrell came up to them at this moment, for which Thea was supremely grateful. It meant she did not need to respond to the baron's disconcerting statement. However, as she asked Anne how she was feeling, another part of Thea's brain mulled over Lord Castleroy's behavior. He was making his intentions crystal clear, as no gentleman would speak thus to an unmarried lady if he were not serious about pursuing a permanent connection with her.

Anne turned to Thea as Lord Castleroy engaged his cousin in conversation.

"I plan to attend a lecture at the Royal Institution later this week given by William Thomas Brande," the younger girl said. "Would you care to join me, Thea?"

"I should like that. Grandmama has given her permission for me to attend the lectures."

"Oh, good! It will feel like old times in Bath. I was sorry not to finish the course of lectures at the Chemical Institution."

Thea lifted her shoulders, smiling. "Fortunately, we have the lectures at the Royal Institution to look forward to."

Lord Castleroy turned his head. "You will be joining us, Miss Grantham?"

"Yes, indeed, my lord. I wouldn't miss it for the world." Thea opened her mouth to speak again but closed it abruptly when she met Sir Percival Ponsonby's eyes over the baron's shoulder. He had just stepped away from Lady Selby and made his leisurely way to them now. "Miss Grantham, I am honored to meet you again." He bowed. "Your servant, Mrs. Worrell, Miss Pellier." He paused a moment and then drawled, "Castleroy."

If Thea were conducting a chemistry experiment, she would note the spontaneous formation of electricity in the atmosphere. The air virtually crackled with it as Sir Percival's gaze swept them all, his brows raised superciliously. However, after a moment, his regard became fixed on Thea's silver scarf. "You have a fine taste in silk, Miss Grantham. Is that French or Italian?"

Thea caught her breath at the intrusiveness of his question. "Neither, my lord. This scarf is of English origin."

He raised those brows again. "Not originally."

"No, but then no silk is originally from England as our climate does not support the cultivation of silkworms, does it?" Her voice was gentle. "I believe raw silk is imported to Britain from Italy, the Ottoman Empire, and the Mediterranean region, but I have no way of knowing from which part of the world this particular silk originated."

Sir Percival leaned back on his heels. "I believe you have misunderstood my meaning, madam. I am not speaking of the origin of the raw silk imported for British manufacturers but rather finished silks which come to our shores in rather . . . er . . . creative ways." His gaze returned to her scarf. "As an arbiter of fashion, I can assure you that your scarf did not come from England's green and pleasant land."

Thea was about to respond when Lord Castleroy spoke, "I believe Lady Longmore is trying to attract your attention, Miss Grantham."

She looked over Sir Percival's shoulder to see that her grandmother was indeed looking around the room, presumably for her. However, Sir Percival was obscuring her from view. "If you would excuse me, sir," she murmured before sweeping the rest of the assembled group with a smiling glance and stepping away.

"Ah, there you are, my love," Grandmama said as Thea approached her. She stood beside a bespectacled young man with a serious demeanor. "I'd like to introduce Mr. Frederick Fotherby to you. He is the younger brother of my godson, Sir Charles Fotherby, and is also recently arrived in London. Frederick, my granddaughter, Miss Grantham."

"It is a pleasure to make your acquaintance, ma'am," he said, bowing.

As Thea rose from her curtsey, she made a careful study of Mr. Fotherby. Alexandra had spoken with great fondness of Sir Charles, who had recently married Stanford's sister, Lady Letitia, describing him as the most gentlemanly of gentlemen. Mr. Fotherby, with his diffident manner and shy smile, seemed to be cast in a similar mold.

"Mr. Fotherby shares your love of chemistry, Dorothea," her grandmother continued. "When I informed him that you and Miss Pellier were planning to attend some lectures at the Royal Institution, he very kindly offered to accompany you."

"How lovely." Thea smiled at him before turning to her grandmother. "I believe Lord Castleroy will be escorting his sister, Grandmama."

"Excellent. A party of four will be ideal. I know many mothers and daughters attend the lectures without a male escort, but I shall feel more at ease knowing that Frederick is with you."

"Have you attended any of the lectures before, Mr. Fotherby?" Thea asked.

"I have. I am also a member of the Royal Society."

"My father was a member of the Society." Thea sighed. "It is a pity that ladies are not allowed to join it. But thankfully, we are encouraged to attend the lectures at the Royal Institution."

Lady Longmore nodded. "Your father told me, Dorothea, that it was Sir Humphry Davy who encouraged female participation at the Royal Institution, although he was criticized for it in some quarters."

Mr. Fotherby spread open his hands. "Well, I, for one, am most grateful for Sir Humphry's inclusion of women in his lecture room as the lady author of *Conversations on Chemistry* was my first instructress on the subject. Her book is an excellent guide for all beginners, not just female students, and had she not attended the lectures, we would not have had the benefit of her teaching. Have you read *Conversations*, Miss Grantham?"

"Yes, indeed. It is an excellent piece of work, and it is one of the reasons I became interested in chemical science."

"May I ask what your other reasons were, ma'am?"

Thea glanced at her grandmother, but when she merely gave an encouraging nod and not the reproving frown Thea half-expected, she carried on. "Well, my father was a chemist and instructed me in the subject. He attended quite a few of Sir Humphry's demonstration lectures. He told me that crowds of up to a thousand gathered at times to hear him speak."

Mr. Fotherby inclined his head. "I was a member of one of those crowds as a schoolboy when my brother took me along, so I can vouch for Sir Humphry's brilliance." A sudden smile lit up his pleasant features. "And last night, I was fortunate enough to experience the next best thing to personal instruction from the great man. His latest paper, an interesting account of the formation of mists, was read aloud at a meeting of the Royal Society."

"Oh! That must have been so interesting." Thea frowned a little. "I heard that Sir Humphry is abroad at present?"

"He wrote this paper when he was in Rome, but I am unsure if he is still there."

"Well, I hope Mr. Brande's lectures at the Institution will prove to be as interesting as Sir Humphry's."

Lord Castleroy came into Thea's line of vision at that moment, stopping beside her.

"Fotherby," he said with a nod.

The younger man bowed just as Lady Longmore said, "I believe you have agreed to accompany your sister to the Royal Institution later this week, my lord? I have asked Mr. Fotherby here to take Dorothea."

"We could make up a party, ma'am, as my cousin, Mrs. Worrell, also wishes to attend the lecture. Will you be joining us, your ladyship?" he asked politely.

"Oh, dear me, no!" Grandmama looked horrified. "Chemistry holds very little interest for me. I leave that sort of scientific endeavor to my granddaughters." She cleared her throat. "I must say that it is a relief that Dorothea has made the acquaintance of gentlemen who do not view her interest in the subject with disapproval."

Lord Castleroy gave a small bow. "Miss Grantham puts many gentlemen to shame with her knowledge of natural philosophy. It is a pleasure to engage in conversation with her."

"My granddaughter shared her brother's lessons to great effect. Possibly to *too* great an effect," she said dryly.

The baron laughed. "Well, I, for one, admire her superior understanding."

"Something for which I am most grateful, Lord Castleroy. It

quite sets my mind at rest that my granddaughter can pursue her interests in London in the company of fellow enthusiasts." Her gaze settled on Thea. "Although, as I have told her, it can only play a small part in her life now. The Season, once it is in full swing, has a way of swallowing up all one's spare time."

"Indeed." The baron looked around Lady Selby's crowded drawing room. "The *ton* is back in force tonight." He paused before saying quietly, "'All the world's a stage, And all the men and women merely players.' *En avant.*"

CHAPTER SEVENTEEN

THEA LOOKED AROUND the lecture room in the Royal Institution, amazed at the variety of people in the audience. Grand ladies and gentlemen rubbed shoulders with mothers admonishing their children to be quiet, while several women with a distinct air of the bluestocking about them were interspersed amongst flamboyantly-dressed dandies and more soberly clad men of scholarly appearance. It truly was a heterogeneous group of people.

Thea froze when her gaze rested on Sir Percival Ponsonby, but fortunately, he wasn't looking in her direction, and she quickly turned her head away. She hoped he wouldn't spot her in the crowd.

She sat between Mr. Fotherby and Miss Pellier, whom she had introduced upon her arrival in Albemarle Street, while Lord Castleroy and Mrs. Worrell took their places on the other side of Miss Pellier. As they waited in the steeply-sided hall for the lecture to begin, Mr. Fotherby informed Thea that the large establishment also consisted of a library, a laboratory, and various other rooms reserved for scientific purposes.

Thea listened to her companion's easy conversation and interspersed the odd comment here and there as she waited for Mr. Brande to make his appearance. Eventually, a dark-haired, neatly dressed man of about thirty walked into the hall and took his place standing behind the sizeable wooden desk in the center of the platform.

He waited for the murmuring of the crowd to settle down before starting his lecture: "Our topic today is an analysis of the oxidation of iron, which is a metal that has been in use since ancient times." He went on to give a detailed explanation about this chemical process, dwelling specifically on how to create a dye known as Prussian blue.

Thea listened closely to the rest of the lecture, taking copious notes. A feeling of excitement settled over her as she recalled the splendor of the Prussian blue paper-hangings in the drawing room in Bath. If she could experiment with the ingredients which constituted this unique shade of blue, she could attempt to stain white silk with the dye.

As Thea looked down the row, she encountered Lord Castleroy's bright blue eyes. She half-smiled at him before gazing in dismay at the man seated beside him, who had fallen asleep and was actually snoring! When Thea gave further study to the occupants in the hall, she spotted quite a few gentlemen who had nodded off during the lecture while a fair number were engaged in taking snuff, perhaps in a feeble attempt to ward off sleep. Certainly, the loud snort the gentlemen in the row across from her made as he breathed in the powdered preparation of tobacco from his snuffbox was loud enough to startle him to greater wakefulness, as well as several of his neighbors slumbering beside him.

In stark contrast, the women in the lecture hall listened attentively to Mr. Brande, and many ladies were taking notes.

Thea was still puzzling over the different responses between the male and female members of the audience as she left the hall after the lecture ended. She became separated from Mr. Fotherby in the press of people, and as Thea stepped into the corridor she looked around in vain for him. Therefore, she was relieved when she spotted Lord Castleroy a short distance away.

"The others have already left the building, Miss Grantham,"

he said, coming up to her. "I am afraid my sister becomes anxious in crowds, and she escaped immediately. Fotherby and Mrs. Worrell accompanied her."

"Oh, poor Anne. A crowd like this can be overwhelming."

"Indeed, and Anne is not accustomed to being in the company of so many people." He offered his arm. "Did you enjoy Brande's lecture?"

"I did, thank you," she said, placing her hand on his sleeve. "But I was quite shocked to see how many gentlemen fell asleep! Why come to a lecture like this if you have no interest in paying attention? I only saw ladies taking notes."

Lord Castleroy drew Thea out of the way of a couple of schoolgirls making straight for them, their heads bent low. "I'm afraid there is a prevailing attitude that men do not need to take notes in public lectures because if they are serious men of science, they should already be familiar with the subjects taught to women and children. And the men who do not have any scientific inclinations will naturally evince unconcern about the content of the lectures, as their primary reason for attending the Royal Institution is not to learn but to see and be seen. The Institution is considered a fashionable venue in many circles."

Thea shook her head as she looked around the congested area. "I find it strange that some people perceive scientific matters as entertainment."

He nodded at the fashionably dressed ladies, fops, and dandies milling about, looking very much as if they were on the strut in Hyde Park. "It is well known that *ton*-ish people attend the lectures to discover new theories to introduce at their next *conversazione*. The Institution is a place of amusement for many rather than one of serious learning."

Thea stared up at him. "But the content of Mr. Brande's lecture was excellent. In fact, I have taken extensive notes as I wish to make Prussian blue dye at home."

The baron shepherded her through the throng of people. "Most of the lectures are of a very high standard. However, the

Institution has become a victim of its own popularity. Because it is now depicted as a place of fashion, any serious-minded men and women who attend the lectures to gain learning are dismissed as having the same shallow interest in scientific subjects as the more frivolous subscribers."

As Lord Castleroy ushered her through the door, Thea stepped out into the sunlight and came face to face with Sir Percival Ponsonby, speaking to Miss Pellier. The baronet's eyebrow rose exaggeratedly high as he studied the notebook in Thea's hand.

He bowed. "Do I behold a scientific lady?"

"Sir Percival." Thea dipped into the briefest of curtseys.

The baronet nodded at Lord Castleroy before returning his attention to Thea. "How diligent of you to take notes, Miss Grantham."

Not caring for the ironical note in his voice, Thea gave a tiny shrug. "They can prove useful when one wishes to recall the content of a lecture."

"And why should a young lady wish to recall such tedious information?" A nasty little smile played about his thin lips.

"Oh, a passing fancy, no doubt." She refused to give him the satisfaction of reacting to his jibes.

His brows drew together, but a gentleman exited the Royal Institution and hailed him at that moment, and Thea moved away with Miss Pellier and the rest of their party.

Miss Pellier looked over her shoulder and shivered as they walked to their carriages. "Sir Percival recognized me from that visit he paid Father before he died. I don't care for him at all. He has such a sneering manner."

Lord Castleroy frowned. "It is best that you avoid him if you can."

Miss Pellier grimaced as she stopped in front of the Castleroy carriage. "I fully intend to."

Mr. Fotherby had brought Thea to the Royal Institution in his curricle. Her grandmother's home was only a short distance from

Albermarle Street—not even half a mile. So when Mr. Fotherby had offered to drive her to the lecture, Thea had taken her courage in her hands and accepted his invitation. Noticing the open equipage, the baron came to an abrupt halt.

"You came in Fotherby's curricle, Miss Grantham?"

She gave a slight nod.

He took a step closer and lowered his voice. "Were you all right?"

Thea glanced at the younger man, who was taking his leave of Miss Pellier and Mrs. Worrell, before turning back to the baron. "I managed. But I felt somehow safer with you holding the ribbons." She sighed. "However, I must grow accustomed to driving with other gentlemen."

"Must you?" His voice was teasing, but the expression in his eyes was not. The combination caught her off guard.

"I . . ." She swallowed, unable to think of a thing to say.

Lord Castleroy drew her to one side as the silence stretched between them. "I have been meaning to discuss something with you, Miss Grantham. May I call on you tomorrow morning? Perhaps we could walk in the garden in Berkeley Square. It might be easier to speak there uninterrupted."

When she hesitated, he gave her his slow smile. "A footman will accompany us, of course."

Pulling herself together, Thea inclined her head. "Very well, my lord."

"Excellent. I have already waited too long to speak to you."

Mr. Fotherby came up to Thea then and handed her up into his waiting carriage. She murmured her goodbyes to the Castleroy party before settling back in the seat. Her stomach gripped in fear as she waited for Mr. Fotherby to climb up beside her, but she clasped her hands in her lap and stared straight ahead.

As Lord Castleroy had said, it helped to keep her eyes open. When she shut them tightly, she imagined all sorts of horrendous obstacles thrown in their path. But when she was able to see the way forward, it lessened her fear of the unknown.

Perhaps this was, in some odd way, a metaphor for life. Refusing to see the road ahead had kept her trapped in a prison of fear for years and years.

It was a sobering thought.

CHAPTER EIGHTEEN

THEA STUDIED HER shoes with great concentration as she waited in the drawing room for Lord Castleroy, frowning as she considered the tips of her slippered toes. Usually, when a gentleman requested a private audience with a lady, it was to make her an offer of marriage. Since his arrival in London, Lord Castleroy had made it clear he was courting her. But, until now, Thea had avoided thinking about a possible proposal from him. Instead, whenever the idea crept into her mind, she cast it aside, not wishing to engage with the prospect. However, now it loomed large before her, bearing down upon her with the greatest of weight.

Her feelings for the baron were conflicted. She found him attractive, but his company never failed to disturb her so profoundly that she wished to run for cover after their encounters. Her desire for a peaceful life devoid of deep emotion was still paramount. And although she liked Lord Castleroy, she did not like how he made her feel. He constantly challenged her, chipping away slowly, relentlessly at her defenses. She released her breath slowly. Had he done so with a blunt-edged instrument, she would have dismissed him without a second thought. However, Lord Castleroy had used a more dangerous weapon to break through her walls—one of sympathy, chivalry, and kindness. And it had utterly disarmed her.

First, he offered his friendship, and then, when she had been in desperate need of help, he stepped in with practical assistance. Thea had felt his lordship's support over these past few weeks like a firm hand beneath her elbow, and it had enabled her to surmount the terror which seemed set to dash her grandmother's hopes for her Season before it had even begun.

And without realizing it, Thea had slipped from a state of wariness into an easy relationship with the baron that she would most definitely miss if she were to lose it. But lose it she must if his lordship made her an offer of marriage today. Her fear of falling in love was even greater than her fear of driving in open carriages. Both involved being open to the unknown and breathing air that quickened your senses as the wind rushed past, pinkening your cheeks, and making you come startlingly to life.

But both were full of risk. Even the risk of the carriage still unsettled her, as accustomed to it as she'd grown. The risk of love was infinitely more dangerous, and she couldn't contemplate opening herself up to such an uncertain state. Not now, not when she had finally won such hard-earned peace of mind. Her grip on life was firmer now after years of struggling in sinking sands that threatened to drag her into an abyss from which she would never arise.

Why would she wish to open herself up to renewed uncertainty? A connection with Lord Castleroy would mean deep involvement of mind, body, and soul. She could not contemplate making herself so vulnerable to him—not after finally, desperately gaining her balance.

Perhaps she was a coward, shrinking from life. But she would rather be a coward and in control than risk all on the unpredictability of human relationships. She liked to feel the ground firmly beneath her feet, and falling in love was more like walking on air. And she wasn't the floating type.

The drawing room door opened at that moment, and Leighton ushered Lord Castleroy inside. The baron walked a few paces inside and bowed. "Good day, Miss Grantham. Ready for our walk?"

Thea picked up her bonnet, which lay on the sofa beside her, and tied the strings under her chin. "I am now," she said, trying to inject a brisk, businesslike note into her voice. However, the sound that emanated from her throat sounded more like the squawking of a dying duck, and she winced. This didn't bode well.

When they entered the hallway, she placed her hand on Lord Castleroy's arm, and he escorted her outside. He must have had a word with Leighton as Simon, the second footman, walked on ahead and unlocked the garden gate before stepping back to allow them to pass.

Lord Castleroy led her onto the path under the plane trees, and they strolled along, with Simon following at a discreet distance. They finally halted at a statue of a man on horseback, and the baron indicated a nearby bench. "Would you care to sit here, Miss Grantham?"

She sat down and contemplated the magnificence of the statue. "Do you know who this is meant to be?"

"King George III romanticized as Marcus Aurelius." He took his seat beside her.

"Ah. I haven't ventured this far into the Square's garden before, so it is the first time I have seen it."

"One man masquerading as another. Something I am not unfamiliar with."

Thea frowned as she turned slightly in his direction. "What do you mean?"

His expression was unusually somber. "I wish to speak to you about my grandfather's silk mill."

"Oh?" She couldn't keep the surprise out of her voice.

He stretched his arm along the back of the bench, frowning. "Our association with a silk mill is not something Anne and I discuss in polite circles. My sister is aware that doing so could affect her chances of contracting an eligible alliance." He turned to look at her, but it was as if he didn't see her. "When my father died a few years ago, I inherited part of my grandfather's mill—the portion that had been my mother's which had transferred to my father upon her marriage. We had never communicated with my mother's side of the family, as my father cut off all contact after their marriage. I knew it grieved my mother, but she was helpless to do anything about it while he was alive." He paused for a moment. "When I learned of my inheritance upon my father's death, I paid my grandfather a call. His two sons had died, and he was trying to manage the mill alone during a very bad time." He stared straight ahead, deepening the line between his brows. "Since the war, the silk industry in Macclesfield has been in a slump, and my grandfather was concerned about the livelihood of his mill workers. He appealed to me for help. And so, I set about trying to assist him with the business even though it would have made my father turn in his grave. I also took my mother and Anne to see him, and they spent a deal of time with him before her death."

"I am glad your mother saw her father again," Thea said quietly. "I don't like to speak ill of the dead, my lord, but how terrible that your father cut your mother off from her own family."

"My father needed my grandfather's money to save his estate from his gambling debts. However, he did not wish our noble name to be associated with trade." His tone was somewhat ironic.

Thea shook her head. "It always surprises me how Polite Society tolerates certain vices. Losing a fortune at the gambling tables is perfectly acceptable to the *ton*, but working for your living is not. It is an odd scale of values."

"Indeed. My grandfather thought he was doing right by my mother when he consented to her marriage as he believed she was marrying well. But she was never entirely comfortable with her position in Society and retreated to the country." His jaw tightened. "My mother took more interest in her children than most aristocratic ladies do, and in one area, she was adamant. She refused to send me to Eton until I was fourteen. She valued her family relationships above anything, and I can see in many ways that I was not brought up like my peers."

"Which is why you feel that you are one man masquerading as another."

"Yes." He massaged the back of his neck before turning to her. "Which brings me to what I wish to discuss with you, Miss Grantham." He paused. "I need your help. My grandfather provides employment not only for his mill workers but for women and children in Macclesfield, who wind and twist silk in their homes. Entire families are employed in doubling and weaving the silk before it's returned to the mill in its full-weight form. And, as handlooms surpass power looms for more delicate fabrics, my grandfather also employs outworkers to make these intricate pieces on their looms."

He sighed. "But since the war ended, the silk industry in Macclesfield has declined. As a result, there isn't enough work, and some families have sunk into poverty." He rose to his feet and walked a short distance away before turning back to look at her, his gaze steady. "My grandfather has a dyeing shed attached to his mill. If we patent the staining techniques you use, local embroiderers could finish the stained silk items from their cottages, and the silk products could be sold from my grandfather's shop in the Burlington Arcade, which is about to open."

Thea gazed at Lord Castleroy in silence. Eventually, she opened her mouth before shutting it again. "I don't know quite know what to say, my lord."

He stepped closer. "You don't have to give me your response now. But please take the time to consider my plan."

"When did you first come up with the idea?"

He sat beside her again. "In Bath. When I discovered that you had stained and embroidered your shawls, I realized the commercial possibilities of your work."

"Oh." For some reason, Thea felt as if a boulder had hit her. Suddenly, she saw every encounter they had ever had through a different lens.

"You have had this idea in mind for a while, then." Her voice was flat.

He bowed. "When I returned to Macclesfield, my grandfather told me about the dire situation of his workers. He is a non-conformist, a Methodist, and has strong ideas about serving the poor. He asked for my assistance."

"Ah." Thea swallowed. "And our . . . friendship, my lord? What of that?" She tilted her head to one side.

His eyebrows drew together as he searched her face. "Our friendship is a completely separate matter, my dear."

"I see," Thea murmured. But her stomach coiled into a tight knot as she looked away.

His revelation put a completely different complexion on things.

CHAPTER NINETEEN

JAMES REALIZED HIS mistake too late. He had been so focused on outlining his idea to help his grandfather that he hadn't thought about how Thea might interpret his actions. James had decided to court his love slowly and with care, as she was clearly not of a mind to accept a proposal from him at present. Therefore, he had decided to wait until later in the Season, when he could be more sure that she reciprocated his affection, before asking for her hand in marriage. But the guarded expression on her face revealed she believed he had been paying attention to her only because he wanted her expertise to register his patent.

His suspicions were confirmed when Thea rose to her feet and, without looking in his direction, said in a low voice, "I should like to return home now."

Her voice sounded formal, and she refused to meet his eyes when he stood. And, although she placed her hand on his proffered arm, she made vague replies to his attempts at conversation as he led her back along the path. Then, as the gate came into sight, she quickened her pace, clearly in a hurry to get away.

Lady Longmore's footman followed close behind them, and soon they were back at the house.

"May I take you driving in the Park tomorrow?" James asked as the front door swung open.

She met his gaze fleetingly. "Very well. I shall give your proposition some thought and let you know my decision."

"Thank you." He frowned. "I'm afraid—."

But he never finished the sentence. Lady Longmore entered the hallway, and Thea moved away with a bright smile that didn't quite reach her eyes. "Goodbye, Lord Castleroy."

He wanted to talk to her, to reassure her that his offer of friendship had not been clouded with ulterior motives. However, after a smiling look in his direction, Lady Longmore began speaking to her granddaughter about an engagement they were due to attend later in the day, and the moment was lost.

With a brief bow in the ladies' direction, he took his leave and descended the stairs. He would have to wait until tomorrow to clear things up.

When James called at Longmore House the next day, Thea appeared even more distant. She allowed him to hand her up into the curricle, but she did not speak until they entered the Park. Not that this was unusual for her. When he took her for a drive, she usually sat immobile, striving, no doubt, to keep her composure. A short while later, James drew the curricle to a halt and handed over the ribbons to his groom. "Let us walk on the grass, Miss Grantham, so you can be more comfortable."

He helped her down from the conveyance and studied her aloof features before tucking her hand into his arm. After walking a little way, Thea came to a halt and turned to face him, dropping her hands to her side. "My lord, I have given your idea careful thought, and I am afraid I have some reservations. I brought a copy of Elizabeth Fulhame's book to London as I still use it for my experiments. In the introduction, she states that she published this record of her work to prevent others from plagiarizing it. She also states that she wished to apply for a patent but never attempted it as she believed it would be in vain. I am not sure why, though. Do you have any idea?" She raised her fine brows in query.

He nodded. "In general, registering a patent in England can

be a long and difficult process. But I have high hopes of succeeding as my grandfather has registered one in the past."

"Oh. I see." Her brow wrinkled as she opened her reticule and drew out a slip of paper. She glanced up at him. "I wrote Mrs. Fulhame's exact words down to share with you. May I?"

At his nod, she studied the page in her hands before saying in a clear voice: "'I publish this essay in its present imperfect state, in order to prevent the furacious attempts of the prowling plagiary, and the insidious pretender to chymistry, from arrogating to themselves, and assuming my invention, in plundering silence: for there are those who, if they cannot by chymical, never fail by stratagem and mechanical means, to deprive industry of the fruits, and fame, of her labors.'" She raised her eyes, meeting his gaze. "This clearly indicates Mrs. Fulhame's opinion on people who might attempt to take credit for her work."

He frowned. "I assumed Mrs. Fulhame had died as she published this essay many years ago and hasn't published anything since."

"Her book was published in 1794, not so long ago. Five and twenty years, in fact." Thea opened her reticule and placed the page back inside. Then, after fiddling with the strings, she hung the small bag over her wrist once more. "I shall only entertain your request, Lord Castleroy, if you promise to investigate what has become of Mrs. Fulhame. If she is still alive, you will need her permission to proceed, not mine."

"You are correct, Miss Grantham. I should not have assumed that she had died. I shall make inquiries."

Thea released her breath in a puff. "Thank you, my lord. I was concerned you might be offended by my suggestion."

Raising his brows, he murmured, "Mercuriality is not one of my faults, Miss Grantham."

"No." She inhaled deeply. "If I were to compare you to a metal, it would certainly not be mercury."

His lips twitched. "I am intrigued as to what metal it might be."

Flushing a little, she pressed her lips together. "That remains to be seen, my lord."

"Indeed." He studied her shuttered face for a moment. "Would you care to walk on?"

She nodded and placed her hand on his arm. But, as they strolled along, she made somewhat stilted remarks in response to his conversational gambits. The ease between them was gone. James had been making slow and what he hoped was steady progress in his attempts to win her love. Yet now, her smile was a social mask as opposed to the spontaneous expression of warmth he had seen on recent occasions.

He was a fool not to have realized the possible interpretation she might give to his proposed plan. But unfortunately, he had limited time to accomplish his aims, as the people in Macclesfield were suffering, and he had not wished the grass to grow under his feet while seeking a solution.

But now, singularly aware of his misstep, he needed to think carefully about how to regain the ground he'd lost. He suspected, though, that mere words would not reassure Thea. Instead, he would have to show her in some other way that his attentions had been sincere. But how?

He looked up and frowned when he saw Sir Percival approaching them, a woman on his arm. Lady Dedham. Like Sir Percival, the viscountess was eager to set the *ton* on fire with her sartorial choices. But as Lord Dedham rarely came to Town, preferring to remain on his estate in the wilds of Yorkshire, his wife came to London without him, and Sir Percival was her cicisbeo of choice.

"My dear Castleroy." Sir Percival bowed. "And your ever charming companion." He turned to the viscountess. "May I present Miss Grantham to you, Lady Dedham?"

The older woman, dressed in shades of purple and lavender with an enormous poke bonnet perched upon her head, pursed her lips. "Miss Grantham. How delightful." She darted a look at her escort before returning her attention to Thea. "Sir Percival told me about your unique taste in scarves, Miss Grantham." Her gaze swept Thea's person from head to toe before settling unswervingly on her silk fichu, with its pattern of blue spots bordered with orange and purple. She took a step closer, her winged eyebrows snapping together. "What an unusually colored fichu, my dear. Patterned silk?"

James felt Thea stiffen beside him, but she merely curtseyed and made a non-committal sound that he didn't quite catch.

The viscountess wagged her finger at Thea. "Naughty, naughty, Miss Grantham! Have you been near an Indiaman recently?"

Thea gazed at Lady Dedham in silence. "I have no idea what you mean, your ladyship."

"Oh, I think you do, my dear!" The older woman gave a throaty laugh. "And rest assured, I don't blame you for being tempted. Imported India silk handkerchiefs can be made into the most beautiful fichus."

"I don't have any knowledge of East India silks, Lady Dedham."

Sir Percival flicked a speck of dirt off one of his enormous sleeve cuffs. "Oh, dear, oh dear. Our young lady is determined to be coy." The baronet proceeded to scrutinize the delicate silk fabric covering the upper part of Thea's chest. James gritted his teeth, resisting the urge to plant the other man a facer for the insolent nature of his appraisal.

"Would you care for a short lecture on East India silk, Miss Grantham?" the baronet continued with his thin smile. "As I recall, you are interested in . . . er . . . lectures."

"Another time, Ponsonby," James cut in. "I need to return Miss Grantham to her grandmother's house."

"Ah, yes. The estimable Lady Longmore." Sir Percival's lips curled. "Her ladyship has always appeared the soul of respectability. But I suppose temptation can strike us all, even the old and upright. Especially when one wishes to launch yet another granddaughter into fashion. You don't look very much like your older sister, do you, Miss Grantham? Your grandmother is perhaps considering a different approach."

James's eyes narrowed as he felt the muscles in Thea's arm clench. Sir Percival appeared to be baiting her. No other explanation existed for the challenging light in the man's eyes and the sneering expression on his face. It made no sense why the baronet should have chosen to target Thea with his poisonous verbal arrows. There must be something more to the matter. And, frustratingly, until James understood the nature of the other man's remarks, he could do very little to defend Thea. As it was, James felt as if he were stumbling around in the dark.

Thea's voice was composed as she replied, yet James could feel her trembling beside him as she dipped into a slight curtsey. "My grandmother's approach has always been one of love and care. Good afternoon, sir. Your ladyship."

James gave the baronet a cool, measured look, and it was only when Sir Percival broke eye contact that James took his leave of Lady Dedham.

As he led Thea back to his curricle, James frowned at her bowed head. She said nothing as they walked to the carriageway, but when he helped her up into his equipage, her eyes were huge in a face pale with distress.

James set his mouth in a straight line as he climbed into the driver's seat. He was determined to get to the bottom of this.

Chapter Twenty

WHEN THEY RETURNED to Longmore House, Lord Castleroy escorted Thea inside. But he did not take his leave of her. Instead, he asked Leighton, who hovered in the hallway, if Lady Longmore was at home. When the butler indicated that his mistress was in the drawing room, the baron nodded in the direction of the stairway. "I should like to have a word with Lady Longmore, Miss Grantham, if you would care to join us?"

Thea swallowed her annoyance. After that horrid encounter in the Park, she did not wish to converse with his lordship. Instead, she wanted to retire to her room to give Sir Percival's threatening words proper consideration before telling her grandmother about the unpleasant encounter. But now, with Lord Castleroy evidently intent on learning more about the baronet's odd attitude, she was in a quandary. Thankfully, a scandal over Edward Ponsonby's attempt to kidnap Alexandra had been avoided. Yet, it appeared Sir Percival was not averse to hinting at it. He might have mentioned it to any number of people, including Lady Dedham—something which could not be ignored.

So, stifling a sigh, Thea led the way up the stairs to the drawing room, where her grandmother was seated near the window, reading a book. She set the novel down on a rosewood side table upon their entrance and smiled at her granddaughter and Lord

Castleroy. However, the expression on Thea's face must have alerted her to the fact that something was amiss because she sat up in her chair and said, with a quick frown, "Whatever is the matter, my love?"

Thea sat in an armchair across from Lady Longmore while Lord Castleroy walked to the fireplace and stood with his back to it, arms crossed. After glancing at the baron, Thea returned her attention to her relative. "We met Sir Percival and Lady Dedham in the Park, Grandmama. Sir Percival hinted at . . ." She looked at Lord Castleroy and then stopped, gripping her hands together in her lap.

Her grandmother wrinkled her brow. "I don't quite follow you, my love."

"I am afraid Miss Grantham may not wish to speak frankly due to my presence." Lord Castleroy straightened. "However, after witnessing Sir Percival's barely veiled hostility in the Park today, I could not leave Miss Grantham without having a word with you, ma'am. Especially as it was due to me that he was introduced to your granddaughter in the first place." He paused. "Please know, ma'am, that I would be pleased to render any service you may need, especially with Stanford absent from Town."

Grandmama inclined her regal head. "Thank you, Lord Castleroy. How very kind of you." She pressed her lips together, a deep line between her brows. "I had hoped the scandal would not come out, especially as Alexandra is now married to Stanford. But these things have a way of getting about, and I should prefer you to hear the details from me as opposed to someone else if Sir Percival is indeed intent on spreading rumors." She shook her head slowly. "The incident casts Sir Percival's cousin, Edward Ponsonby, in a very negative light, so I do not believe Sir Percival will wish to do anything more than hint at it. But unfortunately, this can sometimes be even more damaging as people tend to fill in the missing details with their imaginations." She waved at the sofa across from the chair where she was seated. "Please do sit down, my lord."

As Lord Castleroy lowered his tall frame onto the seat, Grandmama continued, "Last Season, Edward Ponsonby offered for Alexandra, but she turned him down. However, being in desperate need of funds, he made a plan to kidnap her from Vauxhall Gardens to carry her to Gretna Green to marry her for her fortune. Fortunately, Stanford's tiger recognized my granddaughter and told the duke what he had witnessed, and Stanford rescued her a short while later."

The baron frowned. "I know Edward Ponsonby, and I'm not in the least surprised at his actions. What a terrible ordeal for your family, ma'am."

"It was. Stanford banished Ponsonby to the Continent and told him never to return. I assume he met up with his cousin, who has been living in France these past few years. When I heard that Sir Percival had returned to England, I was most distressed as I know he has a poisonous tongue."

"He will not wish to become an enemy of Stanford by spreading such tales about. Ponsonby may have only been needling Miss Grantham as he knows she is a safe target—guaranteed not to spread what he says any further."

"Indeed," Grandmama said slowly. "Which is reassuring, of course, but most vexing. Such unchivalrous, ungallant behavior shows Sir Percival as a man beneath contempt."

"Yes." Lord Castleroy rose and headed over to the window to stare outside. "I would like to confront him about his ungentlemanly conduct. However, by doing so, I could cause more harm than good as I am not your relation. It is best that he believes the scandal has not spread beyond the family circle."

Grandmama pressed her lips together. "And what of Lady Dedham?"

Lord Castleroy shrugged. "I doubt Sir Percival has told her the full story as it casts his cousin as a villain."

"Let us hope so." Her grandmother tapped the arm of her chair with one beringed finger. "I have often noticed that when one reacts too quickly to a crisis, it can be detrimental. It is better to wait and see what transpires rather than make a grand fuss. I only hope you are correct in your summation of the situation, Lord Castleroy."

"I was at school with Sir Percival, ma'am, so I am familiar with his character. He is the sort of provocative person who thrives on innuendo, spreading seeds of dissent. But he tends to avoid direct challenges. It does not play into his somewhat slippery style."

Thea shivered slightly. "Sir Percival reminds me of a snake with those unblinking eyes and venomous tongue. Even his name is sibilant."

"Unfortunately, he thrives on gossip." Lord Castleroy crossed the room to her, stopping a few feet away. "Try not to allow it to distress you, ma'am."

"I won't."

He studied her, a frown in his eyes. "I must leave now as I wish to set in motion the investigation you requested. I trust it shan't take long."

"I look forward to hearing what you discover, my lord," she said formally.

He bowed then and took his leave. After the door closed behind him, Grandmama's bright gaze alighted on her. "And what investigation is this, Dorothea?"

How best to explain it to her grandmother? The older lady knew little about chemical science and even less about the processes Thea used to stain her silk cloths. She drew in a deep breath. "Lord Castleroy plans to patent Mrs. Fulhame's staining techniques, Grandmama. She is the lady chemist whose experiments I follow. When his lordship learned how I create my shawls, he saw the commercial possibilities of my work, and he asked my permission to patent my technique. However, I informed him that he must discover if Mrs. Fulhame is still alive as she invented all the processes, not me."

"Commercial possibilities?" Grandmama's eyes nearly protruded from her head.

"The silk industry in Macclesfield has been in a slump since the war ended, and so Lord Castleroy's grandfather asked for his lordship's assistance to bring his business about." She lifted her shoulders. "When Lord Castleroy noticed my shawls, he conceived the idea of creating similar items and selling them in his grandfather's new shop."

"His grandfather's *shop*? I have never heard anything more fantastical in my life, Dorothea." She remained silent for a moment. "I believe I shall have a word with Lord Castleroy. You cannot become mixed up in trade."

"Please don't speak to him, Grandmama," Thea said quickly. "Anyone with access to her book can follow Mrs. Fulhame's experiments. If Lord Castleroy discovers her whereabouts, he will deal directly with her. It will have nothing to do with me."

"Hmm. I suppose so. But he has been paying such marked attention to you, and this revelation puts his intentions in doubt." She tapped her finger on the arm of her chair once more. "Although he *does* appear very fond of you, Dorothea." She directed a sharp glance at her granddaughter. "Do you believe him to be sincere?"

Thea shifted in her chair. "He does seem very committed to helping his grandfather."

"Not in regard to his grandfather!" Her grandmother shook her head. "Do you believe him to have been sincere in his interactions with you?

"I don't know what to think."

"Well, give it some thought, my love. Lord Castleroy has been all but haunting our doorstep these past few weeks. I know it was ostensibly to help you overcome your fear of driving in open carriages, but in my experience, men rarely act out of pure altruism in their dealings with young women."

Thea glanced down at her hands. "He offered me his friendship, Grandmama."

Her grandmother opened her mouth and then shut it. "I

suppose friendship is a good place to start an association with a gentleman," she said carefully. "But it rarely ends there, Dorothea. Not during the London Season."

"Yes." She sighed. "I've been reluctant to see that."

The older lady frowned. "Why is that? Surely you wish for marriage?"

"I wish for peace of mind."

Her grandmother tilted her head to one side. "The two are not incompatible, my dear."

"Perhaps not." Thea gave a tiny shrug. "But the road to marriage frequently casts one's feelings into turmoil. I do not wish for that." She swallowed. "I . . . I . . . struggle with that sort of disturbance."

Her grandmother's eyes softened. "I know."

Thea's breath caught in her throat, and she looked away. She had warmed herself at the smoldering coals of Lord Castleroy's friendship while closing her eyes to the danger that they could burst into open flame at any point—or be smothered to death. Either way, this sort of connection with the baron was not feasible.

CHAPTER TWENTY-ONE

THEA REGARDED HER image in the mirror with narrowed eyes. Should she wear her favorite gold shawl to the first ball of the Season? Wary of the attention her silk creations had received from Sir Percival and Lady Dedham, Thea had ceased wearing them. Yet, this evening, when she donned her dress of gold lama net over a white tissue slip embroidered at the hem with gold lama flowers, she knew at once that the golden shawl would finish off the ball gown perfectly.

She nibbled on her lower lip as she continued to study her reflection. And then, lifting her chin, she adjusted her gloves. She would wear it. Why should she allow Sir Percival and his unpleasant companion to frighten her into not wearing her treasured creations?

She turned on her heel and left her bedchamber to meet her grandmother, waiting downstairs in the drawing room for her with Frederick Fotherby.

Grandmama had asked the son of her dearest friend to escort them to Lady Lynmouth's ball in Grosvenor Square, and he smiled now as Thea entered the room, greeting her warmly. A moment later, Leighton announced that their carriage awaited them, and Mr. Fotherby escorted them outside.

When they entered the ballroom fifteen minutes later, Thea gazed at the floors chalked in intricate floral patterns before raising her eyes to the enormous chandelier hanging in the center of the room. This, along with a number of girandoles, lit up the large space, which had been splendidly decorated with flowers and foliage.

As Thea glanced around at the elegantly dressed ladies and gentlemen, it became clear why Grandmama had gone to such lengths to provide her with an appropriate wardrobe. The *beau monde* had come out in force to Lady Lynmouth's ball, and it seemed that everyone was garbed in the finest apparel. To keep up this level of sartorial splendor from day to day must cost a small fortune. No wonder it was so expensive to sponsor a young lady for a London Season!

Thea picked guiltily at a loose thread on her glove. Her grandmother's largesse would be wasted if she did not accept an offer of marriage by the end of the Season. Although she hadn't given much thought to this before, she saw now how wrong it had been to have accepted this financial outlay on her behalf when she hadn't set her sights seriously on finding a husband.

Her thoughts turned inexorably to Lord Castleroy. She hadn't seen him since he assured her he would seek out Mrs. Fulhame. And although Thea hated to admit it, she missed him. She glanced surreptitiously around. Perhaps he was here tonight. It felt like an age since she had last spoken to him, and she was both amazed and disturbed by the unmistakable gap he'd left in her life.

Thea had met up with Anne and Mrs. Worrell for a walk in the Park a few days ago, but Anne had not mentioned her brother except to say that he had left London the week before. Thea, not wishing to appear curious about the baron's movements, had not questioned her friend further, but she was in an agony of suspense as to whether he had found Mrs. Fulhame.

Her gaze alighted on Anne and Mrs. Worrell just before she spotted Lord Castleroy standing a few feet away beside Lord Lynmouth. Her heart began to pound, and she stilled her shaking hands as Mr. Fotherby addressed a comment to her. *He's here!*

He's returned to London. I'll speak to him soon. The thoughts crowded in Thea's head, jostling with one another.

And she realized in that moment she was lost.

She had fallen in love with Lord Castleroy.

Her careful plan to remain aloof from deep emotion had been shattered, and there was no turning back. She could only move forward. But how? Too many chains weighed her down to proceed freely.

A deep voice came from behind her: "Good evening, ladies. Fotherby."

Thea dipped into a curtsey as her grandmother and Mr. Fotherby engaged in civil conversation with Lord Castleroy. But Thea kept her gaze lowered, desperately afraid her face might reveal her secret. But eventually, she had to look up, and when she met his eyes, those blue smiling eyes, her panic calmed, and she knew it would be all right. Somehow it would be all right. The sense of reassurance she always felt in his presence wrapped around her, and she exhaled slowly.

Mr. Fotherby turned to say something to her grandmother, and Lord Castleroy stepped closer. "Miss Grantham. I trust you are well?" The intent way he searched her face showed his question was not just a polite platitude, that he meant it.

Thea nodded, still in a state of tumult, and wondered how she could be so sure of her love for him when she was as yet unsure of his motive for pursuing her.

But, on some level, she did know. And it had nothing to do with reason. Instead, it was something else, an instinctive trust in her bones, a knowledge he would never hurt her. "I am very well, thank you," she replied softly.

"I am glad to hear that." A smile tugged at his lips. "I found her, you know."

"Mrs. Fulhame?"

His smile broadened. "Who else?"

"Oh!" Thea pressed a hand to her chest. "Where, my lord?"

"In London of all places. I left the Capital in search of her after a member of the Royal Institution gave me incorrect information regarding her whereabouts. After traveling around the country on a wild goose chase, I ended up back here. Mrs. Fulhame is living retired from Society in Cheapside. She is eager to meet you."

"You told her about my work?" Thea breathed.

"Of course. She was delighted that a 'fellow mariner,' as she termed it, was continuing on the scientific path she had laid out. May I call on you tomorrow to take you to see her?"

"Yes, please." Thea clasped her hands in front of her. "I never thought I would ever meet my heroine."

"A dream come true, then." He leaned slightly closer. "I hope it is the first of many for you, my dear."

She glanced away only to meet Sir Percival's cold eyes over Lord Castleroy's shoulder. A small smile curled his lips, and Thea averted her gaze. What a pity he was in attendance this evening. As she turned, a sandy-haired young gentleman, neat as a new pin in his evening clothes, approached their party and greeted Mr. Fotherby, who smiled. "Atherton! Wonderful to see you, old chap. Are you still acting as Bakewell's secretary?"

The young man nodded, and Mr. Fotherby introduced him to Thea's grandmother as Mr. Marcus Atherton, the youngest son of one Squire Atherton, who owned the estate neighboring the Fotherby country seat in Berkshire.

"I am acquainted with your mother, Mr. Atherton," Grandmama said with a smile before introducing him to Thea.

The newcomer's gaze became fixated on Thea's shawl as she sank into a curtsey. However, after a moment, he appeared to recollect himself and looked away just as Lord Castleroy stepped to one side to speak to an acquaintance.

Thea sighed. Yet another person who couldn't hide their reaction to one of her shawls. Perhaps she should cease wearing them altogether.

"I hope you find London to your liking, Miss Grantham?" Mr. Atherton said.

"Thank you, sir, I do," she murmured. "It is my first visit to the Metropolis, and I find that there is never a dull moment. I have a score of places I hope to visit."

"Indeed. I have resided in London for over three years now, and I can attest to the fact that there are still several places I have yet to see." His sandy-colored brows drew slightly together. "Although, in general, I favor museums and places of cultural interest more than parties."

Mr. Fotherby shook his head and said in a low voice, "Truth be told, I am surprised to see you at a ball."

His friend grimaced. "A social education is just as important as a cultural one my mother was wont to say. After many years of avoiding the London scene, I have come to realize the truth of that statement."

"Well, I, for one, am very pleased to hear that." Mr. Fotherby grinned. "I've always valued your opinion on all things political, and now I can look forward to some sensible conversation during the social rounds."

Mr. Atherton looked around the crowded apartment. "Quite. I can see that this does not seem like a setting for sober-minded conversation."

When he stepped away a short while later to seek out his partner for the upcoming country dance, Thea said, "What a pleasant gentleman!"

"Atherton's a good chap. He's always wanted a political career and will no doubt go far as he has a good brain and friends in high places, including your brother-in-law, as a matter of fact."

"He knows Stanford?" Thea's eyes widened. "But surely he is much younger than His Grace?"

"The Dowager Duchess of Stanford is Atherton's godmother. She and Mrs. Atherton were childhood friends, I believe."

"Ah." Thea pressed her lips together. "Although London is a large city, the world we move in is very small. Everyone seems to be connected to everyone else."

"Yes. And it's particularly daunting when so many of the

matchmaking mamas have known one since the cradle. Should we join this set, ma'am?"

They walked onto the floor together, and Thea smiled when she spotted Anne with a gentleman she did not recognize. "Oh, there is Miss Pellier!"

Mr. Fotherby followed her gaze before clearing his throat. "I was wondering if I could escort you and Miss Pellier to another lecture at the Royal Institution, Miss Grantham."

"That would be delightful, sir. We both enjoyed the last one. I am sure Miss Pellier would wish to attend another."

"Excellent. I shall broach the subject with her."

The movement of the dance began, and Thea gave her attention to her steps. But, as she progressed down the line, her gaze collided once more with Sir Percival's, who stood to one side, watching her. She shivered a little and glanced away. Something in the way he looked at her made her skin prickle.

When the country dance ended, she was on tenterhooks that the baronet would approach her. However, upon her return to Lady Longmore, it was Lord Castleroy who stepped forward, not Sir Percival, and she accepted the baron's invitation to join the new set with alacrity.

His eyes gleamed as he led her onto the floor. "You are a keen dancer, Miss Grantham? Never before have you accepted one of my invitations with such enthusiasm."

"Er . . ." She raised her eyes to his. "Well, actually . . ."

He sighed. "I knew there would be a 'but.'"

"Not a 'but,' Lord Castleroy. No, indeed! I am truly pleased to dance with you. It is only that . . ." She bit down on her bottom lip. "I am relieved your invitation rescued me from a possible advance from Sir Percival. He keeps looking my way this evening, and I find it most disconcerting."

The amusement faded from his face. "I am sorry he is making you feel uncomfortable. Shall I have a word with him?"

The couple at the top of the set began to dance, and Thea dropped into a curtsey as Lord Castleroy bowed before they progressed down the line. She spoke quietly as they moved closer to complete a figure. "Perhaps it would be best not to say nothing for now. I do not wish to provoke him, and maybe he will leave me alone if I ignore him."

He frowned as he took her hands in his to lead her down the center. "Very well. But I don't like it."

Thea blinked up at him. James's touch was electrifying—like a current shooting straight up her arms. She couldn't get her brain to work.

What a very odd sensation.

Giving a small shake of her head, she attempted to clear her mind, but it did not help at all.

Falling in love was a crazy business.

CHAPTER TWENTY-TWO

LORD CASTLEROY CALLED the following day to take Thea to see Mrs. Fulhame in Gracechurch Street. He drove her there in his curricle, and Thea was so distracted by her recent discovery that she had fallen in love with him that she barely noticed the three-mile journey to Cheapside as her thoughts spun in a hundred different directions.

However, she was brought back to reality with a painful bump when they entered the busy shopping district, and the baron swerved to avoid a gig that veered in front of them.

"I'm sorry about that." He shot a quick look at her, his brows drawn together.

A wave of faintness threatened to engulf Thea, but, gripping her hands together, she managed to ward it off. "It wasn't your fault," she said shakily. "He lost control of his horse."

"Horses often take fright on crowded streets such as these, but fortunately, the risk of a serious accident is small when we're forced to travel at such a snail's pace as this."

"I don't think I shall ever be wholly comfortable with driving in London," she said in a small voice.

"The fact that you are a passenger in an open carriage today in such a chaotic part of London is a testament to your courage. May I tell you how much I admire you?"

He met her eyes fleetingly before returning his attention to the road. Thea sat quietly beside him, heartened by his words, warmed by his sudden smile. How hard it was to resist him.

She frowned down at her hands. Although Lord Castleroy seemed sincere in his affections, a nagging voice of doubt in her head refused to be silenced. Would he have paid so much attention to her had he not been intrigued by her shawls? The baron had noticed her silken creations from the very first day he met her and had pursued her ever since. How likely was it that a handsome man like Lord Castleroy would have developed a *tendre* for such an ordinary damsel as she? It seemed too good to be true.

On the seat beside her, she had brought a selection of her stained silk items wrapped securely in a large woolen shawl. She planned to show them to Mrs. Fulhame. Picking them up now, she placed them securely on her lap as her thoughts turned to how the older lady would receive her samples.

Mrs. Fulhame had written in her essay that the possibility of making cloths of gold, silver, and other metals by chemical processes had occurred to her in 1780. She had spoken to her husband, Dr. Fulhame, and some friends about the project, but it was deemed improbable. However, despite this discouragement, the lady chemist proceeded with her scheme. And after some time, she realized the idea to some degree, using her experiments.

Now, in 1819, nearly forty years later, Thea had followed the steps outlined in Mrs. Fulhame's more successful experiments and, in doing so, created works of art using her scientific principles. A remarkable thought.

Upon entering Cheapside, Thea peered this way and that as she took in her surroundings—a busy shopping district filled with warehouses, fashionable shops, and inviting-looking coffee houses. She turned her head at a strange rattling sound, and her gaze came to rest on the doorway of a shop that was thronged with people. Through the shop's open door, she could see several busts, decorated with patchwork and feathers, that seemed to be dancing atop the rocking beam of a weaver's loom.

A voice rang out: "Here you may be served with all patterns and sizes, from the foot to the head, at moderate prices . . ."

"What on earth are those?" She pointed at the moving figures.

Lord Castleroy glanced at the shopfront and smiled. "That shop is owned by an imaginative hosier named Romanis. He attaches the busts of famous men to the upper parts of the machinery of a loom. Then, when the machine starts working, the figures move back and forth to the rattling sound made by the shuttle."

She craned her neck as they traveled on. "What an ingenious idea! They appear to be greeting passers-by."

Lord Castleroy halted beside a church with a charming steeple. "Bow Church," he said as he handed the reins to his groom. "I'll leave my curricle here as I believe there may be an obstruction ahead. The traffic has come to a complete halt."

He jumped down and walked around the carriage to help Thea alight. Then, after tucking her hand into the crook of his arm, he led her past a bookseller's window, where they waited for some time to cross the street. However, the road was three or four deep in carriages, stuck in what appeared to be a never-ending procession, and it took some time.

Thea was relieved to traverse the busy thoroughfare on foot. Being stuck in his lordship's curricle in this crowd of conveyances would have been a nightmare.

As they left the crush behind them, Lord Castleroy drew to a halt in the street and knocked on the front door of Mrs. Fulhame's house. It swung wide after a few minutes, and a servant ushered them inside. After stepping into a tiny vestibule, Thea and Lord Castleroy were led upstairs to a modest drawing room, where a grey-haired lady sat on an upright chair near the window. When Thea advanced inside, the woman rose to her feet and studied her with bright eyes in a lined face.

"Good day, Mrs. Fulhame," Lord Castleroy said. "May I present Miss Grantham to you?"

As Thea curtseyed, Mrs. Fulhame indicated a couple of arm-chairs. "How pleased I am to meet you, Miss Grantham," she said in a low, pleasing voice. "Lord Castleroy has told me all about your work. Pray sit down."

Thea unwrapped the parcel of shawls and placed them neatly on a nearby table. "I was delighted when his lordship told me he had arranged this meeting with you, ma'am."

Mrs. Fulhame looked down at the table. "These are the silk shawls you made using my experiments?"

At Thea's nod, the older lady slowly shook her head. "Lord Castleroy said they were a sight to behold, and I can see he did not exaggerate."

"Allow me." Lord Castleroy picked up the delicate garments and handed them to Mrs. Fulhame before taking his seat.

Thea held her breath as Mrs. Fulhame examined her crea-tions. Eventually, their hostess held up the fichu Lady Dedham had remarked upon. "I remember this experiment, Miss Gran-tham. Is it not the one where one immerses silk in a solution of nitro-muriate of gold? I was pleased with my results, but yours are even better. These colors are lovely!"

Thea nodded. "It is indeed that experiment. I was surprised when someone recently mistook it for an East India handker-chief."

Mrs. Fulhame stretched her arms out, examining the silk from a distance. "I am not surprised. It is the unusual patterns of the East India handkerchiefs that are so appealing, and this pattern of yours is equally unique." She set the fichu down. "In Asia, they print by hand, you see, and also use a method known as 'tie-dyeing' to create their designs. Consequently, there is a vast difference between East India silk and English silk."

"You are very well-informed about the silk industry, madam," Lord Castleroy said, a faint question in his voice.

Mrs. Fulhame nodded. "I hoped my silk staining methods would achieve commercial success all those years ago. Indeed, my husband, Dr. Fulhame, made inquiries on my behalf and discovered that English silk manufacturers, ascertaining the popularity of contraband East India handkerchiefs in this country, attempted to create similar items on their looms. But the mechanical printing methods they used failed to achieve the same effect. Indeed, their results were only pale imitations of the originals as the patterns they printed were too unvarying and dull compared to those produced by hand."

Thea leaned forward in her chair. "I have enjoyed experimenting with these colors, ma'am, although I must admit that most of my shawls are stained silver or gold. I have only recently started experimenting with color."

"My interest primarily lay in that direction as well." Mrs. Fulhame folded the fichu and set it back on the table before picking up Thea's silver scarf. "How beautifully this has been stained! And the embroidery is exquisite."

The corners of Lord Castleroy's eyes creased as he looked across at Thea. "Miss Grantham has contrived to combine chemistry with artistry."

The older lady nodded. "Indeed. And I once combined chemistry and geography, using my staining methods on maps. The rivers were set in silver while the cities shone in gold. It came out very well, I must say."

"Another good reason to register your patent, Mrs. Fulhame," Lord Castleroy said.

She shook her head. "It is such a difficult process that I have no desire to commit myself to it. Before he died, my husband applied for His Majesty's royal letters patent for his invention of a new method to manufacture lead, but he was unsuccessful." She tilted her head, eyeing Lord Castleroy with a quizzical expression in her eyes. "You are unusual in your support of women in scientific endeavors, my lord. Many of my acquaintance have attempted to blight the unprotected petals of the scientific world rather than help them grow."

Lord Castleroy glanced across at Thea. "Oh, I greatly admire unprotected petals, ma'am, and would never wish to blight any of them."

"A commendable sentiment," Mrs. Fulhame said tartly. "Some men are like mules, inordinately obstinate in their refusal to acknowledge the worth of females attaining knowledge in their preferred area of learning."

The baron raised his brows. "But books like *Conversations on Chemistry*, which a woman wrote, make it quite acceptable—and even encouraged—for women to practice science in these days."

"In the home, perhaps," Mrs. Fulhame said. "However, women are not encouraged to pursue their theories in their chosen scientific field, let alone oppose the opinions of established men of science as I once did."

"You have ceased your chemical science experiments, ma'am?" he asked.

Her face was expressionless. "I am afraid my finances no longer permit me to perform them."

He bowed. "I hope . . . indeed, I insist that you accept financial remuneration for your invention should the submission of the patent prove successful."

Mrs. Fulhame remained silent for a long moment. Eventually, she inclined her head. "Thank you, sir. It means the world to me, especially as you were under no obligation to seek my permission."

"I must admit that it was Miss Grantham who brought it to my attention."

The older lady smiled at Thea. "Thank you, my dear. I tried to steer a female ship for many years upon the choppy waters of masculine selfishness in science. I am pleased now to pass on the navigation of this particular vessel to you."

"I shall do my best to be a trustworthy mariner, ma'am," Thea said gravely.

"Oh, I believe you will be." She smiled at Lord Castleroy. "Particularly with such a trusty Captain at your side."

Thea froze. "Um . . . I—we are not . . . that is . . ."

Mrs. Fulhame glanced from Thea to the baron and then back

again. "Oh! Forgive me, Miss Grantham. I assumed that you and Lord Castleroy were betrothed."

Thea's cheeks warmed. "We aren't."

Mrs. Fulhame folded her hands in her lap. "Ah," was all she said. But somehow, this short word seemed to hold a wealth of hidden meaning.

Thea dared not look at Lord Castleroy. But then, as if drawn by an invisible magnet, she turned her head and met his eyes. And the intense expression in their depths was nearly her undoing. She rose swiftly to her feet and began gathering her shawls together. "Thank you very much for your time today, Mrs. Fulhame. It was an honor to meet you."

Her hostess stood. "Please feel free to visit me at any time, Miss Grantham. I should dearly like to discuss chemistry further with you."

"I would be privileged to do so." Thea stilled and then looked across at Mrs. Fulhame. "Thank you, ma'am. For everything. Your experiments opened up a whole new world to me when I very much needed it."

The older lady smiled. "It is indeed a great pleasure, my dear. Chemistry has always been a source of great joy for me. I am pleased I succeeded in opening up it to you as well."

As Thea left the room with Lord Castleroy, the thought intruded that there might be another source of happiness open to her, a source she hadn't wished to consider before.

She needed to think about it.

CHAPTER TWENTY-THREE

THEA WANDERED DOWNSTAIRS to the library. The warm weather of the day before had given way to a miserable, cold day. Rain splattered on the windows, and the wind howled outside—perfect weather for curling up on the sofa in the library with a good book.

Fortunately, Grandmama had decided to stay at home today rather than venture outside to make morning calls. And so Thea had a free day to slow down from the frenetic activity that had swallowed up all her time over the last few weeks.

She wandered along the library shelves, running her fingertips over the spines of the books, breathing in that familiar scent that belonged only in places where print was on paper. Spotting a book of poetry by Mary Anne Taylor, she removed it from the shelf. When she opened the volume, her gaze came to rest on her mother's name, inscribed on the front page.

Thea pressed her lips together as a wave of emotion swept over her. The little things always caught her off guard, those unexpected moments reminding her of all that had been lost. Like Lord Castleroy's mother, Thea's mama had been fond of Mary Anne Taylor's writing and taught her several of her poems when she was a young girl.

When Mama died, Thea had searched high and low for this book. If only she had known that Grandmama had taken it back to London with her all those years ago!

She took the book of poems over to the sofa and sank against it, staring straight ahead. How strange to hold this volume in her hands again. She remembered her mother smiling at her as she read from its pages. Mama would recite a poem every night to Thea before she went to bed, even if it was only a verse or two. She had treasured this time listening to her mother's lilting voice with its pure, musical quality bringing the words to startling life.

As she paged through the book, she found a sheet of folded paper tucked in between two pages. A letter? Opening it, she smoothed out the edges and saw it was addressed to her mother:

My beloved Elizabeth,

How grateful I am that we can now exchange letters. Our betrothal has brought me a wealth of joy, such that I almost fear for our happiness. Can it be that it rests solely upon the fickle whims of Fate? I am afraid to grasp our love too tightly, fearing it may flitter away as something too perfect for this sorry world.

But let me not dwell on such things. Superstition does not sit well with me, and it is best to walk a confident path, accepting all life has to offer with open hands and with thanks.

Please accept my gift of Reflections *by Mary Anne Taylor. I know she is a favorite of yours. And when you peruse her verses, dwell with joy on these words from "The Dedication to Spring." They encapsulate all that I feel during this, the spring of our love:*

"Joyous Spring, coming with hints of light,
Filling hearts with faith and enduring delight.
Courage reborn, and confidence strengthened,
All hopes renewed as days are lengthened."

With all my love,
Henry

Thea blinked back tears as she set the letter to one side. Her father had loved her mother so much. She read the letter again, this time more slowly. How poignant that Papa had written that he feared for their happiness. A single tear ran down her cheek. Loving someone that deeply meant living on a perpetual knife's edge as your happiness depended entirely on someone else's existence. To make yourself vulnerable in that way, to trust Fate not to steal away the object of your affections—surely it was the hardest of things.

Thea paged absently through the book and stopped when she came upon another poem Mrs. Taylor had written about spring. But this one wasn't joyous. Instead, it was titled "An Elegy to Spring."

How cruel the earliest blossoms fare,
That Spring in vain attempts to spare.
The hope of revival in a heart,
Spent and riven with false start.

Like some wanderer, clothed in sack,
Bent in spirit, curved of back,
The hope of light now washed away,
By driving rain and fading day.

Thea closed the book with a sigh. So often, the first blossoms of spring were destroyed by a sudden cold spell. Although they bravely made their appearance when the seasons changed, it was as if Nature resented these most fragile of flowers and sought to remind them that such delicacy and sensitivity did not belong in such a harsh world.

It was all very well to marvel at the first snowdrops of the season, which seemed to thrive in icy conditions, but other spring blossoms were not as hardy and could not survive the wintry blasts that so often followed the first mild weather of the year.

How did you know which sort of flower you might turn out to be? You could resemble the characteristics of the more resilient snowdrop or be a less hardy plant altogether. Her father had turned out to be the latter and had not endured the frost of his wife's early death. He had been devastated by the loss, giving up his grasp on personal relationships and eventually disappearing into his world of scholarship.

Thea feared very much that she might be just like him. And, if she did share a similar makeup, how could she, in all fairness, inflict herself upon a husband and children?

Papa had recovered some interest in his scientific endeavors after Mama's demise. But it had taken some time for him to regain any awareness of the external world. And he had never fully returned from the distant place he had retreated to, leaving his children to suffer from his state of frozen inertia.

Although Thea had felt the stirrings of hope within her recently, she knew that should she allow Lord Castleroy into her life, there would be no half-measures. He would give much but also ask for much in return. Could she survive being transplanted from her safer, shielded spot to this much wilder setting?

Because he would not allow her to stay uninvolved. That look in his eyes yesterday precluded that. She gave a tiny shake of her head as she tried to assimilate the notion that he appeared to be enamored of her. For so it seemed.

I greatly admire unprotected petals and would never wish to blight any of them.

Those words had been deliberate, the expression in his eyes sincere. Surely he could not have feigned this interest in her? She had pondered his pursuit, suspecting of late that his determination to save his grandfather's mill had prompted his attentions to her. However, it was becoming harder and harder to reconcile this calculating version of Lord Castleroy with the man she was getting to know.

Thea rose to her feet and wandered over to the window, looking out at the rain-soaked Square. She faced a choice at this juncture that would determine the course of the rest of her life. Such an important decision required much rational reflection. She was not of a mind to give in to romantic follies or to pursue silly sentimentality. Instead, she needed the surety that she was equipped to deal with the kind of life she would lead at the baron's side should he offer for her. She had not wished to consider the prospect before, resolutely pushing aside all such thoughts. However, it was not in her nature to venture into unknown territory without some sort of methodology to guide her way.

What sort of chemist would she be if she did that?

She needed to consider all possible outcomes.

Thea might have fallen in love with Lord Castleroy, but love was not enough to create a contented life. In fact, it often had the opposite effect. The memory of Papa's utter heartbreak was seared into her mind, serving as a sad reminder of the transience of life and how nothing was certain. He had indeed been a wanderer, clothed in sack, never fully present in this world ever again. She hoped she wasn't like her father, but she did not know.

She didn't know.

CHAPTER TWENTY-FOUR

Alexandra had written a letter advising Lady Longmore and Thea that she and Stanford would travel to London later than planned as they had been unavoidably delayed at Stanford Court. When they eventually arrived in the Capital at the end of the following week, Alexandra immediately sent a footman to Berkeley Square to advise Lady Longmore of the fact. They brought with them Aunt Eliza, who had been to visit them at the Court and would be stopping for a few nights in London on her return journey to Grantham Place. Although it was already late in the afternoon, Thea begged her grandmother to accompany her to Grosvenor Square.

Hastening ahead of the older lady, Thea entered the elegant drawing room and embraced her older sister. "I'm so pleased you've finally arrived, Alex! It feels like an age since I last saw you. Did you have a good journey?"

"I did, thank you, although traveling always wearies me." Alexandra tilted her head as she considered her sister. "You seem a little pale, dearest. Are you enjoying the Season?"

Grandmama entered the room then at a more stately pace with Aunt Eliza at her side, so Thea did not reply. However, after she had greeted her aunt and inquired after her health, she turned her attention back to her sister.

"Now tell me, dearest," Alexandra patted the space next to

her on the window seat as she resumed their conversation. "Is London to your taste? I've been concerned that you may find it quite chaotic."

Thea pondered the question as she sat down. "Strangely, I haven't found it too overwhelming. It helps that Lord Castleroy and his sister, and Mr. Fotherby all share my interest in chemistry. We've been to the Royal Institution a couple of times to listen to the lectures. And I've even met Mrs. Fulhame, the author of *An Essay on Combustion.* So I have had a delightful time in that regard."

"How wonderful that you met her! What is she like?"

"Very clever and well-informed—particularly in regard to the silk industry." Glancing across at Aunt Eliza, Thea lowered her voice. "Mrs. Fulhame has given Lord Castleroy permission to register a patent for staining cloths with metal salts. He took me to meet her, and I showed her my shawls."

"Oh, Thea. How exciting!" Alexandra's eyes brimmed with enthusiasm. "Stanford mentioned that Lord Castleroy's grandfather owns a mill in Macclesfield in Cheshire. Is that why he wishes to apply for a patent?"

She nodded. "The silk industry in Cheshire has suffered since the war ended, and Lord Castleroy's grandfather hopes to revive it by patenting the technique Mrs. Fulhame pioneered."

"I am so pleased that your hard work is finally being recognized. Will you be involved in the venture?"

"I'm not sure of the finer details. After Lord Castleroy obtained Mrs. Fulhame's permission, he left London for Macclesfield to discuss the project with his grandfather." She glanced across at Lady Longmore. "Grandmama does not wish me to be connected to trade. If I do play a role in this enterprise, it will not be publicly known."

"I am sure Lord Castleroy will wish to consult you about the process. I have read Mrs. Fulhame's book, and her experiments seem somewhat complicated."

"If his lordship employs chemists to do the work, all they will need to do is refer to the silk-staining experiments in Mrs. Fulhame's essay. Lord Castleroy won't need me to advise him."

Alexandra drew her brows together. "I disagree. If it were so easy to refine the process, someone else would have attempted to do so by now. That book was published many years ago."

"Mrs. Fulhame explained to me how resistant some of the men of science were to her original ideas. Perhaps that's why no one has used her experiments for commercial purposes thus far."

Alexandra pulled a face. "I suppose they struggled to take the theories of a scientific woman seriously. Was a paper about Mrs. Fulhame's work ever presented at the Royal Society?"

"In her book, Mrs. Fulhame mentions that there was once a possibility of having a scientific memoir presented to the Society, but events persuaded her not to pursue that method. She published her *Essay* instead."

"Poor Mrs. Fulhame." Her sister sighed. "It seems that she has walked a difficult and unrewarding path."

"Fortunately, Lord Castleroy plans to reward her for her invention should the patent succeed."

Alexandra sat up straighter. "Lord Castleroy has promised to remunerate her? How very good of him!" She paused for a moment. "But then, he is a good man, according to Stanford."

"His Grace appears to be on very good terms with Lord Castleroy."

"They were at Eton together and have been friends ever since. Lord Castleroy has implemented the same methods on his estate that Stanford introduced to bring more prosperity to his tenants. And he is also assisting his grandfather in his endeavors to help the poor in Macclesfield. A gentleman with a conscience." A sparkle appeared in her eyes. "What do you think of him, Thea?"

"I like him very well." Thea folded her hands in her lap.

"And . . ."

"And nothing."

"Hm. I won't press you. But should you wish to discuss his

lordship with me at any time, I have a listening ear. Do remember that."

Aunt Eliza came over at that moment, and Thea sighed in relief when Alexandra gave up her seat to their aunt. Much as she loved her sister, she did not wish to speak to anyone about Lord Castleroy. Not while she was still so unsure of her own mind.

Thea was listening to Aunt Eliza's account about the recent happenings at Grantham Place when the door opened, and the Duke of Stanford entered the room with Lord Castleroy at his side.

Thea's gaze fixed on the baron for a fraught moment before she rose to her feet and curtseyed. In the clamor of greetings, she regained her composure and was calm enough when Lord Castleroy approached her a few minutes later. Aunt Eliza had stepped away to speak to Grandmama, and Thea now stood alone at the window.

"Miss Grantham, how fortuitous to find you here. We are making up a party to Richmond Park tomorrow morning if it is a clear day. Mr. Fotherby wanted to drive my sister there, but I have suggested an aquatic expedition on the Thames to save you the distress of going such a long way in an open carriage. I also have invited Stanford and Her Grace to join us."

"Um, that sounds delightful, my lord." Thea removed her spectacles and began to polish the lenses with a small cloth she withdrew from her reticule. Somehow she felt that if she didn't look at him, he wouldn't be able to see her. Not properly.

A nonsensical notion, of course. But comforting.

Lord Castleroy remained silent for a few minutes before saying softly, "I am sure they're clean by now."

She paused mid-shine. Then, clearing her throat, she popped her glasses back on her nose. Now she was forced to look at him. Holding her breath, she met his amused eyes. How disconcerting he was. She always felt so gauche in his presence, her usual self-possession gone. "Anne mentioned Mr. Fotherby's invitation to Richmond when I visited her yesterday, but she made no mention of your return."

"I wasn't sure when I would be returning to London."

"Ah." Thea began to fiddle with the bridge of her spectacles before forcing her fingers to her side. Her fidgeting was getting out of hand. "Did you have a good trip to Macclesfield, my lord?"

He indicated the window seat, and she sat down. "It was very successful."

"Your grandfather is well?" Her voice came out unnaturally high as he sat beside her. He was so . . . near.

"He is very well. Thank you." Lord Castleroy's voice was grave, but his blue eyes twinkled.

"Good. Good." Thea wracked her brain for something to say. Perhaps it was best to head back to the more stable ground of chemistry. "Is your grandfather in agreement about the patent, Lord Castleroy?"

"He is. We are starting the process of applying for a patent. It can take some time, but we hope to begin manufacturing the stained silk cloths as soon as possible to provide desperately needed employment for the local workers." He drew his brows together. "If you would let me know the more successful of Mrs. Fulhame's experiments, I shall employ chemists to stain the cloth. I only hope they prove to be as competent as you."

"I am sure once the chemists are familiar with the experiments that produce the best results, they will manage very well." Thea raised her shoulders in a small shrug. "I truly believe that if a man had invented this process, it would have become a commercial venture years ago." Thea rested her chin on her hand. "How ironic that in the end, it was I, another lady chemist, who ventured to explore Mrs. Fulhame's experiments."

"Indeed. Something for which I shall forever be grateful. My grandfather's mind has been set at rest, as he is convinced the silk shawls will sell very well in his shop in the Burlington Arcade."

"Even though I cannot mention my involvement in the scheme, my lord, I shall be delighted to see them on sale. Will you take me there?"

"Yes, of course, if you are still in London. It will be some time before they become available. But at least we are starting the process."

Thea swallowed hard at his proximity. And then, as she breathed in his faint scent of sandalwood and soap, her pulse began to race. Such a heady combination. She exhaled slowly.

Her retreat to the safer ground of chemistry was a complete fallacy because quite a different sort of chemistry seemed to be exploding between them, setting in train a chain of reactions she had never expected.

No procedure existed for this.

CHAPTER TWENTY-FIVE

LORD CASTLEROY ARRIVED early the following day for their outing to Richmond Park. "We don't wish to miss the morning tide," he said as he ushered her outside. He indicated a basket in his curricle. "I've brought a cold collation for a picnic at Richmond Hill. And Stanford has arranged a visit to Syon House."

"It sounds delightful, my lord." Thea smiled up at him as he climbed into the driver's seat. Her stomach no longer clenched in fear when she sat beside him in his curricle. The change wrought in her since the start of the Season was profound. She would never have believed it possible to overcome such a deep-seated fear.

When they arrived at the Thames, Lord Castleroy took some blankets and a basket from the curricle and placed them in the boat, where Anne and Mr. Fotherby were already seated. As Thea climbed into the sailing vessel, she wrinkled her nose at the somewhat pungent smell emanating from the river before settling underneath the boat's awning, grateful for the protection. She had never been particularly fond of sitting in direct sunlight. Her skin was too fair.

As they waited for Stanford and Alexandra to arrive, Thea chatted to her friend while Mr. Fotherby conversed with Lord Castleroy. It had become evident over the past few weeks that

Anne was enamored of Mr. Fotherby. And he appeared to return her sentiments as he had asked her to dance with him twice at the last ball they had attended, and he took every opportunity to drive with her in the Park. They had even started attending lectures together at the Royal Institution without always inviting Thea. And, although Thea was delighted for her friend, she also felt a trifle adrift, as if other people were moving onwards with their lives while she remained trapped in limbo. Thea shoved the thought aside with a frown—she was determined to live in the moment today and not dwell on her troubles.

Mr. Fotherby addressed a comment to Anne, and Thea looked away, studying the variety of wherries, barges, and cutters floating on the water. Traffic upon the river rivaled that in the streets of London, but Thea felt much more comfortable here, sitting in a boat. Thank goodness she hadn't needed to brace herself for a long carriage drive. Lord Castleroy had been very thoughtful to consider her wishes by suggesting a boat trip to Richmond instead. She nibbled on her bottom lip. He was always thoughtful.

Alexandra and Stanford joined them then, and after they had settled into the boat, they cast off. Thea looked at the passing scenery and did not participate much in the conversation, happy to be outdoors and away from the constricting confines of city life. She hadn't realized how much she had missed country living. But being on the water now gave her a sense of freedom she had missed these past few months. How she cherished this escape from the formal activities that had consumed her days since the beginning of the Season!

They landed near Richmond Hill, and Lord Castleroy took the picnic basket and the blankets to a nearby group of elms and oaks, which provided some welcome shade. Thea strolled away on the grass with Alexandra and Anne until they came to a wood where deer grazed peacefully. The men, engrossed in a debate about some parliamentary matter, approached them a short while later, and they all returned to the picnic spot.

Thea halted under the trees, her brows raised. Someone had arranged some chairs around a table laid with proper knives, forks, a tablecloth, and even fine linen napkins.

She had assumed they would sit on the blankets the baron had brought along. When she mentioned this to Alexandra, her sister laughed. "That was Castleroy's original plan, but my husband cannot abide lounging on the ground." She nodded at a liveried footman standing nearby. "Stanford arranged for Edmund to set this up."

"How lovely." Anne gazed at the laden table. "Although it is a little chilly under the trees." She removed the fichu Thea had made her from her reticule and, with a slight shiver, placed it around her shoulders.

Thea glanced across at her brother-in-law, who stood in conversation with Lord Castleroy. Dukes lived life on a different plane from the rest of society, it seemed. So much for hoping to escape to a more countrified existence! But as she sat on the chair Lord Castleroy pulled out for her, her lips curved ruefully. The seat was very comfortable. And she had never been very good at balancing plates of food on her knees.

They ate a delicious repast of roast beef, ham, cheese, rolls, stewed fruit, and plum cake. The servants then cleared away the meal, and their party made their way to the town, passing the Star and Garter Inn before going on to Isleworth on the opposite shore.

"I want to show Alexandra the market gardens," the duke said. "I believe they are celebrated for their produce. We shall go on to Syon House later."

"Would you like to see the market gardens, Miss Grantham?" Lord Castleroy asked. "Or would you prefer to go directly to the house?"

"I'd like to go to Syon." She wrinkled her brow. "Wasn't Catharine Howard imprisoned there for some time before her execution in the Tower of London?"

"She was," Lod Castleroy replied. "And Lady Jane Grey also

resided at Syon House before she went to the Tower."

"A distressing history," Thea said gravely. "I hope Syon House has been a happier residence for its more recent female inhabitants."

Anne and Mr. Fotherby accompanied Thea and the baron, and they passed a church with a tower grown over with ivy before walking the short distance on the great road to the mansion.

They passed through a colonnaded gateway before making their way up a flight of steps to the Duke of Northumberland's seat. As Thea stepped into the hall, her eyes widened as she looked around the massive oblong chamber with its black and white marble floor and splendid marble statues. Eventually, her gaze came to rest on a bronze cast of a gladiator in the throes of death. Grimacing a little, she exited the room and entered a vestibule containing several Ionic columns topped with golden statues. Looking up, Thea noticed the gilt ceiling, and when they moved into the drawing room next door, that ceiling was also luxuriously gilded.

The walls there were hung with rich three-colored silk damask. Thea wandered over to the side of the room to examine the coverings more closely. "These hangings are splendid." She indicated the silk damask as Lord Castleroy came up beside her.

He stepped closer, inspecting the wall more carefully. "I read in the guidebook *Picturesque Rides and Walks* that these hangings are the first of this sort to be made in England. My grandfather has been thinking of creating similar silk wall coverings using your staining methods." He glanced around the magnificent apartment. "I thought it might look a trifle ostentatious as I have no taste for gilded splendor in my homes. But golden walls would not look out of place in a room like this."

A short while later, Anne and Mr. Fotherby left the drawing room, and Thea and Lord Castleroy followed them into a gallery with a splendid array of paintings, including portraits of several noble-looking gentlemen. After stopping to examine a couple of the canvasses, Thea walked to the end of the room, where the others awaited her at folding doors that opened into the garden.

She raised her gaze to Lord Castleroy's face and then glanced away. The uncompromising set of his square jaw unsettled her. Had he noticed her determined efforts to avoid all discussion of a personal nature today? She had been quite distant in her interactions with him since he picked her up this morning. But she didn't know what else to do, not when her resistance to him felt as if it were hanging by the veriest thread.

As she stepped outside, Lord Castleroy explained that the garden was separated into two parts by a river. "It flows into the Thames," he said as they came upon a bridge leading from one part of the grounds to the other.

Anne and Mr. Fotherby wandered off to view a Doric column with a statue of a Greek goddess at the top, just as Lord Castleroy indicated a nearby greenhouse with a lightly Gothic front.

"Part of the greenhouse is formed by the only remaining walls of the monastery that used to stand here," he said quietly. "Would you care to go inside?"

At her nod, he turned, and she followed him through the door of the structure he held open. She wandered to the far end and carefully touched one of the old stone walls. "I like the idea of blending the old with the new." She looked up at him. "Isn't it heartening to know that these walls still endure centuries after they were built and that they, in quite another way, still nurture and protect life, even though attempts were once made to destroy them?"

He stepped forward, smiling a little. "Why, Miss Grantham. You sound quite romantic."

"I am not completely devoid of sentiment." She crossed her arms and moved back, but the wall was right behind her, and she couldn't retreat at all.

"I did not say that you were." He took another step. "Indeed, I believe you might be quite the opposite."

He was looming over her now, and she tilted her head back

to meet his gaze, striving for calm. "I am not sentimental, my lord."

"Sentimentality and sentiment are not the same thing. One is affected feeling, while the other is pure emotion, without any sense of cloying pretension."

She swallowed. "An . . . an interesting distinction."

His eyes, those deep blue eyes, narrowed as he studied her. "You feel things deeply."

She stood as unmoving as the statues she'd just seen in Syon House and then gave a jerky nod.

"And you find it easier to shut off emotion than to live in a state of responsiveness."

"It . . . it feels safer that way." She studied her folded arms and then looked up. "It's too painful to allow emotions free rein. I learned that at a young age."

"It is possible to unlearn things, to change entrenched ways of being." His voice was gentle.

Thea was silent before saying jaggedly, "But I don't know how."

He raised a hand, touching her cheek. "May I show you?"

Somehow she nodded, even though a loud voice rang in her ears, commanding her to do the opposite. Instead, she shifted slightly forward, removing the distance between them. She remained rigid, faintly trembling, and then his arms were around her, pulling her closer, so close. His eyes blazed with a startling light as he lowered his head to hers, and she stilled.

Thea hadn't known what to expect, but it wasn't this slow, unhurried kiss as if his lips had all the time in the world to become acquainted with hers. She'd been as tightly strung as a bow when he first took her in his arms. But now her muscles eased, her limbs seemingly losing the ability to hold her upright. She leaned nearer, needing his support. And, as soon as she did, his kiss deepened, her breath mingling raggedly with his as she was swept into a realm of sensation she'd never experienced before.

She drew back after what felt like an eternity and took a few calming breaths, gradually returning to reality. Blinking around at her surroundings, she set her slightly askew spectacles straight again. What on earth was she doing? She'd given no thought to her reputation when she'd welcomed his embrace. If they had been caught in such a compromising situation, Lord Castleroy would have been forced to offer for her, and she would have had to marry him.

How heavenly that would be.

Thea dismissed the betraying thought and stepped neatly around him.

She needed to get away.

CHAPTER TWENTY-SIX

THE REST OF the afternoon passed in a blur for Thea, and she did her best to keep well away from Lord Castleroy. Stanford had arranged for a coach to take him and Alexandra back to London from Syon House as they had an early evening engagement they needed to attend. Desperate to avoid a boat trip in close proximity to the baron, Thea begged a seat in the duke's carriage, leaving Lord Castleroy, Anne, and Mr. Fotherby to travel back to London by water.

Thea felt a little guilty abandoning her friends, but she couldn't spend any more time in the baron's company. Not today. Not until she'd come to some sort of decision about how she wished to go on.

A sense of inevitability existed about that kiss. On some level, she had known it might happen if ever they were ever alone together. And yet she had gone into that greenhouse with him, tempting Fate, almost as if she had wished for it to occur. Which she probably had. She sighed. No use in lying to herself.

Thea gazed out of the coach window at the passing scenery. How tired she was of living in constant fear, of living in pain. Something within him had always beckoned to her, some quality that made her think she could be happy with him, that love did not always end in tragedy, leaving an aftermath of sadness in its wake.

"Are you all right, Thea?" Alexandra touched her arm.

She gave a tight smile. "Yes. Just a little weary. It's been a long day."

Her sister considered her thoughtfully, but she did not probe deeper, for which Thea was profoundly grateful. Instead, Alexandra began speaking about the beautiful market gardens she had seen in Isleworth, expounding on them at some length until Stanford's coachman set Thea down in front of Longmore House.

Just as she bid farewell to her sister, Alexandra met her gaze squarely. "If you ever need to speak about it, dearest, I'm here."

Thea gazed after the coach as it moved off and then shook her head as she entered the house. Impossible to keep secrets between sisters.

The next day, Thea set out quite early in the morning with Anne to Bond Street to buy a length of net. Thea was to attend her first Almack's Assembly of the Season later this week, and she wanted to fashion a simple reticule to match her ballgown. She had made the plan with Anne yesterday, and they set out together now on foot, with Simon following a short distance behind to carry any purchases they might make.

Thea frowned when she passed a shabby young man standing near the garden gate. She had spotted him in the Square a couple of days before when she'd gone out with Grandmama on a morning call. Although Thea sometimes struggled to recall people's names, she rarely forgot a face. And although the young man had been dressed in much smarter clothes the last time she had seen him, she was convinced it was the same person.

Thea had heard the news of some recent burglaries in Berkeley Square. Hopefully, the stranger wasn't loitering to gather information about the inhabitants of the various houses in order to attempt another housebreaking.

She put the man out of her mind as she left the Square. No use worrying about it and allowing it to spoil her morning. She decided she would tell her grandmother about the dawdler when she saw her later, though, and perhaps she could alert the authorities. When Thea returned home, she had quite forgotten about the man and her earlier plan. However, as she looked out of her bedchamber window that afternoon before changing her dress, she spotted him again on the other side of the Square.

This time Thea told her grandmother about the man when she went down to the drawing room before dinner. The older lady did not appear too concerned, but she did ask Leighton to ensure that all the doors and windows were securely locked before they went out to the opera later that evening.

Thea dressed with care for her first Almack's Assembly the following evening. Madame Bouchet had designed a dream of a frock of fine net embroidered with white double Indian roses worn over a pale blue slip. Thea's headdress was a simple wreath of white roses intertwined in her pale red hair, which had been braided and twisted around the top of her head.

Thea studied the selection of shawls Wilson had laid out on the bed, her brows drawn together. Wearing one of her metallic-stained scarves this evening would not be wise if she did not wish to invite comment from Sir Percival and Lady Dedham, who were bound to be there as well. So, picking up her favorite Norwich shawl instead, she smiled at her maid and left the room.

Thea hadn't seen Lord Castleroy since their excursion to Richmond Park. She knew from speaking to Anne that he hadn't left Town, so perhaps he was avoiding her after their scandalous encounter in the greenhouse. He would be at Almack's tonight, though, escorting his sister to her first assembly in those hallowed portals. Thea's stomach turned over at the thought of being in close proximity to him again.

When she entered the ballroom with Grandmama, Thea immediately spotted Lord Castleroy standing to one side with his sister and Mrs. Worrell. She met his gaze before looking away, feigning an interest in the assembly rooms she had heard so much about. Almack's was less grand than the private ballroom in Stanford House Alexandra had shown her the other day. But the finely dressed people circulating here did not match their somewhat plain surroundings. Or so they believed. So often, select groups of people, with their set rules and regulations about what mattered and what didn't, had an ethos of exclusion that people in other spheres of society did not know—or even care— much about. However, in their own small world, the *ton* played their games, reigning supreme. And that was all that really mattered to them.

Mr. Atherton came up to Thea to ask her for the first dance, and Thea accepted his invitation with pleasure. Her retiring nature made it quite hard for her to sparkle at Society events, and she numbered only a few gentlemen among her acquaintances in London. As they performed the movements of the country dance, Mr. Atherton conversed with her about some of the more interesting churches he had visited in the Metropolis. However, when they came together to form a figure, he changed the subject. "I believe you have become something of a leader of fashion, Miss Grantham."

She opened her eyes wide. "A leader of fashion? You must be mistaken. I am no such thing."

"No, indeed, ma'am—I am not mistaken. There is talk in some circles about your rich silk shawls, which are said to be of the first stare. And, indeed, even I, a complete ignoramus when it comes to matters of apparel, noticed the quality of the shawl you wore the other evening."

Thea swallowed. Thank goodness she had decided to wear her Norwich shawl this evening. To think that people besides Lady Dedham and Sir Percival, who was a complete dandy, were talking about her silk creations was disconcerting. "Ah, yes," she said after a moment. "A few people have complimented me on that shawl."

"Can you tell me where you bought it, Miss Grantham? I am looking for a birthday present for my mother, and I believe a shawl such as yours would answer perfectly."

Fortunately, the movement of the dance separated them at that moment, and when they reunited, Thea had regained her composure. "I'm afraid that it was acquired in Bath," was all she said. No need to elaborate further.

"Ah," Mr. Atherton said. "A pity." He cleared his throat. "I was speaking to Miss Pellier before you arrived. When I complimented her on her scarf, she told me it was a gift from you. Was that scarf also acquired in Bath?"

Thea did not answer, as they had reached the top by now, where they led off before progressing to their respective sides of the line again. Thank goodness the separation prevented her from having to reply, as she didn't know what to say.

While Lord Castleroy was engaged in the process of seeking a patent for Mrs. Fulhame's chemical methods of staining, he would not wish for other people to know about his plans in case some other party also decided to apply for His Majesty's permission. The last thing the baron needed was a race for registration. Mrs. Fulhame's book of experiments had been available to the public for many years, and it was in the realm of possibility that someone else might have the same idea as Lord Castleroy should they discover how Thea made her shawls.

She needed to make it clear to the few people in London who did know her secret that it would be best not to speak about it to anyone. Hardly anyone knew of her work, so it was doubtful people outside of her immediate circle knew how she made her shawls. Aunt Eliza came to mind, and Thea repressed a grimace as she automatically performed the final steps of the dance. Her aunt's tongue ran on wheels, and she might have easily said something to someone while she was in London.

On the other hand, Aunt Eliza considered her niece's work detrimental to her chances of becoming a social success, so hopefully, the older lady hadn't spoken of Thea's chemistry work to any of her friends. However, when Aunt Eliza returned to the Capital for her niece's coming out ball, Thea would be sure to ask her relative to keep a still tongue in her head.

The dance came to an end, and Mr. Atherton led Thea back to her grandmother, where he took his punctilious leave.

Thankfully. Thea was surprised he had questioned her so closely about her items of personal apparel. Surely it wasn't quite the thing to do so? She drew her brows together as she considered the matter and then set it from her mind when Mr. Fotherby came up to ask her to dance.

After that, Thea never missed a dance, and she was grateful not to be left at the side of the rooms with the chaperones and dowagers. Her connection to the Duke of Stanford must have ensured her popularity tonight. He was considered a leader of Society, after all, and she was his sister-in-law.

Thea returned to her grandmother's side when the strains for the first waltz sounded. She hadn't received permission from a Patroness of Almack's to dance it, as yet, and was therefore required to stand it out. However, just as Thea was contemplating the few ladies who had already been granted the favor, Lady Sefton approached Grandmama with Lord Castleroy at her side. The comfortable-looking lady was one of the less forbidding Patronesses of Almack's and a great friend of Lady Longmore. Now, seeing the unmistakably conspiratorial look which passed between the two ladies, Thea's stomach performed a somersault. Grandmama must have asked Lady Sefton to suggest Lord Castleroy as a suitable partner for her granddaughter, thereby giving Thea permission to dance.

And that's exactly what transpired. Lady Sefton gestured in the baron's direction. "You may dance your first waltz at Almack's with Lord Castleroy if you so desire, my dear."

If you so desire . . .

What an unfortunate choice of words. Thea's face flamed as she encountered Lord Castleroy's glinting eyes. However, she recollected herself enough to thank Lady Sefton for granting her permission before being led away by the baron.

She stepped into his arms without a word, and they circled the room in silence, not saying anything, not needing to say anything. They waltzed in perfect harmony as if they had performed these steps a hundred times before.

When the dance ended, Lord Castleroy drew her to one side. "I need to travel to Wiltshire tomorrow, Miss Grantham, but I hope to call on you when I return. May I?"

She held her breath for a moment. And then, flattening her gloved hands against the edge of her gown, she tilted her head, a smile trembling on her lips. "You may, my lord."

"James," he murmured before pressing her hand and saying in a low voice, "*Await love's appointed hour . . .*"

He bowed then and walked away, and as Thea stared at his retreating back, the rest of the verses from "A Summer Song" by Mary Anne Taylor echoed in her mind:

When warmth is lavished on the flower,
And rest imparted in the bower,
Joy bestowed upon the lover,
O! This time of blessed Summer.

❧

CHAPTER TWENTY-SEVEN

AFTER THE ASSEMBLY at Almack's, Thea walked around as if she were in a dream. Against her better judgment, she had encouraged James to pay his addresses to her even though she had believed until that evening that she was still weighing up her choices. In reality, however, her decision had been made some time ago. She just hadn't allowed herself to accept it until now.

Her heart flooded with joy as she thought of James's imminent return to London. Her life was about to open up in ways she hadn't ever considered possible. And all because of love. Somehow, the powerful emotion had transformed the arid landscape she had been walking upon into something lush, verdant, and alive. Something beautiful. And she finally felt ready to set aside her fears so she could focus on a future filled with promise.

She spent the week James was away attending lectures at the Royal Institution with Anne and Mr. Fotherby, shopping with Alexandra, and going to parties every evening. She did not wear her homemade shawls on these occasions, and after some consideration, she dropped a word in Anne's ear about the inadvisability of wearing the patterned shawl she had recently given her. Lady Dedham's assumption that Thea had obtained her fichu illegally from Asia shocked her as she had not realized the extent of the illegal trade in East India handkerchiefs. After considering the matter, she broached the subject with her brother-in-law over dinner at Stanford House one evening.

"Do you know anything about the illegal trade in silk handkerchiefs, Stanford?" she asked after the first course had been cleared away. "Lady Dedham assumed that one of my scarves had been smuggled in from India. I was astounded."

The duke smiled wryly. "It is well known that Lady Dedham only wears foreign silk. And I find it rather rich that she accused you of the same crime she's guilty of herself. No doubt she broached the subject with you as she wanted to know where to purchase such a scarf herself."

"She did appear unduly interested in it and asked me if I had fashioned it from an East India handkerchief."

A line appeared between Stanford's brows. "Those handkerchiefs are seized in vast quantities in the Port of London and other ports. The attraction is in their affordability, and everyone seems to desire them, regardless of social status or wealth."

"I knew that French silk was popular in London, but I did not realize India silks were equally sought after."

"There is great demand for them. Men use them as neckties or cravats, and they're large enough for women to use them as head scarves and shawls. But they have also become a magnet for thieves. A fair number of trials at the Old Bailey have something to do with stolen silk handkerchiefs."

"I had no idea," Thea said, shaking her head.

"I'm afraid it has been a problem across England for decades. But more so in the Metropolis as this is where culture and trade combine. I'm afraid the Revenue is defrauded of vast sums of money every year."

Alexandra spoke: "Speaking of smuggling, I had the oddest conversation with Mr. Atherton yesterday, Thea. He asked me if I knew where you had obtained the shawl you were wearing the other night. He said he was looking for a birthday gift for his mother."

"He told me the very same thing!" She tapped the edge of the table with one finger. "I didn't tell him that I make my own shawls as I don't wish to speak to anyone about my experiments until Lord Castleroy has applied successfully for his patent."

Stanford leaned back, his brows drawn even closer together. "A wise idea. The silk industry is very competitive. If word gets out that Castleroy intends to apply for a patent, other interested parties might decide to do so as well."

"That's what I thought," Thea said.

Grandmama shook her head. "It is a good thing that I kept quiet about your chemistry work before you came to London, Thea. I did so for a completely different reason, of course."

Alexandra chuckled. "Poor, Grandmama. First, it was my horticultural interests you had to contend with, and now it's Thea's chemistry."

"Indeed. And soon, it will be Abigail's astronomy." Grandmama's voice was somewhat gloomy.

"Have you had a letter from Abby recently?" Alexandra asked. "She has been a very poor correspondent of late."

"Abigail scrawled me a few lines a fortnight ago," Grandmama said. "But, according to your Aunt Longmore, she is having a splendid time."

"Abby wrote to me last week," Thea murmured. "She says she is very busy attending various engagements. I am glad she is enjoying herself. She was always more sociable than Alexandra or I were."

"Hmmm." Grandmama pursed her lips. "I hope your aunt is keeping a close eye on her. Abigail can be a little headstrong sometimes, and your Aunt Eliza isn't there to keep her in check." She paused for a moment. "Speaking of Eliza, she will be coming to Town for your coming out ball, Thea. But we won't see all that much of her as she will be staying with her sister in Wimbledon."

The conversation moved on to other topics, but when Thea returned home later that evening, she frowned a little as she remembered Mr. Atherton's comments to Alexandra. He was going to great lengths to acquire a shawl for his mother's birthday. It was decidedly odd.

Thea stepped out of the house the next day to meet Anne in Gunter's across the Square. They met there at the same day and time every week for a chat, and Thea always looked forward to it.

She peered around for the shabby man, but he wasn't anywhere to be seen, and she breathed a sigh of relief as she hastened across the Square. Wilson followed closely behind her. Her maid would wait outside the famous tea shop until Thea was ready to return to Longmore House. Although it was only a short walk, Grandmama was a stickler for such things and would not allow her granddaughter to go about unattended, particularly as so many members of the *ton* stopped at Gunter's to partake of their delicious offerings.

After Thea entered the shop, she spotted Anne and Mrs. Worrell seated at a table near the counter. Crossing the crowded space, Thea greeted the two ladies before sitting in the empty chair next to Anne. A hovering waiter took their order, and Thea engaged her companions in conversation until their order of jasmine rose ices arrived.

They all stopped speaking as they consumed the delectable treats, which tended to melt very quickly. Thea finished hers first and glanced rather absently around the tearoom. Her gaze swept past a gentleman with a somewhat familiar face, and she frowned a little before sneaking another look at him. Had she been introduced to him at an evening party? She didn't wish to make the social solecism of accidentally giving someone the cut direct.

Returning her attention to her companions, Thea pressed Anne's arm when Mrs. Worrell stood to greet a nearby acquaintance. "Do you recognize that gentleman, Anne? The one standing in the corner with brown hair and the dark green coat? He seems so familiar, but I can't quite place him. I fear I may have caused him offense as I looked directly at him without acknowledging him."

Anne shifted her chair slightly to get a better view. But, after surreptitiously viewing him for a few minutes, she shook her head. "I'm afraid I don't recognize him, Thea. But I am not the right person to ask. Other than Frederick—." She blushed. "Er . . . I mean Mr. Fotherby, I am acquainted with very few gentlemen in London."

"I suppose you don't need to be acquainted with anyone else," Thea said, smiling. "Mr. Fotherby appears very enamored of you."

Anne darted a look at her chaperone before returning her attention to Thea, lowering her voice. "May I tell you something in confidence, Thea? Frederick has asked me to marry him! He is waiting for James to return to London before making me a formal offer."

"Oh, Anne! I am so pleased for you. This is wonderful news!"

Her friend sighed softly. "I'm so happy. The happiest I have ever been. I never expected such a love, you see, as I'm no beauty. But from the moment I met Frederick, there was an instant connection between us, a sense of knowing."

Thea nodded, furrowing her brow slightly. She had experienced just such a connection upon first encountering Lord Castleroy. But she had ignored it, not wanting to acknowledge his impact on her.

Thea opened her mouth to respond just as the gentleman in the dark green coat stepped into her line of vision again. She froze and raised a hand to her forehead as faintness swept over her. She did recognize him. Although he was now dressed in the garb of a gentleman, this was the same young man who had been loitering around her home for the past few days. Just who was he?

When Thea left the tea shop a short while later, she was put in mind of the man again when she looked back and saw him speaking to Sir Percival Ponsonby. She hadn't noticed the baronet entering the tearoom, and now she hastened away, not wanting him to spot her.

CHAPTER TWENTY-EIGHT

WHEN THEA RETURNED home, she mentioned the matter to Lady Longmore, who was in the drawing room reading a novel she had borrowed from the circulating library. "Are you certain it was the same man?" she asked, closing the book.

"Yes. Each time I've seen him, he has been dressed differently. But I remember his face. He has a distinctive jawline."

"How very odd." Grandmama rhythmically tapped the cover of her book. "Perhaps he is involved in some political element. There has been a great deal of unrest in London in recent years due to opposition to the Corn Laws. Berkeley Square is home to any number of gentlemen with influence in British politics."

"It could be that," Thea replied, a thread of doubt in her voice. "But the first time I noticed him, it was because he was carefully observing Longmore House. That's why I gave him a second look."

"Hm." Grandmama's grey brows drew together. "And he was conversing with Sir Percival in Gunter's? I will have a chat to Stanford about it. Perhaps he'll have a suggestion as to what we should do."

At that moment, the door to the drawing room opened, and Leighton ushered Mr. Atherton inside. Thea's heart sank. She had no wish to speak to this man again. He asked far too many awkward questions. However, she pasted a polite expression on her face and engaged in her share of the conversation until Mr. Atherton said with a smile. "May I take you for a drive in the Park, Miss Grantham? It has turned into such a fine day. My curricle awaits me outside."

Thea stiffened. "Oh! I . . . I will be driving in the Park with my grandmother later this afternoon, sir. But thank you."

"Do go out with Mr. Atherton instead, my love." A sheepish expression crossed Grandmama's face. "I am right at the end of my book, and I'm longing to finish it."

Thea repressed a sigh. When her grandmother was nearing the final chapters of the numerous novels she perused, she was a hopeless case, frequently hiding away from everyone until she had finished her latest story. Thea was convinced that the frequent naps her grandparent took were just excuses to indulge her voracious novel-reading habit. She turned to their visitor. "I should be pleased to accept your invitation, then, sir."

"Excellent!"

Mr. Atherton took his leave of Lady Longmore before escorting Thea out of the room. His bays were being led up and down the street by a groom, who drew the pair to a sudden halt when they exited the house.

Thea had only ever driven with Lord Castleroy and Mr. Fotherby, and she felt the familiar clutch of fear in her stomach when she took her seat beside this new, unfamiliar driver. However, she drew in a deep breath, which calmed her immediately, and sat beside him with tolerable composure.

However, unlike Lord Castleroy and Mr. Fotherby, who gave their full attention to their horses when they drove through the busy streets of London, Mr. Atherton maintained a stream of conversation, even though Thea only gave him monosyllabic responses. Moreover, he frequently glanced down at her as he spoke, which stretched her nerves.

They were just about to enter the Park when a riderless horse galloped out of the gates, right into the path of Mr. Atherton's bays.

Everything seemed to slow down before her eyes as the horse, with its bunched muscles, raced straight in their direction. Thea opened her mouth to scream, but no sound came out.

The stallion was nearly upon them when he changed direction at the very last minute. Mr. Atherton's horses, however, were already rearing in their traces, and chaos reigned as her companion tried to calm them. But he wasn't able to do so, and the carriage began to tilt to one side.

Thea jumped out of the vehicle mid-tilt just before it tipped completely over.

She twisted her ankle painfully as she landed on the street and sat dazed in the road for a few moments before staggering to her feet just as a concerned gentleman and his wife approached to ask her if she was all right. Thea recognized the couple, Sir George Painswick and his wife, from a ball she had attended the other evening.

When she turned around and saw that Mr. Atherton had survived the accident and was attempting to calm the horses with the aid of his groom, Thea accepted Sir George's offer to take her home. Mr. Atherton gave a brief nod when Sir George told him of his intentions, and Thea limped away to her rescuers' carriage, which their coachman had drawn up on the side of the road.

"Do you know what happened?" Lady Painswick anxiously asked as Thea lowered herself onto the opposite seat.

"That horse must have thrown its rider." Thea's voice sounded as if it were coming from a long distance away.

"My poor Miss Grantham," her ladyship said. "It must have been terrifying to see that animal coming straight at you. Thank goodness it ran off in the other direction before it became entangled with those poor horses."

Thea swallowed past the painful knot in her throat. "I hope someone has managed to stop that stallion. He is a risk to himself and others."

Sir George frowned. "Are you quite well, Miss Grantham? You look excessively pale."

Lady Painswick scrabbled around in her reticule and removed a bottle of smelling salts. "Perhaps these will revive you, my dear." She proceeded to wave the salts under Thea's nose. They helped a little but not much. Nothing could really help.

The coach drew up outside Longmore House a short while later. Sir George insisted on accompanying Thea inside, giving her his arm as she climbed the stairs to the drawing room, with Lady Painswick following close behind.

"My poor dear!" Her grandmother searched Thea's face as she rose to her feet. "What on earth has happened? You look like you've just seen a ghost."

A ghost. Thea stared at her grandmother, unblinking. How strange that Grandmama had used that world.

When Thea made no reply, Sir George relayed what had happened. Grandmama sank onto the sofa and raised a shaking hand to her cheek. But, drawing her cloak of good breeding almost visibly around her, she rose to her feet once more and thanked the couple for their kindness.

After Simon saw them out of the room, Thea sank onto the sofa and stared straight ahead. Her grandmother settled beside her, chafing her hands and making comforting tut-tutting sounds almost as if Thea were a little girl again. After a while, she said quietly, "You've injured your foot, my love? You were limping when you entered the room."

"It's my ankle. I sprained it when I jumped down from the vehicle."

The older lady nodded briskly. "I shall ask Dr. Wainfleet to call so he can have a look at it."

She rang the bell then, and when Leighton entered the room, Lady Longmore requested a tray of tea. "You must drink a cup, my love, and then lie down. You've suffered a terrible shock, and you need to rest. Especially as . . ." She hesitated. "It must have brought back bad memories. But let us speak of this tomorrow."

Thea accepted the cup of tea Grandmama handed her and took a few sips before setting it aside. If she attempted to drink anymore, she would cast up her accounts. She couldn't stomach anything at present.

Grandmama looked at the barely touched cup of liquid and sighed, but she did not press Thea to finish it. Instead, she took her granddaughter's arm and drew her gently to her feet, assisting her through the door and upstairs to her bedchamber. Grandmama rang the bell for Wilson, who hastened into Thea's room five minutes later. After giving the maid some instructions in a lowered voice, Grandmama pressed a kiss to Thea's cheek. "Get some rest, my love. You will feel better when you wake up."

Wilson helped Thea change into her nightgown before giving her an arm as she hobbled to her bed. After drawing the curtains, her maid padded quietly from the room, leaving Thea alone. Blessedly alone.

Drawing the counterpane up to her chin, she stared up at the canopy. How could she have stepped into the living nightmare she had suffered from for so many years? It was inconceivable, unimaginable, heartbreaking.

So utterly heartbreaking.

Fate had played a nasty, perverse trick on her, as if it was determined to blast the budding hope in her heart, leaving her right back where she had started, all the progress she'd made in vain.

CHAPTER TWENTY-NINE

Dr. Wainfleet called the next morning to examine Thea's ankle in the drawing room, where she was resting. It was quite swollen and bruised but fortunately not broken. "Hmmm." The middle-aged physician leaned back on his heels, stroking his chin. "A few weeks' rest, and you should be fully recovered, Miss Grantham. No dancing for the next while, of course, but now that I've wrapped your ankle, you should be able to walk with relative ease. Is it very painful when you put pressure on it?"

Thea took a few tentative steps. "It's much better now, thank you."

"Excellent. You are fortunate that you did not break that ankle after jumping from such a height." He considered her, frowning. "You seem very pale. Should I give you something for your nerves? It must have been a distressing experience."

"I don't need anything, thank you," she said quietly.

"Well, if you change your mind, Miss Grantham, do not hesitate to ask."

He turned to Lady Longmore, who had sat quietly in a corner of the room during the examination. "Thankfully, it appears to be a mild strain."

Grandmama's brow was furrowed. "My granddaughter's coming out ball is in six weeks. The invitations have already been sent out. Should we change the date?"

"If Miss Grantham rests her ankle, she should be able to dance by then. But perhaps not for the whole evening."

"Very well. Thank you, Dr. Wainfleet."

After the physician left the room, Grandmama sighed. "I am glad it isn't worse, my love. Although it is a pity that you won't be able to dance for a while, especially with the current rash of coming out balls."

"I shan't mind, Grandmama."

She shook her head. "Well, I suppose it is what it is."

Mr. Atherton called later that day. When he entered the room, he apologized profusely for the incident the day before and inquired about Thea's health.

"I am well, thank you, sir, except for a slightly strained ankle."

"I am pleased to hear that." Mr. Atherton sat on the chair Thea indicated and pulled at the chain attached to his quizzing glass.

"Did anyone catch the runaway horse?" Thea asked.

"Fortunately, yes. Apparently, Mr. Henry Walter was thrown from his horse while riding in the Park. His friends retrieved his stallion after you had already left with Sir George." He cleared his throat. "Pray accept my sincere apologies for abandoning you yesterday, but my attention was fully occupied in trying to calm my bays."

"There is no need to apologize, Mr. Atherton. Of course, you needed to attend to your horses."

"A most unfortunate accident." He pulled harder on the chain. "I say, Miss Grantham, I was hoping that you could assist me. Unfortunately, I haven't had any success finding a shawl for my mother in that particular shade of gold you wore the other evening."

"What a pity," Thea murmured.

He stared at her for a moment. "Yes. Yes, well, I suppose I shall need to look for something else."

She made no reply, and after a few minutes of lackluster

conversation, Mr. Atherton rose and took his leave.

Grandmama chuckled as the door closed after him. "I must say, my love, that you have perfected the art of deflecting unwanted questions."

"Unfortunately, I've had much practice as I have had to deal with far too many questions such as this since my arrival in London."

Lady Longmore rose to her feet. "I never suspected that your shawls would draw so much attention. It has been most disconcerting. I've had several dowagers approach me recently, asking me about them. It appears the taste for contraband silk is as strong as ever."

"We underestimated the interest it would attract."

Grandmama crossed to the door before turning back. "Indeed. But fortunately, no one has any idea that you made them, so they can only speculate. You truly have set everyone in a bustle, Dorothea!"

"It was never my intention, Grandmama." She bit her lip. "Perhaps I shouldn't have shown them off as I did. I'm afraid my vanity got the better of me."

"I don't see why you should hide your light under a bushel. Although I do see the sense of concealing it now until Lord Castleroy receives his patent." Just before she exited the room, her grandmother turned back. "I need to discuss the week's menus with Cook. Is there anything in particular that you fancy for your dinner tonight? You only picked at your food last night."

"There is nothing, thank you. I am afraid my appetite has deserted me."

The older lady sighed. "And with good reason. Such a shocking thing to happen."

When the door closed after her, Thea stared into space. A strange numbness seemed to have settled in the region of her heart, dulling the anguish which had burst forth yesterday. She picked up the novel Grandmama had been reading, but the antics of the heroine, who had just escaped from a nunnery, did not hold her attention, and when the door opened again fifteen minutes later, she was ready to cast it aside.

But when Lord Castleroy strode into the room, Thea gripped the book tighter, pressing it to her middle, using it as if it were some sort of shield. She wasn't ready to face him yet. She didn't think she would ever again be ready.

"My dear, I have just spoken to your grandmother. She told me about the accident. How are you?" He took her hands in his, searching her face.

"I . . . I don't quite know, my lord."

He pressed her fingers. "All that matters now is that you are safe. Well and safe. May I?" He indicated the space on the sofa beside her.

At her nod, he sat beside her. But she still had that odd frozen feeling, as if she were observing the scene from under very deep water.

Lord Castleroy took her hands in his again and looked down at her, his eyes intent. "I have been counting the hours since I last saw you, Thea. When you indicated that you were open to receiving my addresses, it was as though I'd been given the stars on a silver platter. Darling Thea, will you do me the honor of becoming my wife?"

She gazed up at him and then drew her hands away, holding them stiffly in front of her. "I'm afraid, my lord, that I cannot answer you right now. I don't feel quite myself."

He frowned. "I'm afraid I am completely at sea."

"Did Grandmama not tell you the details of the accident?" Her voice felt as if it were coming from far away.

"Just that you had fallen and injured your ankle."

She swallowed painfully. "It was . . . more than that."

"What exactly happened?" He leaned closer, his arm brushing hers.

"Mr. Atherton asked me to drive with him in the Park. Just before we entered the gates, a horse, a riderless horse, came bearing down upon us, causing the carriage horses to startle. I leaped from the curricle."

He took her hands in his again, chafing them as Grandmama had done yesterday. Yet she still felt cold. She wondered if she would ever be warm again.

Her voice was unsteady. "It felt like a reenactment of my mother's accident. Instead, this time it was a horse, not a dog." She paused for a moment. "I thought I was getting better, but now I see I haven't changed at all. I am as afraid as ever." She withdrew her hands, shifting away. "I'm no snowdrop, my lord, thriving in adverse conditions. And I think you need the qualities of a snowdrop to be a good wife."

He remained silent for some time. Finally, he said, "I'm not looking for a snowdrop, Thea. They only flower for a brief while before the plant dies back after the fruits have opened. I prefer daisies."

"Daisies?" She twisted in her seat, gazing up at him.

"They're far more cheerful and seem to welcome the sun instead of staring down at the frozen ground. Besides, snowdrops are poisonous." His eyes smiled.

"I was speaking in metaphorical language, my lord," she said with dignity. "You are making light of my concerns."

"I would never do that." His jaw set slightly. "But I will challenge you when I don't agree with you. You're not the judge of my happiness, Thea. And when you attempt to act nobly for my own good by giving me up due to some false idea that you are irreparably flawed, I grow somewhat frustrated. You say that you are not strong enough to face adversity, but most of us struggle, which is why we choose to battle the headwinds of this life with a loving partner at our side."

Her eyes widened. "You struggle? But you appear so confident, so sure of yourself. I've often wished for that sort of strength." She rubbed her hands up and down her arms.

"There are various types of strength," he said quietly. "Yours is just different from mine."

She looked away. "You truly believe I'm strong?"

"There is strength in gentleness and in a mind that seeks knowledge. You have both."

"But I feel so broken," she whispered. "I have for so long."

He took her hands in his. "Look at me, Thea."

When she reluctantly raised her eyes to his, he said, "My grandfather traveled to Asia as a young man and brought back a piece of porcelain, which he gave my mother upon her marriage. It was a strange piece. As a boy, I used to study it often, puzzled by the fact that it had cracks mended with lacquered gold. I asked my mother why she kept a repaired piece in such a prominent position in her sitting room." He pressed her hands. "She told me flaws can be beautiful and that, once properly mended, the restored cracks can make an object even stronger."

His words slowly sank in. "You truly think I'll mend?"

"Are you not an expert in working with gold?" His grin was lopsided.

A smile flickered on her lips, and then she sighed. "Please allow me some time, my lord. I need to be sure before I give you my answer."

He pressed her hands again before releasing them. Then, rising to his feet, he looked down at her, his expression suddenly remote. "I trust this time it's not *adieu*, my dear."

And on these words, he left the room.

CHAPTER THIRTY

WHEN JAMES STEPPED out of Longmore House, he stared frowningly ahead. He had walked to Thea's home from his residence in Grosvenor Square, and now, after deliberating for a moment as to whether he should continue to his club or return home, James set off in the direction of Castleroy House. He passed a man in the street who looked vaguely familiar but did not give him a second thought, preoccupied as he was with his recent meeting with Thea.

Now, as James stopped in the street to greet an acquaintance, he spotted the man again, some distance behind him. The fellow appeared to be following him, and James's brows snapped together as he walked on. Pickpockets abounded in London, and it was necessary to always be on one's guard. He was a fool to have paid so little attention to his surroundings. Shoving thoughts of Thea aside, James turned into his street. After he had walked a few more steps he halted and pretended to wave at a friend across the street. Out of the corner of his eye, the man came into his field of vision and stopped dead.

He was definitely being followed. And suddenly, James knew why the chap seemed familiar. When he'd come out of his front door last week, he had noticed someone standing in the road with his hat pulled low. The furtive pose had made James take a second look, and he had observed a lantern jaw and shabby clothing. Although the fellow's battered hat still concealed half of his face, there was no doubt in James's mind that it was the same person.

James turned around in a leisurely manner again, not wanting to alert the man to the fact that he had recognized him. Then, quickening his pace, he continued down the street. Why would someone be watching his house and following his movements? Could it be that another mill owner had got wind of his plan to register the patent? He walked on, his muscles tensed. It seemed unlikely, as very few people knew about Thea's silk-staining work. Still, there was a possibility that someone had somehow discovered his plans, as he had already begun the process of applying for the patent. Word had a way of getting out about such things, which could lead to attempts at espionage, especially as the silk industry was in such a dire state.

James had visited a master weaver in Spitalfields the other day, and he had been dismayed at the squalid conditions present in London's traditional silk district. The roads were unpaved, and the stench in the air turned his stomach as there was a complete lack of sewers and drains in the city's eastern part. He had entered the weaver's house, which was small and damp, and no doubt the cause of the man's wracking cough.

Old Joseph had shaken his head as he recalled more prosperous times. And indeed, the once bustling district was now clothed in eerie stillness, with only an occasional loom heard clacking away and many of the houses exhibiting sheets of paper instead of glass panes in the windows.

Ironically, the attempts to safeguard the industry in London had, in fact, ruined it. The Spitalfields Act of 1773 strictly controlled the prices master weavers could pay journeymen for each piece of silk rather than allowing prices to fluctuate as market rates did. So in leaner times, rather than journeymen benefiting from set high prices for their work, instead, masters who needed to reduce the prices they paid for labor simply employed fewer journeymen. Steep fines for violation made ignoring the Act impossible, so many people lost their work.

Consequently, it wasn't long before silk manufacturing came largely to a halt in London, and in recent years production had moved to the countryside, where the Act had no jurisdiction. Most of the remaining silk manufacturers in the Metropolis had abandoned making anything but the fancy and expensive silk pieces that could only be purchased by the very wealthy whose tastes and desires were always shifting. And this was the market that James's grandfather wanted to expand into.

He had requested his grandson to track down any remaining master weavers in London who could partner with him in this new endeavor, and Joseph had been the first weaver James had approached. The old man's delight at the prospect of steady work had been sobering, and James hoped more than ever that his patent would succeed—not only in bringing the Macclesfield workers back to prosperity but also in restoring the livelihoods of some of these skilled craftsmen.

James pondered all this with half a mind as he stayed alert to the man who still followed him. When he arrived at Castleroy House, he entered without a backward glance and went straight to his study. He sat at his desk and leaned back in the chair, his hands linked behind his neck. The story of the Lombe brothers was a cautionary tale about the extremes to which some people would go to pursue profit in the silk industry. In bad times, people became desperate. And times were very bad.

The person trailing him must have heard about the patent. James couldn't think of any other reason for someone to track his movements. He unlinked his hands and placed his elbows on the desk, sighing faintly. Although he didn't like the idea of leaving London right now, it was the only way to make the trail go cold. He would need to halt his efforts to seek out more master weavers and retreat to Castleroy for a while. And, perhaps in his absence, Thea would be able to see her way more clearly.

Her accident had shaken her badly. If only he could take all her fears upon his shoulders. But unfortunately, battles of the mind needed to be fought alone, and they often offered up the strongest of adversaries—one's own thoughts. Witnessing her mother's death at a young age had caused Thea to recoil from the world. And there was no guarantee that she would ever decide to return and embrace life fully.

His mother had retreated from adversity in a similar fashion. Although she had never complained about her husband, James knew their marriage wasn't happy. His father had resented his need to "marry down" to save his estates and hadn't kept his dissatisfaction a secret. James's mother had always felt like an outsider, kept at arm's length by the members of the *ton*, until she had eventually stopped visiting London, spending most of her time at Castleroy, where she found solace in nature, poetry, and her children.

"Life has a way of offering unexpected consolations," she told him once when he was reluctant to return to Eton after a holiday at Castleroy. "Light cannot be hidden, and it silvers the darkest of clouds. Always look for that light, my son."

He remembered her words during those first few years at school, where he had felt like a fish out of water. And he had found some consolation, including his friendship with Stanford, which had successfully shut down the other boys' disparaging remarks about his mother's family. Once when Percival had made a taunting remark about James's impure bloodlines, Stanford, who had received an extensive education about the well-to-do families in England, had remarked coolly that before Percival made any more disparaging comments, he should look back two generations into his own family tree.

Percival had looked horrified and immediately left the common room. Stanford had later told James that Percival's grandmother had once been arrested for stealing a card of lace from a linen drapers shop in Bath. She was eventually acquitted of the crime, no doubt because she was a gentlewoman, and the punishment of transportation or hanging was considered too severe for someone of her status. But before the lady's trial, she had spent six months in jail, a most embarrassing thing for a genteel family to contend with.

Percival had mostly left James alone after that, but he had always been aware of his resentment and knew that Percival would embrace any opportunity to insult him.

James's thoughts returned to Thea. He had sensed she did not wish for deep involvement when he met her, but he had pursued her despite that sure knowledge. Her vulnerability had appealed to his protective instincts, and he had been determined to win her love, like some knight errant of old, attempting to gain the favor of his lady love by proving his chivalric virtues. How ironic that his quest had been doomed from the start as he could not rescue her in the way he wished.

And why did he wish it? If Thea had been eager to receive his attentions, would he have even pursued her? A difficult question to answer. Her reserve had been reassuring to him in some odd way as it meant he did not need to become too engaged himself. And although he had challenged Thea to face her fears, had he ever faced his?

He gripped his hands together and lowered his head, staring at the polished wooden surface of the table.

The truth was he hadn't. Like Thea, he still felt detached from the circle he moved in. They were both wanderers, orbiting the circumference of their worlds without wishing to enter the center, feeling safer on the periphery.

How strange that he hadn't seen this before.

The person one chose to love often said more about oneself than it did about them.

It was a sobering thought.

CHAPTER THIRTY-ONE

THEA LEARNED FROM Anne the next day that Lord Castleroy had left Town again. The news came as a surprise as the baron had only just returned, but Anne informed her that an urgent matter had arisen which had necessitated his return to Castleroy.

After his proposal, Thea felt at sixes and sevens, unable to focus on anything for more than a couple of minutes. Even her chemistry work suffered as she kept losing concentration, making the simplest mistakes.

Feeling thoroughly discontented, she decided to pay Mrs. Fulhame a visit a few days after James's departure. The older lady had urged her to call again, and it would be lovely to discuss her experiments in more depth. It would also serve as a welcome distraction from the torment of her circulating thoughts.

Wilson accompanied her in the carriage and waited in the hallway for her mistress as Thea made her way upstairs.

Mrs. Fulhame's smile was welcoming when Thea entered the drawing room. "Alone this time, Miss Grantham? I rather took to your baron."

Thea blushed at the frank nature of this comment as she took the seat Mrs. Fulhame indicated. "He isn't my baron," she said quietly.

"Isn't he? He certainly gave that appearance. But then, it's no business of mine."

Thea opened her mouth and then shut it. Mrs. Fulhame had the kind of face that invited confidences, but Thea did not like to talk about her personal affairs, especially to a virtual stranger. But perhaps she could relieve the weight on her mind by speaking more broadly about her concerns.

So, after inquiring about the older lady's well-being, she said, "Sometimes I wish that the experimental nature of scientific work could be applied to other realms of experience. It is so reassuring to be able to follow a procedure to determine an outcome."

Mrs. Fulhame bent her head. "Indeed. But sometimes, the correct procedure is difficult to determine! When I started my experiments, I imagined that only a few would be necessary to solve the problem I posed. But experience soon showed me that a very great number were required."

Thea studied her toes for a moment before looking up. "Why is it that it's only in chemical science experiments that we are able to observe all the possible combinations before committing to the one that works best? Imagine if we could test how various elements combined in alternative areas of life before making important decisions."

"Hm." Her hostess studied her with bright eyes. "Scientific experimentation aims to build an understanding of the natural world. We revise as we go and always question what has been discovered once new ideas are put forward."

Thea's shoulders drooped. "So, why does this philosophy not apply beyond the world of chemical science?"

"Are you certain it doesn't?" Mrs. Fulhame leaned slightly forward. "Whatever the realm, should we not always be seeking and investigating the truth? And when any opinion or belief is found wanting, we must be willing to surrender it, remaining ever open to new or more reasonable ideas. Sensible people do this all the time."

"I suppose scientific training is an excellent way to guard against lazy thinking."

"Indeed, my dear. But the other realms of experience you refer to may not be governed only by thinking. Once one throws other elements into the mix—like human nature—events cannot be so easily controlled. A difficult thing for a chemist to accept, perhaps."

"Very difficult."

Her hostess smiled. "And when the elements of youth, love, and passion combine, it can be an explosive mixture."

Thea half smiled. "I've had a few chemical explosions in my time, Mrs. Fulhame, but I can honestly say that they weren't nearly as hazardous as the experience of falling in love."

"Hazardous yet glorious. And something worth guarding if it comes your way." She met Thea's eyes for a speaking moment before turning the conversation to the latest lecture demonstration at the Royal Institution, which she had attended. Thea had attended the lecture as well, but she hadn't seen Mrs. Fulhame there, and she was delighted to discuss the particulars of the presentation with her.

Half an hour later, Thea rose from her chair and made her farewells, promising to call on Mrs. Fulhame again when she had the opportunity.

"I shall look forward to that." Sadness flickered in the old lady's eyes. "I rarely have the opportunity these days to discuss my interest in chemistry with fellow enthusiasts. It has been delightful to do so today."

As Thea drove back to Longmore House in the carriage, the knot which had settled in her stomach since Lord Castleroy's proposal eased somewhat. After the accident, all she'd wanted to do was crawl into a hole and lick her wounds. But today, she was finally ready to emerge from her retreat and face the facts of the matter. Her lips curved into a wry smile. Or perhaps it was more accurate to say the *feelings* of the matter. Either way, hiding away as she had been doing was the coward's way out, and she had taken that way for far too long.

Anne was awaiting her in the drawing room when she entered Longmore House. "Lady Longmore said that you would return at any moment, so I stayed."

Her friend looked a little pale, and Thea studied her face with concern. "Is anything the matter? You don't look well."

Anne sank back onto the sofa again. "It is only that . . . well, a very strange thing happened this morning. I don't wish to tell Cousin Jane about it in case it gives her a nervous spasm, but when I went downstairs this morning, I saw a note being shoved under the front door. I thought it was odd that someone would deliver a letter in such a way, so I quickly opened the door and looked outside. I saw a man running away down the street."

Thea took the piece of paper her friend held out and read it:

To the lady of the house:

The Thameside quays between London and Richmond belong to us. And we investigate all trespassing on our territories. Whichever shopkeeper supplied you with East India scarves will pay a high price for receiving goods from another source. If you yourself are the supplier of silks to the lady in Longmore House, you will stop immediately if you don't wish to pay with your life.

Thea dropped like a stone onto a nearby chair. "This is terrible!"

"I've been trying to understand what this letter means." Her friend raised a shaking hand to her cheek. "The only time I've ever been to the Thames was when we went to Richmond the other day. On the way there, the weather was warm, so I needed no covering. But later in the day, during lunch, I slipped on your fichu, and when we returned on the water, I was wearing it. Perhaps, a member of a smuggling gang saw it and assumed I had bought it from a shopkeeper selling contraband silk on the River."

"That must be it. But why would they assume that you're supplying me with silk shawls?"

"They must know somehow that we are friends. And as you didn't return on the water with us but traveled back in the carriage with the duke, suspicion fell on me instead. James was telling me the other day that smuggling gangs in London guard their territories fiercely. Perhaps they've been spying on us to gather information about your shawls."

Thea shivered. "I've noticed a man loitering outside our house. And then, the other day, I saw him in Gunter's, but that time he was dressed as a gentleman."

Anne's eyes widened. "He must be following you to ascertain where you obtain your silks. However, he must know by now that you haven't gone to any suspicious locales." She pressed her lips together. "And . . . he would have observed my comings and goings to your home, and suspicion must have fallen on me as a possible supplier as I returned to London on the boat wearing your fichu. If a smuggler was watching us, he would have noticed I wasn't wearing the fichu on my arrival at the River but only on my way back."

"The smugglers must think you're buying contraband goods for both of us, Anne!"

Her friend shook her head and sighed. "If it weren't so awful, I would laugh. What a ridiculous thing to think about two gentlewomen!"

"It isn't that strange." Thea contemplated the letter once more before looking up. "Grandmama told me that when she was young, one of her mother's acquaintances was stopped by a Customs officer after a trip on the Continent. Apparently, the lady had concealed a quantity of French silk in her high head wig, which the officer then duly seized. It was quite a scandal at the time among their group of friends. And well-to-do ladies are still buying contraband silk. Lady Dedham wears nothing else!"

"I wonder where she buys it?"

"Grandmama told me that Society ladies have visited the East India ships for years. They arrive back home looking considerably plumper in appearance than when they left."

"While other ladies sail down the Thames on pleasure trips with nefarious purposes in mind. Apparently." Her friend's voice was dry.

"Oh, Anne! I feel dreadful that it was my fichu that drew the smugglers' attention to you!"

"It's not your fault." She nibbled her bottom lip. "I shall send James an urgent letter to tell him what's happened. He'll know what to do. But in the meanwhile, I admit I'm rather nervous about leaving home. To think that those criminals have been spying on us turns my stomach."

"Will you tell Mr. Fotherby about it?"

"I'll do so when he returns to Town. He's visiting his brother, Sir Charles, at present. In the meanwhile, would you keep this to yourself until I hear back from James?"

"Yes, of course. But perhaps I should tell my grandmother?"

"As the suspicion has fallen on me rather than you, Thea, you should be safe enough. I'm definitely not telling Cousin Jane! She'll go into a decline if she finds out."

Thea nodded. "I'll wait until Lord Castleroy returns, and then he can speak to Grandmama."

"I hope James will be able to return soon." She hesitated. "He wasn't quite himself when he returned to Castleroy House after seeing you. Did you have a falling out?"

Thea sighed. "No, not a falling out. But I was in a bad way after my accident, and I wasn't . . . quite myself either."

Anne studied her gravely. "Please don't break his heart, Thea. He's desperately in love with you, you know. I was hoping . . ." She came to a halt. "But I shouldn't be speaking to you about this. James would hate it."

Thea sat in frozen silence for a moment. "Has—has he confided in you?"

Anne gave a small shrug. "He doesn't need to. I can see." She frowned. "He's always been the best of brothers, and he's so considerate to those in need. But he doesn't think of himself. He's been tirelessly helping Grandfather to restore his business, as he knows the extent of the economic woes in Macclesfield. I just wish someone would take care of *him* for a change!"

Her friend's voice was fierce, and Thea winced, remembering how James had supported her as well, coming to Longmore House every day to help her face her fear of driving in open carriages. But, only aware of her own chaotic feelings, she hadn't given proper consideration to his actions, almost taking them for granted.

How selfish she had actually been, concerned only for her own well-being while disregarding his. Had she even thanked him properly for his kind actions? Regret coursed through her when, after some reflection, she realized she hadn't. Grandmama had thanked him, but Thea, caught up in all her woes, hadn't even bothered to express her appreciation for the effort he had expended on her behalf.

And, suddenly, her desire to isolate herself from other human beings to prevent herself from being hurt seemed more than cowardly—it was also ungenerous and miserly. To always take from others but never to give? What kind of life was that? Could she, in all honesty, say she loved James when she didn't bother to consider his feelings, his needs?

Love was not something that should flow in one direction.

Blinking back tears, Thea pressed Anne's arm. "I hope that someday it will be my privilege to take care of your brother."

Anne's face lit up. "So you do love him, Thea?"

"I do."

"Oh, how wonderful!" She kissed her cheek. "Truly, it's the most splendid news."

When Anne left a short while later, Thea sank onto the window seat, feeling as if a great weight had lifted from her shoulders. It had taken her far too long to realize the error of her thinking. And now, all she wanted was to see James again, to hold him in her arms, to share her newfound understanding with him.

The sooner he returned to London, the better.

CHAPTER THIRTY-TWO

THEA'S INJURED ANKLE gave her an excellent excuse to stay at home rather than attend Lady Elizabeth Lavenham's coming out ball that night. Settling in the drawing room with her embroidery, she sighed in relief, delighted to have an evening to herself, free from the pressure of curious eyes and hushed whispers. And smuggling spies.

Thea sighed. She had no desire to go anywhere while the possibility existed that her movements were still under observation. She dropped her sewing onto her lap, staring straight ahead. Poor Anne! She still couldn't believe her friend had received such an awful letter. It seemed utterly fantastic. Hopefully, when James returned, he would sort everything out. But, in the meanwhile, it was best that she avoided going out as much as possible.

Unfortunately, Thea could not avoid the musical evening she and Lady Longmore had been invited to the next day, even though she voiced her wish not to go out.

"You will be seated the whole time, my love, so you'll be comfortable enough," Grandmama proclaimed when Thea expressed her reluctance to leave the house. "Avoiding all parties until your ankle heals is a dreadful idea. You will miss half the Season!"

"Very well."

At her subdued tone, her grandmother glanced at her sharply. "Is anything the matter, Dorothea? You've been very preoccupied today."

"I'm just a little tired."

"Missing Lord Castleroy, no doubt."

Thea met her grandmother's quizzing gaze. "I suppose I am."

Grandmama studied the giant ruby ring on her third finger. "When Lord Castleroy called the other day, he asked me for a private interview with you. I must admit I was expecting a betrothal announcement later that day. Instead, he left Town, and you've been as quiet as a mouse about what transpired."

"I . . . well, I asked Lord Castleroy to give me some time before giving him my answer. After the accident, I felt dreadful. I wasn't in a state to answer him."

"Ah." Grandmama pressed her fingers together. "And are you ready to answer him now?"

"Yes," she said simply. "I shall accept his lordship's proposal when he returns to London."

"Oh, my love!" The older lady beamed. "This is marvelous news! I am quite delighted." She paused for a moment, shaking her head. "You're not one to wear your heart on your sleeve, I must say, so I confess I wasn't entirely certain what your response to the baron would be. Although anyone can see that you make an excellent couple."

"Truly, Grandmama?"

She tilted her head to one side, smiling a little. "Lord Castleroy has a certain expression in his eyes when he looks at you, almost of wonderment. It is quite charming to see."

"Oh!" Thea felt her cheeks heat. "I wish he hadn't gone away."

"Well, don't mope, my love. He will be back soon enough."

When Thea limped into the large drawing room at Caversham House the next evening, she moved in the direction of the gilded chairs set out in rows in the center of the room for the guests. After some deliberation, she chose a chair on the end of the first row near the musical instruments, so that she wouldn't need to stand up to make way for other guests looking for their places.

The concert was due to begin in twenty minutes, and Thea looked around the elegantly decorated apartment to see how many people she recognized. Her gaze rested on Sir Percival, standing some distance away in conversation with Lady Dedham. Thea inclined her head coolly in response to his elaborate bow and suppressed a grimace. Somehow the baronet contrived to make a polite gesture look like an insult.

Her gaze traveled on until she met Mr. Atherton's eyes. He smiled and began to make his way across the room to her. Oh, dear! She pressed her fingertips firmly together. She really didn't want to speak to him tonight. But unfortunately, she had no choice in the matter.

"Miss Grantham! I have been meaning to call on you again. May I?" At her nod, he sat beside her, his brow slightly furrowed. "How are you faring after your unfortunate injury?"

"My ankle is a trifle painful, but it will mend. I hope your horses have fully recovered?"

His frown deepened. "They'll do. But it was a nasty accident, and I'm very sorry it resulted in injury to you."

"These things happen, Mr. Atherton. Indeed, we are fortunate that the consequences were not more severe."

"Yes." He paused for a moment, frowning down at his knuckles. Finally, he raised his head. "I hope this isn't presumptuous of me, Miss Grantham, but I dare say you've marked my interest in your exceptional silk shawls. You see, I am active in political circles, and smuggling is an enormous problem for His Majesty's government. My employer is deeply involved in trying to prevent it. As his secretary, I have access to certain information." He cleared his throat. "I was concerned that you might have—inadvertently, of course—purchased some contraband silk when you arrived in Town. However, when I broached the matter with your brother-in-law yesterday, he explained in the strictest confidence that you make your silk shawls yourself using chemical processes. I must say I admire your talent and industry, Miss Grantham. Your work is remarkable."

She raised her brows. "So you *weren't* looking for a present for your mother?"

He had the grace to look embarrassed. "My mother's birthday is in a little while yet. However, I assure you she would be delighted if I could purchase one of your shawls as her gift."

"I am afraid they aren't for sale, Mr. Atherton."

"I feared so. It is a pity, as your silks would sell very well if they were ever available commercially. Indeed, after the stir they have already caused amongst the *ton*, I predict they would become the rage."

Catching a movement out of the corner of her eye, Thea turned her head and stifled a gasp. Sir Percival hovered nearby, inspecting a harp of all things. How long had he been crouching there? She hadn't seen him move across the room. He must have circled the periphery to get to this side. Very suspicious.

As her posture stiffened, Mr. Atherton looked around. Lowering his voice, he said, "I don't think he's close enough to hear us."

"I trust not." She pressed her lips together. "Please don't mention my silk staining work to anyone, Mr. Atherton."

"You can rest assured, Miss Grantham. I told His Grace that I would keep the knowledge to myself. And I give you my word as well."

"Thank you."

He bowed then and made to rise but then sat down again. "One more thing. I have reason to suspect that your unusual shawls have come to the attention of rival smuggling gangs who believe them to be contraband silk. I cannot say more about it at this time, but please be on your guard."

His grave look caused Thea's breath to catch in her throat. But then his expression lightened, and when he walked away a moment later, Thea wondered if she had read too much into that sudden flash of disquiet in his eyes.

Thea remained seated, feeling like a flightless bird, alone and unable to take wing and remove herself from the range of anyone who might wish to target her. If only Grandmama would stop chatting to Lady Sefton!

However, Lady Longmore was caught up in her conversation and evidently not inclined to return anytime soon. When a couple of musicians began tuning their instruments, Thea breathed a sigh of relief. Hopefully, the concert would start soon so that she could avoid any more tête-à-têtes.

But Thea's hopes were disappointed when a strong waft of perfume assailed her nostrils, and Lady Dedham stopped beside her chair. "Miss Grantham," she said with her overly friendly smile. "How delightful to see you this evening."

Thea inclined her head. "Lady Dedham. Forgive me for remaining seated, but I have an injured ankle."

"How unfortunate," the older lady said. "A curricle accident, was it not? Mr. Atherton's curricle?"

"Yes."

Lady Dedham sat next to her. "Well, if you would take some friendly advice, my dear, I wouldn't spend too much time in that man's vicinity. He's a killjoy. Indeed, I believe he only frequents Society events to sniff out who's wearing foreign silks so that he can report us to the Customs House. I'm surprised he's welcomed into the homes of so many Society hostesses. I, personally, won't allow him to set foot in my home. That man is worse than a bloodhound. Has he been bothering you about your foreign silks?"

"He has no need to." Thea's voice was cool. "I don't own any foreign silks."

Her ladyship prodded Thea's arm with her fan. "Come now, my dear. You're doing it much too brown! It is as clear as the nose on your face that your shawls are imported. We've all been speculating for weeks about where you found such a treasure trove. Won't you share your little secret with me?"

"You're under a misapprehension, Lady Dedham. I am sorry

you don't believe me, but I am telling you the truth."

"*I* believe you, Miss Grantham," a soft voice drawled.

Thea's head jerked up. "Sir Percival."

Lady Dedham glanced from Thea to the baronet before placing her hands on her hips and shaking her head. "Percy! You were saying to me only yesterday that Miss Grantham must have discovered a new distributor of silk in London, as her shawls are so different from anything you've seen before."

"I've changed my opinion."

"Well, I think you're wrong." Her look was arch. "It is as clear as day that those shawls are handmade. No Englishman could produce anything of that quality."

"Perhaps an English*woman* could, though," he said softly, his thin brows raised.

Thea's heart sank. He must have overheard her conversation with Mr. Atherton.

"Oh, Percy!" Her ladyship sighed. "You're speaking in riddles again." She turned to Thea. "I swear I have no patience with gentlemen when they attempt to be clever. Do you not agree with me, Miss Grantham?"

Lady Longmore returned then, sparing Thea the necessity of making a reply. The concert was about to begin, and the guests started trooping toward the chairs to take their places. Lady Dedham rose to her feet with a trilling laugh. "Forgive me, Lady Longmore. I didn't mean to steal your seat."

Sir Percival offered Lady Dedham his arm, and Thea averted her gaze as he and the viscountess moved off.

"Are you all right, my love?" Grandmama asked as she seated herself.

Thea nodded, not wishing to alarm her grandmother. But she was far from all right. How could she be in a reasonable state when her carefully guarded secret was out?

CHAPTER THIRTY-THREE

THEA REMAINED AT home the next day, hoping against hope that James would walk in the door at any moment. But he didn't. And by the evening, no word had come from him or Anne. Grandmama was out most of the day making morning calls and shopping, and when she returned late in the afternoon, she was exhausted and retired to bed early with a headache.

As the interminable day drew to a close, Thea hobbled upstairs. She had asked to have her dinner sent up on a tray as she couldn't abide eating alone in the dining room, prey to her revolving thoughts.

If she heard nothing from James or Anne by midday tomorrow, Thea would send a note to Castleroy House, asking for news. Having a plan of action made her feel a little better, but she still struggled to fall asleep, lying awake for hours staring at the canopy.

When she went downstairs the next morning, Thea sat in the drawing room. However, she found it impossible to concentrate on her embroidery. Tossing it aside, she picked up a copy of *La Belle Assemblée*, but the fashion prints were uninspired, the poetry dull, and the theatre reviews full of pretension. She tossed the magazine aside and looked up eagerly when Leighton entered and said with a bow, "This letter has just arrived for you, Miss Grantham."

"Thank you," Thea murmured, removing the note from the silver salver. When the butler exited the room, she quickly read it:

Please step outside, Miss Grantham. I desire to speak to you out of earshot of any servants about a very important matter. The gate to the garden square is open. Miss Pellier and I will meet you there. Please come alone.

Yours,
Castleroy

Thea frowned. James must want to discuss the threatening note Anne had received away from any listening ears. Placing the letter to one side, she rose slowly to her feet and sighed. He must have forgotten her sore ankle. She couldn't walk very far on it, but she understood his wish to keep the matter private. Unfortunately, even the most trusted servants might be tempted to discuss such a scandalous piece of news belowstairs.

Thea crossed the room and opened the door, but Leighton was not in the hallway. She hesitated a moment. Perhaps she should inform someone of her whereabouts. But she didn't relish hobbling back inside the drawing room to pull the bell for the butler. Besides, Thea didn't want to waste any more time. James and Anne were waiting for her outside.

She closed the front door behind her and inched tentatively down the shallow stone stairs. Her ankle throbbed, but she focused her attention on the ground, afraid to miss her footing and take a tumble. When she looked up, a coach-and-four was directly in front of her. James must have come straight to Berkeley Square after arriving back from Castleroy this morning.

She stumbled along the cobbles, wincing a little as pain shot up her leg. The carriage obscured the view of the garden gate. As Thea stepped around it, she stopped, peering around. No one was there. She frowned. How odd. Were James and Anne already walking in the garden? But surely they would wait for her? A door squeaked behind her, and suddenly she was gripped by the elbows and dragged into the coach. Her ankle banged against something, and she let out a cry of pain as the door shut behind her.

Thea fell onto the seat and blinked rapidly as her eyes adjusted to the dimness inside. This level of secrecy on James's part was ridiculous. Surely he didn't need to pull her into his carriage to have a private discussion with her?

However, as the conveyance lurched forward, it wasn't James who spoke. Instead, Sir Percival Ponsonby said in drawling tones, "Good morning, Miss Grantham."

Thea's heart pounded as shock robbed her of speech.

"You walked neatly into my trap, didn't you?" The sneer in his voice was undisguised. "I knew I only needed to mention Castleroy's name for you to come running. Or rather, limping."

"But—but, why?"

"I'm following in my cousin Edward's footsteps and taking you to Gretna Green."

She trembled. "You must be mad. You don't even like me. Why would you wish to marry me?'

"Your powers of perception are remarkable, madam. You are correct. Bookish women have never appealed to me. But I'm in a bit of a corner and need to leave the country."

"You want my dowry," she stated flatly.

"That—and your . . . er . . . expertise in staining silk."

She gripped her fingers together. "You overheard Mr. Atherton."

"Indeed." He laughed softly. "It threw a great deal of light on why you were visiting Elizabeth Fulhame the other day."

"*You* sent that man to spy on me!"

He raised his brows. "You noticed him? Rather careless of him, I must say."

"Why was he following me?"

"To discover where you bought your shawls, of course. Little did I know you made them yourself. You would have saved me a deal of trouble if you'd simply mentioned that fact."

"It isn't public knowledge."

"Castleroy instructed you to keep it a secret, did he? I must say, it's very satisfying to steal you from under his nose. That patent of his won't have any protection in a foreign country."

She frowned. "You mean in Scotland?"

"No, no. We shall marry there. But we'll live in France."

"France?"

"Yes. My cousin is living there in straitened circumstances due to the Duke of Stanford's actions. And now that I cannot stay in England, France it must be for me, too. Besides, the French are leaders in fashion. It's the perfect place to sell your shawls. You should be grateful to me, my dear Miss Grantham."

Thea shook her head. "Set me down at once. It will do you no good to force me to marry you. Besides, I doubt you would manage to get your hands on my dowry in such circumstances. And it's pointless to marry me for my chemistry skills. All you need to do is find a copy of Mrs. Fulhame's book and hire a French chemist to follow her experiments."

"Ah, but if it were as easy as that, many others would have attempted to do so. You have determined which of Mrs. Fulhame's experiments work best. I cannot waste time hiring someone to learn what you already know."

"I'll refuse to marry you."

"Oh, by the time we reach Scotland, I believe you will have changed your mind." He gave her a nasty smile, and Thea's heart sank. This man was utterly ruthless. Somehow she had to contrive a plan to get away. If only she were mobile! Her damaged foot meant she couldn't make a run for it at the many hostelries Sir Percival would need to stop at on the Great North Road to Scotland.

She sank into silence, her mind spinning in agitated circles. No one would suspect Sir Percival had kidnapped her as it was such a nonsensical idea. Ironically, it had only occurred to Sir Percival because his dastardly cousin had attempted a similar plan with Alexandra last Season. That plan had failed dismally, as Stanford's tiger had recognized Alexandra and alerted the duke about her kidnapping, and he had come to her rescue. But how likely was it that someone had seen Thea being bundled into the baronet's carriage?

Her stomach heaved at the truly dire situation. The only clue Grandmama had of foul play was the letter Thea had received earlier that morning. It had been delivered straight into Leighton's hands. Surely he would tell Lady Longmore about it when she questioned him about her granddaughter's whereabouts. Thea drew her brows together. She had left the letter on the sofa, so Grandmama would hopefully find it and read it. Then, when she asked Lord Castleroy about it, he would inform her that he hadn't sent it and start his investigations. But this would all take time. And time was something she didn't have.

What if Sir Percival forced himself on her? From what he had intimated, he was already on the run from the Law. So he wouldn't hesitate at such brutal conduct. A shiver of fear ran down her spine at the prospect, and she dug her nails into her hand. To be alone with such a villain and at his mercy was utterly horrifying. The baronet had no respect for women, no consideration for finer feelings. He was a monster to have contrived such an evil plan, and she was trapped in a carriage with him.

Her thoughts turned to James, her darling James. If only she had accepted his proposal instead of putting him off! But she had been in a state of stunned dismay when he called on her, almost paralyzed by disbelief. It was as though she had expected a prize for confronting her greatest fear, like she had made some sort of fatalistic bargain with life. *If I am brave and face up to this bogey, it will never haunt me again.*

However, daring to face her fear didn't necessarily mean that her path would be forever free of that particular trouble. Instead, bravery was something she needed to cloak herself with every day. But after the accident at the Park gates, she had been angry that Fate had failed to reward her courage in the way she had secretly hoped.

What she hadn't realized then was that courage was its own reward.

And now she needed it more than ever.

CHAPTER THIRTY-FOUR

WHEN JAMES ARRIVED back in London, he went straight to Castleroy House to speak to his sister. He clenched his jaw as he read the note Anne had received. The smugglers had made the same mistake James had made at first, assuming the shawls Thea made were contraband silk. James had not expected her work to create such a stir in Polite Society. But now he saw he had been foolish not to predict the possibility that the smugglers supplying the *ton* with illegal silk would be cognizant of any circulating gossip regarding their trade.

And now his poor sister had fallen under suspicion due to her friendship with Thea. How ridiculous it was. Yet he knew better than to take such a threat lightly. After a quick word with Anne, where he attempted to reassure her, James headed to Longmore House to speak to Thea.

When he entered the drawing room, Lady Longmore looked up with a smile. "Oh, there you are, Lord Castleroy. I confess I have been wondering why you have been out so long, particularly as Thea cannot walk far." She peered behind his shoulder. "Has my granddaughter retired to her bedchamber?"

James frowned. "I've only just arrived, Lady Longmore. I haven't seen Miss Grantham."

Lady Longmore picked up a piece of paper from the sofa. "But you sent her this note, Lord Castleroy! I found it when I came downstairs."

He stretched out a hand. "May I see it?"

"Yes, of course." She handed him the folded letter, a line between her brows. "There must be some misunderstanding."

The words punched straight into his gut. He read the note again before looking up. "I didn't write this, ma'am. When did Miss Grantham receive it?"

"It's not from you?" She brought a hand to her cheek. "But—I don't understand, my lord. It makes no sense."

The door opened as she spoke, and the butler ushered Marcus Atherton inside. He bowed in Lady Longmore's direction before turning to James. "Lord Castleroy. I was planning on calling on you right after seeing her ladyship. How fortuitous to find you here."

James nodded at the newcomer but made no reply as he turned to the butler and held up the note. "Did you deliver this letter to Miss Grantham earlier, Leighton?"

"Why, yes, sir. I delivered it a couple of hours ago. A messenger boy dropped it off."

"When was the last time you saw Miss Grantham?" James asked urgently.

The butler appeared taken aback, swaying slightly from side to side as he contemplated the question. "After I delivered the letter, my lord, I needed to go downstairs to speak to Cook. When I returned, Miss Grantham was no longer in the drawing room."

"You didn't hear her go out the front door?"

"No, indeed, your lordship. I assumed Miss Grantham had retired upstairs to rest her ankle."

Mr. Atherton stepped forward. "I have come to speak to Lady Longmore about this very matter, my lord."

Lady Longmore stared from Mr. Atherton to James before she turned to the butler. "You may leave us now, Leighton." Her voice shook.

When the manservant had retired from the room, Mr. Atherton advanced inside, taking the seat Lady Longmore indicated. "I'm afraid I have some bad news, your ladyship." He looked around the room for a moment before settling his gaze somewhere over his hostess's shoulder. "When I learned that your granddaughter had come under suspicion for buying contraband silk, I informed my employer, Lord Bakewell, of the speculation. He had become concerned about the actions of a particularly ruthless smuggling gang in London and arranged for an agent to follow Miss Grantham, as he hoped he would discover where she bought her beautiful silks. The smugglers supply a couple of shops the wealthy patronize, but members of the *ton* are very discreet about where they acquire such items, as you can imagine." He shrugged. "During our investigations, I discovered from the Duke of Stanford that Miss Grantham created her shawls using chemical staining processes. When I informed my employer of this fact, he told me he had received word that Miss Grantham's silks were of interest to smugglers. Therefore, he still wanted her followed in the hope of flushing the smugglers out into the open if possible. He suspected they would trail her in an attempt to find out where she obtained them."

"I cannot believe my ears," Lady Longmore said faintly. "Can this really be true?"

Mr. Atherton sighed. "I'm afraid so. I received word less than an hour ago that Miss Grantham was snatched into Sir Percival Ponsonby's coach right here in Berkeley Square and that he drove away with her. Our agent tried his best to follow the coach, calling a hackney and informing the driver to follow them as far as he could. However, the hackney driver turned back when Sir Percival took the Great North Road out of London."

Lady Longmore shook her head. "You must be mistaken, Mr. Atherton."

"I wish I were, your ladyship." The secretary tapped one hand on the arm of the chair and then leaned forward, clasping his hands in front of him. "We have recently discovered that Sir Percival is the head of one of the largest smuggling rings in

London. He has been under suspicion for several weeks, and last night he was apprehended by a Customs officer during a smuggling operation. He killed the man and is now on the run from the Law. As his actions are punishable by death, he'll probably attempt to leave the country. He must have come up with this as a contingency plan. Your granddaughter is well-dowered, I believe?"

"Yes. But Sir Percival has no liking for her. He would never wish to marry her."

"He is taking her north for some reason. Could Gretna Green be his destination?"

"Dear heavens, no!" Lady Longmore slumped in her chair. "Not again!"

Mr. Atherton's brows rose. "This has happened before, madam?"

She nodded, her face white. "Last year, Mr. Edward Ponsonby, Sir Percival's cousin, attempted to elope with my eldest granddaughter as he wanted her dowry. He was thwarted in his attempt by the Duke of Stanford and was banished abroad."

Mr. Atherton steepled his fingers together. "I'm afraid, I am very much afraid, that Sir Percival may be following in his cousin's footsteps. No doubt that is why he conceived the idea in the first place."

James's blood pounded in his ears. "I'm going after them."

"I thought you would," Mr. Atherton said quietly. "Which is why I've brought along the two agents who have been following Miss Grantham. They are waiting outside. May I beg a couple of places for them in your coach so that they can arrest Sir Percival and bring him back to London?"

"Yes, indeed. An excellent idea. They can come back in his coach with him. But first, I want to know exactly how Ponsonby is connected to the smuggling trade. The more I understand his motives, the better."

"Of course. I am unsure how familiar you are with the public auctions held by Customs and Excise?"

"I know they take place every quarter. But I'm not familiar with the details."

The secretary bowed his head. "Seized contraband goods are sold at these auctions—things like tobacco, brandy, tea, and, of course, silk. Most of what goes to auction can then be sold on the domestic market, but not silk. All foreign silks that are bought must be exported out of the country for sale elsewhere."

Mr. Atherton paused for a moment. "It seems that Sir Percival's primary business is to buy these silks very cheaply at the public auctions and then export them to France—usually Calais or Ostend. He is not the original smuggler of the goods, and he appears to follow all regulations once he purchases them. But once the silks are across the Channel, he simply packages them differently and then smuggles them back into the English market once more using his own methods and network of smugglers. He's made a fortune doing this."

James frowned. "I see. That explains why he spends so much time abroad."

"Indeed. But Sir Percival keeps a tight rein on his business by being present for every auction. Last night, he was caught on a boat on the Thames with smuggled silk. He shot the officer attempting to arrest him and fled the scene."

"And now he has nothing to lose." James released a harsh breath. "He'll take what he can. Including Miss Grantham."

Lady Longmore rose from her chair. "I'm coming with you, Lord Castleroy.

He snapped his brows together. "But your ladyship, we'll be going at a rapid pace and changing horses as often as possible so I can catch up with them. It won't be a comfortable journey."

"I cannot stay in London, waiting for news. I don't care how uncomfortable the journey is. I must come."

Her face was set in determined lines, and James suppressed a sigh. The last thing he wanted was to concern himself over the comfort of an old lady on a long trip. But he couldn't very well refuse. Besides, when he caught up with Ponsonby, he would want a lady with him to act as Thea's chaperone. So, with a nod, he said, "Very well, ma'am. I plan to leave within the hour."

"I shall be ready," Lady Longmore said, hastening out of the room.

James turned back to Marcus Atherton. "Thank you for your swift actions, Atherton. I am in your debt."

Mr. Atherton's smile was wry. "I deeply regret that Miss Grantham injured herself in my carriage. She was very gracious about it, not reproaching me in any way. I am delighted to be of any assistance to her—and you. I suppose I am correct in my supposition that congratulations are in order?" He raised his brows.

"I certainly hope so," James said grimly.

And on those words, he strode from the room.

CHAPTER THIRTY-FIVE

THEA SAT ON the bed in the inn's bedchamber, staring down at the floor. Sir Percival had arranged for her dinner to be brought to her room. He had also hired a guard to stand outside in the corridor for the duration of the night. They had spent three days on the road now, and at every hostelry, Sir Percival informed the innkeeper that Thea was his younger sister and needed to be confined to her room as he was taking her home to their parents after an attempt to run away from boarding school.

Everyone accepted his word without question. Thea had stopped expecting anyone to believe her when she protested that she was being held against her will and was growing very tired of the censorious looks cast her way. However, there was nothing to be done about it. Even if she could have escaped from being held under lock and key, her sprained ankle limited her movements so severely that she couldn't make a run for it. Adding insult to literal injury, Sir Percival also told the people they encountered that she had injured herself while jumping out of a window, making Thea seem even more flighty in their eyes.

She was at her wits' end. No one in London would ever suspect that Sir Percival had kidnapped her. It wouldn't even cross their minds. Any fragment of hope of a possible rescue had long since faded. They were too far away from London by now for anyone to successfully pursue them. And although her virtue was as unimpeached, Thea had been traveling alone with a man for three days now in a closed carriage. Her reputation would be in ruins if this were ever discovered, and she wouldn't be able to show her face in Society again.

She must escape. If she failed to do so, Sir Percival would certainly try to force her to marry him. He couldn't very well put a gun against her head, but she wouldn't put it past him to attempt some other form of coercion.

She hugged her arms around her middle as she recalled the hours and hours she had spent in the close confines of the carriage with him. She spoke as little as possible, and he, in turn, largely ignored her, seemingly preoccupied with his own thoughts. Never in her life had Thea been more grateful for her lack of beauty.

She ate a meal of overcooked beef and cabbage before retiring to bed and sleeping badly, waking with a nasty crick in her neck and a sense of dread in her stomach. It sat there like pockets of gravel, weighing her down.

An hour later, Sir Percival unlocked her bedroom door, and Thea limped down the stairs after him to be bundled up into the carriage once more, the door slamming shut behind her. She glanced across at the baronet now, and a shiver tiptoed down her spine. Sir Percival had such a cruel mouth, his lips thin and turned down at the ends as if he were sneering at all and sundry.

What crime had he committed to be forced to leave the country? It must be something terrible that he needed to leave in such a hurry. She shivered again as she stared out of the window. In any other circumstances, she would have been fascinated to observe the passing scenery. But now, in her state of uncertainty, she failed to appreciate the blur of trees and fields, her mind endlessly turning as she pondered how to get out of her perilous predicament.

She was on the verge of falling asleep, lulled into somnolence by an unexpectedly smooth section of the road, when the coach jerked to a sudden halt. Her eyelids flew open, and a few seconds later, the coach door opened.

Sir Percival straightened in his seat, but before he could do or say anything, James sprang into the carriage.

Thea blinked, unable to believe her eyes. He'd come! Somehow he'd found her! Sir Percival uttered an oath and reached for the sword on the seat beside him. But James knocked the blade to the floor, pointing a pistol straight at him. Behind James, a man stood, also holding a weapon, and he said in a ringing voice, "Sir Percival Ponsonby, I arrest you in the name of the Law! Step outside!"

Muttering another oath, Sir Percival climbed down, the baron following closely behind him. James hadn't met Thea's eyes once, his full attention on the baronet. She couldn't believe James was here, truly here. It seemed unreal. She leaned a little out of the coach, her gaze traveling to the man who had ordered Sir Percival from his carriage. The officer of the Law was aiming his pistol at Sir Percival's heart, his black, wicked heart, and the baronet held his hands up in the air, his expression wary.

Sensing movement, Thea glanced to the side where James's carriage had stopped right behind them. A coachman attempted to calm the restive horses while the guard beside him on the seat pointed a heavy-looking pistol at the men in the road. Evidently, this was a well-orchestrated operation to catch a dangerous man. Thea's eyes narrowed as she studied the guard. *It couldn't be him.* Her eyelids shut before snapping open once again. She stared. No, she wasn't mistaken. It was the man who had followed her in London, the man she had seen speaking to Sir Percival the other day in Gunter's.

And he wasn't aiming the weapon at Sir Percival. Instead, the guard was pointing the pistol straight at James's back. As he raised the gun and aimed, Thea looked frantically around the coach, and her gaze lighted on the only loose object in sight. Sir Percival's sword! She grasped the hilt and picked it up. Then, leaning out of the carriage again, she threw the blade at the guard with a strength born of utter desperation.

"James!" she screamed. "James! Look out!"

The sword flew straight past the guard's head, upsetting the horses and causing the front pair to begin rearing in their traces. James dodged out of the way just as the gun went off with a loud bang.

And then everything was in chaos.

The guard jumped from the coach and started sprinting down the road. James gave chase, catching him around his legs and throwing him to the ground.

James's coachman, meanwhile, was attempting to calm the frightened horses while the beefy-looking Law officer, with a firm grip on Sir Percival's arm, removed a length of rope from his pocket with his other hand and swiftly bound Sir Percival's wrists and ankles before yelling an instruction at Sir Percival's coachman that he needed him to turn the coach around as they would be heading back to London.

Then the officer, leaving Sir Percival lying trussed up in the road like a well-feathered chicken, strode over to James and the villain who had attempted to shoot him. Frowning down at the man lying in the road, he said through gritted teeth, "You traitorous cur! You'll be returning with Sir Percival to London to face the might of the Law for attempting to murder a peer of the realm."

"You're mistaken," the man wailed. "My aim was just a little off."

"No, it wasn't!" Thea called out. "I saw you aiming that pistol at Lord Castleroy. I recognize you from London. You've been following me around, and I saw you speaking to Sir Percival in Gunter's."

James stepped closer as the officer bound the man's hands and feet with yet another piece of twine extracted from his capacious pocket. "He was following me, too. Sir Percival's spy, no doubt, working for Customs and Excise."

At that moment, a white head peered out of Lord Castleroy's coach. "Is it safe to come out now?"

Thea shrieked. "Grandmama! Oh, Grandmama, I'm so happy to see you." She inched herself out of the carriage and hobbled across to Lady Longmore. "Your bones must be rattling after such a speedy trip. I can't believe you've come! You hate traveling fast."

"Of course I had to come when I heard my granddaughter had been kidnapped! I've been in an agony of fear and suspense."

"Who told you I'd been kidnapped?" Thea looked up at her in wonder. "I thought no one would ever guess."

"That officer over there . . ." Grandmama nodded in the direction of the man tying up the guard, "told Mr. Atherton of Sir Percival's actions, and then Mr. Atherton came to Longmore House straightaway to inform me. Lord Castleroy had just called to speak to you, so we set off together."

Thea looked at James, who was now dusting off his coat. "Thank you, my lord. Oh, thank you! I have never been happier to see anyone than when you stepped into the coach."

He glanced up. "Due to a broken axle that needed to be repaired at Grantham, we took longer than I hoped to catch up with you." He came closer. "Has he hurt you, Thea? If he's harmed so much as a hair on your head, I'll . . ." His jaw tightened as he examined her face. However, something in her expression must have reassured him, for the tension in his shoulders visibly eased as he took her hands in his. "You're well?"

"So well," she said softly, smiling into his eyes.

Grandmama cleared her throat. "What are our plans now, my lord?"

James released Thea's hands and turned to the older lady. "I think it will be best to travel to Macclesfield, ma'am, to stay with my grandfather. We're only about sixty miles away, and if we take it in easy stages, it shouldn't be too fatiguing for you. Returning to London straightaway would be very tiring."

Grandmama's brows drew together. "I believe you are right, Lord Castleroy. That sounds like an excellent idea."

The baron turned to speak to the officer, who was now loading the two bound men into Sir Percival's coach. "Will you manage on your own?"

The officer nodded. "I'm from Bradford, my lord. I'll go via my home on our way back and ask a couple of my brothers to assist me on the journey."

"Very well." James placed a hand in his pocket and removed a bulging purse. "This will pay for the tolls and the changes of horses."

The officer accepted the bag of coins. "Thank you, my lord."

James stepped back to his conveyance. "To Macclesfield," he said to his coachman.

The great-coated man tipped the brim of his hat. "Aye, my lord," he said in a gravelly voice as James assisted Thea into the coach.

Fortunately, the horses were now calm, and within minutes, the carriage was in motion, taking them to the mill town famous for its silk.

CHAPTER THIRTY-SIX

THEA DISCOVERED ON the journey to Macclesfield exactly how Sir Percival had been involved in the smuggling industry. "How horrific that he shot a Customs official."

"He's a dangerous man," Grandmama said. "Thank goodness he never laid a hand on you, my love. And, thankfully, for the sake of your reputation, you will be safely betrothed to Lord Castleroy when you eventually return to London."

Thea darted a look from her grandmother to James. Although Thea had told Grandmama that she planned to accept the baron's proposal, she hadn't as yet told *him*.

However, James did not appear surprised at Lady Longmore's statement, and his expression was impassive as the older lady continued: "To refute any rumors, I shall write to my friends to inform them that once you accepted Lord Castleroy's proposal, we decided to leave the Capital to meet his lordship's grandfather, Mr. Sherborne. Everyone knows that you sprained your ankle, Dorothea, and cannot dance, so it was already likely we would retire from the social scene for a while. We shall return in time for your coming out ball."

"That sounds like an excellent plan," Thea said. "My lord?"

He bowed his head. "I am relieved no scandal will attach to your name." His voice was oddly formal, and Thea's spirits plummeted. But the strange moment passed, and soon they were engaged in a discussion about their upcoming stay in Maccles-field.

"I shall show you the town," James said. "But I will need to leave you there as I must visit one of my estates near Derby. I've been putting off inspecting the lands due to the demands of the Season, but I hope to implement the agricultural reforms I instigated at Castleroy. You should be comfortable enough in Macclesfield for a few weeks. I shall return to escort you back to London."

Comfortable enough. How depressing that sounded when she had finally decided to retreat from comfort and embrace change. She studied James's face carefully. Something was amiss, but she couldn't discern what it was. She frowned a little. If only she could speak to him alone! But it wasn't a possibility with Grandmama present, so any private conversation would have to wait.

She tilted her head to one side. "Does your grandfather live in the town?"

"He bought a ruined estate on the edge of Macclesfield some time ago and restored the house. Mulberry Hall is a lovely old place. I'm sure you will enjoy your visit."

"Mulberry Hall?" Her lips curved upward. "Is that an homage to silkworms, my lord?"

"It is." He smiled. "There isn't a mulberry tree in sight, but my grandfather couldn't resist the name."

They stopped at a snug little inn for the night before continu-ing on early the next morning to Macclesfield. By this time, Thea was heartily tired of being confined to a carriage, but she made no complaints. Soon the endless jarring and jolting would be over. Poor Grandmama bore the journey stoically, but the old lady's cheeks were very pale, and Thea cast a few anxious glances in her direction on their final day of travel. She must be under tremen-dous strain as she had never been a good traveler.

Thea was still amazed that Grandmama had come on such an arduous journey. Such concern warmed her heart, especially as

Thea had grown accustomed to a lack of maternal care over the past few years. Of course, Aunt Eliza had done her best to fulfill Mama's duties, but she lacked motherly warmth, and Thea had missed that nurturing love. Oh, how she had missed it.

They drove through the gates of Mulberry Hall late that day. The house, built in stone and framed in timber, was in a U shape, with its arms ending in a couple of charming gables.

Lawns and flower gardens surrounded the house, and Thea looked at the cheerful prospect with delight. Daisies abounded, and she cast a shy look up at James. Had he noticed? When she met his blue eyes, something odd happened to her stomach, and she looked hastily away, studying the garden with fierce concentration.

They entered the hall, positioned in the center between the two wings. As the butler took their outdoor things, James explained that this had once been the Great Hall of the original structure.

"A 16th-century chapel is at the back of the house," he continued. "It was once a convent, and one can almost imagine the nuns at prayer there." He touched Thea's arm. "Remind me to show you."

Recalling what had happened the last time Thea had entered a medieval monastic structure with him, heat crept into her cheeks. But fortunately, the dim lighting in the hall hid her blushes, and she turned hastily away to speak to Grandmama.

A servant led them up to their bedchambers, and Thea looked around the elegantly decorated room with pleasure. The owner of a silk mill would have access to the most beautiful materials to decorate his home. Her gaze came to rest on the pale pink counterpane on the bed, and she stepped closer to examine it, feeling the fine fabric between her fingers. The silk was of an excellent quality.

When she made her way downstairs, the same servant who had taken them up to their bedchambers led Thea to the drawing room, which was much lighter than the hall due to a splendid bow window that stretched from the coved ceiling to the floor, affording a fine view of the lawns and the wood beyond. Grandmama was already there, conversing with an elderly man with pink cheeks and a full head of white hair. James's grandfather, Mr. Sherborne.

Thea stepped forward and then halted at a slight sound behind her. As she turned, James came through the door and offered her his arm. Placing her hand on his coat sleeve, Thea allowed him to lead her to his grandfather.

"I am delighted to make the acquaintance of my future granddaughter-in-law." Mr. Sherborne rose to his feet and bowed in a courtly fashion. "I have heard so much about you, Miss Grantham. Do sit down."

Although his eyes were kind, Thea lowered herself gingerly onto the seat he indicated, concerned that he might ask her about her recent ordeal. But he didn't allude to it, and before long, she was engaged in an easy conversation with him about her silk staining techniques. However, Mr. Sherborne evidently knew about the kidnapping as later he said in a slightly gruff voice, "The rivalries in the silk industry are legendary, my dear. I'm glad you'll soon be James's wife. A single lady is an easy target for ruthless predators."

"Silk appears to bring out the worst in some people."

"Indeed." His eyes settled on his grandson for a moment. "And the best in others." He looked back at her and patted her on the hand. "Before James leaves for Derby, he must show you our mill in Macclesfield. I am sure you will find it of great interest."

"I should like to see it," she murmured.

The conversation during dinner was lively enough, but Grandmama looked fatigued and did not linger in the drawing room after dinner, retiring early to bed. Thea accompanied the old lady upstairs, and after ensuring that she was merely exhausted and not unwell, Thea went to her own bedchamber. Fortunately, she had a nightgown to change into, as Grandmama had had the foresight to ask Wilson to pack clothes for her granddaughter before leaving London. If she hadn't, Thea wouldn't have had a rag to her back.

She had expected to lie awake for ages staring at the canopy. However, within minutes of her head touching the pillow, her lids dropped over her eyes like leaden weights.

The next day when she went downstairs, James was already in the breakfast room. He rose as she entered, and Thea frowned a little when she detected that odd look of reserve on his face again. However, before she could broach the subject of their engagement, Mr. Sherborne walked into the room, and the moment was lost. Repressing a sigh, Thea concentrated on her breakfast, only looking up when James invited her to drive to the mill with him after the meal.

She glanced across at his stern profile as she sat beside him in his grandfather's curricle half an hour later. Why did he appear so unapproachable? She couldn't understand the change in his attitude. They were meant to be betrothed, for heaven's sake, yet his manner was like that of a distant acquaintance.

He turned his head. "Do you know anything about the history of Macclesfield, Miss Grantham?"

Miss Grantham? What had happened to Thea? She frowned a little, but then, remembering that the groom perched behind them, the tension in her shoulders lessened. James wouldn't want to discuss their private affairs in front of a servant. And neither, for that matter, would she. But she did need to speak to him. And soon. She cleared her throat. "All I know is that Macclesfield is famous for its buttons."

"Indeed. That is how the industry began, although those early buttons were most often covered with linen or Angora goat hair. It wasn't until Tudor times, when imported Spanish silk buttons became popular, that the button makers here began using silk instead." As they exited the gates of Mulberry Hall, he went on, "There are dozens of mills here now, but a Macclesfield button man named Charles Roe built the first silk-throwing mill in the town nearly 80 years ago, as the patent that Thomas Lombe had held on the machinery in his mill had finally run out. It was around the same time that my great-great-grandfather also built his mill."

"You have deep roots in Macclesfield, my lord."

"Yes. As Grandfather says, silk is in my blood." He concentrated on the road ahead before pointing at a nearby hillside. "Hollins Wood."

"There's something very charming about holly trees," Thea looked appreciatively at the passing landscape.

"Holly trees aren't only decorative. Their branches are of very hard wood. That's what was used to create the circular bases of the buttons."

"Are buttons still manufactured here, my lord?"

"Unfortunately, the trade declined. Now the mills and their water wheels dominate the town. However, in one way or another, silk has sustained the families of Macclesfield for generations. The River Bollin provides power for the mills as it turns the water wheels, and it supplies the clean water that is vital to the dyeing process. It also helps that Macclesfield's climate is perfect for storing raw silk."

"It's damp?"

"Yes," James said as they entered the town. A short while later, he pointed out a church. "Sunderland Street Chapel, the place of worship for Macclesfield's Methodists. Several silk manufacturers, including my grandfather, are members. The chapel manages the Macclesfield Sunday School, which provides formal education for thousands of children every year on their one day off from work. Grandfather has a heart for the poor and is very involved in the school."

"He is a good man," she said quietly.

He nodded. "The best."

When they came to the mill, he drew the horses to a halt and handed the reins to the groom before helping Thea down from the curricle. "The lower two floors contain the throwing machines, while the top three floors house the winding engines that spin the raw silk."

The mill was a very tall brick building with a pitched, somewhat shallow roof.

As they stepped inside, Thea stopped to fan herself with her hand. "It's so warm in here!"

"For the silk to be processed successfully, the mill must be heated. A fire engine is used to circulate hot air."

"Oh." Thea wrinkled her nose at the excessive noise and the overwhelmingly musty smell, but the workers at the machines seemed oblivious to it. She stole a peevish glance up at James as he explained in exact detail how the mill operated. He should write a guidebook about Macclesfield, so thorough was his knowledge of the silk industry. This endless impartation of dry facts was disconcerting, to say the least.

Due to her painful ankle, Thea was unable to tour the mill, but she observed what she could from the mill entrance before returning somewhat reluctantly to the curricle. What was she to do? James seemed a stranger. But why? As they drove home in silence, Thea wondered if she should ask him why he was behaving this way.

It seemed the only choice open to her. So when they drew up in front of the house, she drew a deep breath. "May I speak to you privately, my lord? Perhaps we could sit under that oak tree?" She indicated a nearby garden seat.

His brows drew together. "Very well. Although I am leaving in less than an hour for Derby."

She stole a glance up at him as she seated herself on the wooden bench. Hopefully, grasping the nettle wouldn't prove to be an excessively painful experience.

She intertwined her fingers as he sat beside her. "My lord, you appear disturbed about something. Am . . . am I correct?"

He glanced down at her. "You could say that."

"But . . . but why? You asked me to marry you. However, now we are betrothed, you seem different. Unhappy. Have you had second thoughts?"

"Have *I* had second thoughts?" He removed his hat and ran a hand through his hair. "How can you ask me that when you haven't even given me your first thoughts."

"What do you mean?"

"When we parted in London, you told me you needed time to consider my proposal as you weren't sure if you wished to marry me. And now, the only reason we're betrothed is that a wedding is necessary to save your reputation. It isn't because you've decided that you want to be my wife."

He rose to his feet, staring down at her. Thea's breath caught at the pain in his eyes, and she twisted her fingers even tighter together. However, before she could say anything, he gave a stiff bow and strode off in the direction of the house, leaving her alone. So, so alone.

She twisted her hands together. How could she not have seen this? She had been utterly blind to his feelings. Her lack of a response that day must have been incredibly hurtful to him. He didn't know that her refusal to answer him then had not been rooted in uncertainty about her love but rather in deep uncertainty about her ability to be a proper wife, a wife capable of feeling the full range of human emotions.

She had decided to end her self-enforced isolation and marry James before she was kidnapped, but he didn't know that. She needed to convey to him the sincerity of her love, even though it must appear as if she were only using him now to save her reputation.

But how?

※ ※ ※

CHAPTER THIRTY-SEVEN

J AMES LEFT FOR his estate in Derby a short while later, and Thea sat quietly in the drawing room with Grandmama, pondering what to do. She released a soft sigh as she leaned back against the sofa, dismissing her initial idea of writing a letter to him. What she needed was time alone with James to explain how she had changed, how she had come to the realization that she no longer wished to close herself off from the world—and from him.

When he returned to Mulberry Hall, she would enlighten him.

However, one week stretched into two, and James did not come back. Thea, restricted to the house due to her healing ankle, spent a great deal of time reading books from Mr. Sherborne's library. But she had endless hours to think, and her thoughts were not happy. How could they be when her beloved did not know that she returned his sentiments?

Mr. Sherborne was a genial host, and Thea discussed her chemical science experiments with him in great detail. But she missed James desperately and found it difficult to concentrate, trailing off on occasion, her brain refusing to cooperate. James's grandfather did not appear to mind, and the understanding in his eyes and the benevolence of his smile showed he was fully cognizant—and hopefully tolerant—of her slightly distracted state.

After her third week of confinement to the house, Thea was itching to *do* something. Fortunately, her ankle was much better, and she was able to walk a short distance in the garden now, enjoying the sweet scent of the flowers and the warmth of the sun on her skin.

Grandmama was also looking much less pale. After a few weeks of rest, she appeared in a better frame for the return journey to London. Thea hoped against hope that James would return in time for her to speak to him before they left for the Capital. However, in the end, he only arrived at Mulberry Hall the day before their date of departure.

He apologized profusely for his long absence, explaining that estate affairs had taken up more time than he'd expected. But Thea, listening to his explanation with a grave expression, wondered if he hadn't used the excuse of work to keep away from her. Heaven knew she had oft retreated in a like fashion to escape difficult feelings. Perhaps she and James were more similar than she'd realized.

They returned in easy stages, which left only a week or so to finalize the arrangements for Thea's coming out ball. Grandmama had sent numerous letters to London over the past few weeks, making as many of the arrangements as possible from afar. And fortunately, as the ball was due to take place at Stanford House, Alexandra was able to take over many of the responsibilities for the grand occasion.

Her sister had written her a lengthy letter expressing her horror at what had befallen Thea. "I cannot believe that another Ponsonby male behaved in this execrable fashion! However, you will be relieved to learn that the wheels of Justice are turning and that Sir Percival will need to answer for his actions for killing that poor Customs official."

When they returned to the Capital, Thea hoped that she would finally be able to speak to her betrothed. But to her dismay, she hardly saw him in the week leading up to her ball. Aunt Eliza was in Town, and although she usually stayed with her sister in Wimbledon when she visited London, she spent the last few days before the ball as a guest at Stanford House, helping with the preparations.

Thea took very little pleasure in the feverish planning. All she wanted was James. Yet he appeared as far away from her as ever, caught up with his own responsibilities upon his return to the Capital, which included overseeing the arrangements for Anne's coming out ball which was to take place the week after Thea's.

When Anne called on Thea the day after her return to Berkeley Square, her friend smiled and shook her head. "Who would have thought that we would both be betrothed before our coming out balls?"

"You're officially engaged to Mr. Fotherby?"

"I am. Finally! Frederick asked James for his permission to marry me yesterday. He has had to wait for an age to speak to him due to James's long absence from Town. But now we are finally betrothed."

"Oh, Anne! Many congratulations. I am so happy for you!"

"And I for you! I still can't believe that I will finally have a sister." Her expression sobered as she examined Thea's face. "How are you after your terrible ordeal, Thea? I still can't believe what happened."

"I am better now. Although, I still have the occasional nightmare. That feeling of being trapped, unable to escape." She looked away, shivering a little.

"Thank goodness James caught up to you. He was beside himself with worry when he heard the news. When I think about what could have happened . . ." Her friend trailed off.

"I know. I try not to think of it. But I am aware every day how close I came to losing everything I hold dear. It puts everything into perspective, especially our more trivial everyday concerns."

However, those trivial concerns persisted in rearing their heads as they finalized all the details for the coming-out ball. Thea was frowning over the list of refreshments Alexandra had ordered from Gunter's when her grandmother walked into the room. "My love! I've completely forgotten about the flowers for the ball. Alexandra has asked me more than once what sort of arrangements you'd like but I've been so busy since our return to Town that it slipped my mind. We must pay a visit to King's Road at once! Come."

When they arrived at the nursery garden an hour later, Lady Longmore fell into earnest conversation with the proprietor about the floral decorations she envisioned for the ball. As Thea listened to her grandmother speaking about the importance of flowers for setting the tone of an entertainment, she suddenly knew what she needed to do. When the older lady turned to her to ask her which flowers she preferred, Thea said in a firm voice, "Nothing but daisies, Grandmama."

"*Daisies*, child?"

"Masses and masses of daisies."

"But. . ." She raised her hands. "They're so ordinary, Thea. You could have your pick of beautiful flowers."

"I have a particular reason for wanting daisies at my coming out ball, Grandmama. Please indulge me. And could you ask the man who'll be chalking the ballroom floors to draw only daisies?"

Her grandmother considered her for a long moment. "Very well, my love. But it will no doubt provoke some comment. Lady Sefton was telling me the other day that you have quickly garnered a reputation in London for unfailing elegance in your dress. No one will expect daisies to be your choice of flower for your ball."

Aunt Eliza had even more to say on the matter when the florist delivered the flower arrangements to Stanford House on the afternoon of the ball. "Dorothea!" She gazed around in horror. "Your grandmother informs me that this is all your doing. *Daisies?*"

Thea glanced at her visibly ruffled aunt before turning her attention to the florist's assistant, who was arranging the bright flowers in the porcelain bough-pot in the fireplace on the far side of the ballroom. "I like daisies, Aunt Eliza."

"It doesn't matter what you *like*, Dorothea. What matters is what people will *think*."

Thea tilted her head. "But that's exactly what I'm doing—considering what someone, in particular, will think."

"You are always far too cryptic for me, Dorothea." Her aunt's voice dripped with disapproval. "Daisies!" she said again in disgust as she swiveled her head to view the dozens of arrangements placed on various surfaces around the room. Her shoulders stiffened when she looked down. "Good heavens! They're even on the floor!"

"I think they look lovely." Alexandra, who had been directing the florist on the other side of the room, came up to them then. "They brighten the ballroom considerably, lending a proper air of celebration to the festivities."

Her aunt sniffed. "Well, I only hope Dorothea won't live to regret this moment of utter madness."

But when Thea stood at the top of the staircase later that evening, waiting for the first guests to arrive, she only felt a sense of joyful anticipation. Surely, surely, once James set eyes on her choice of flowers, he would understand the message she was trying to send him.

He was the first guest to arrive and walked up the grand marble staircase alone, bowing deeply over her hand before turning to greet Lady Longmore, who stood to one side talking to Alexandra and the duke.

"Is Anne not coming?" Thea asked, peering over James's shoulder.

"She will arrive later on with Fotherby." He lowered his voice. "I came early to lend you my support, my dear."

She smiled shyly at him before whispering in her grandmother's ear. Then, upon that lady's quick nod, she turned back to James. "I have something I'd like to show you, my lord. In the ballroom."

He raised his brows slightly before offering her his arm as

they approached the ballroom's magnificent double doors. A footman flung them open, and they stepped inside, the only occupants of the splendid room, which was dominated by an enormous crystal chandelier in the center of the gilt stucco ceiling.

James's gaze traveled around the room before coming to rest on her face. She held her breath in expectation, not saying a word. Waiting. Just waiting.

The corners of his eyes creased. "Daisies, Thea?"

Her nod was solemn. "I remembered what you said about them—that they welcome the sun instead of staring down at the frozen ground. I chose them because of you." Her lips trembled into a smile. "I love you and truly, truly want to marry you. I didn't know how else to show you the sincerity of my feelings after . . ." She swallowed hard. "After I learned what you believed in Macclesfield."

He searched her face, a curious light in his eyes. Then, taking her hand, he drew her across the room to a couple of French doors that opened onto a balcony. Shutting the doors behind him, he pulled her close, lowering his head to within inches of hers. "Darling Thea," he murmured before finding her lips in a kiss so heated it stole her breath.

Her hands crept up his chest, eventually coming to rest on his shoulders as he deepened the kiss. And then her world became him, only him, until, in the vague recesses of her mind, she remembered where they were and why exactly they were here tonight.

"James!" She drew back slightly. "James . . ."

"Mm?" His lips were now on the sensitive skin just beneath her jawline.

"You're making me late for my coming out ball!" She pushed against his shoulders. "We'd better go back inside. What—what if someone discovers us out here alone?"

He raised his head, his eyes gleaming in the moonlight. "What can they do, my darling girl? Force us to become betrothed?"

"Oh, James!" She shook her head, smiling.

He gave a low laugh but acquiesced to her wish, tucking her satin-gloved hand into the crook of his arm and leading her back into the ballroom, decked with flowers as bright and wonderful as the love they had discovered together.

"Darling daisy arriving with the Spring, awakening to beauty and love's sweet offering," he murmured, gazing down at her. And Thea, recognizing the words from "The Awakening", smiled up at him, her heart in her eyes. Little had she known when she accepted his offer of friendship that it would grow into this love, this deep, enduring love, which had wrapped her in a silken cloak replacing the sackcloth.

As she walked across the room with her beloved, she recognized the blessing of having her grief turn into dancing, clothing her in pure gladness.

And she would never take it for granted.

The End

Author's Note

Elizabeth Fulhame

Elizabeth Fulhame was a pioneering British scientist whose book *An Essay on Combustion with a View to a New Art of Dyeing* and Painting, wherein the Phlogistic and Antiphlogistic Hypotheses are Proved Erroneous* describes the process of catalysis and photoreduction.

She was married to a physician called Thomas Fulhame and published her book under her married name Mrs. Fulhame. Elizabeth Fulhame's maiden name is unknown, and her birth and death dates are also unknown.

After 1810, Mrs. Fulhame disappears from the historical record.

The Baron and the Lady Chemist is set in 1818/1819 when Elizabeth Fulhame may still have been alive. I therefore felt it was possible to include her in my story. And, although my book is a work of fiction, I tried, as much as possible, for Elizabeth Fulhame's dialogue in *The Baron and the Lady Chemist* to reflect her published views.

*I have changed the spelling from "Dying" to "Dyeing" to help prevent any confusion for readers unfamiliar with this work.

Acknowledgements

Many thanks to my highly skilled editor, Courtney Brown.

Works Consulted

Brande, William Thomas. *Manual of Chemistry.* (From the second London Edition) New York, 1821.

Davy, Humphry. *A Syllabus of a Course of Lectures on Chemistry, Delivered at the Royal Institution of Great Britain.* London, 1802.

Farrell, William. "Smuggling Silks into Eighteen-Century Britain: Geography, Perpetrators, and Consumers." *Journal of British Studies* 55, no. 2 (2016). https://www.jstor.org/stable/24702001.

Fulhame, Mrs. *An Essay on Combustion, With a View to a New Art of Dyeing and Painting. Wherein The Phlogistic and Antiphlogistic Hypotheses are Proved Erroneous.* London, 1794.

Griffith, Sarah. *Businessmen and Benefactors: The Macclesfield Silk Manufacturers and their Support for the Town's Charitable Institutions, 1750-1900.* (PhD diss., University of Liverpool, 2006) http://hdl.handle.net/10034/81282.

Hassell, John. *Picturesque Rides and Walks, with Excursions by Water, Thirty Miles round the British Metropolis; Illustrated in a Series of Engravings, Coloured after Nature: with an Historical and Topographical Description of the Country within the Compass of that Circle, Volume 2.* London, 1818.

Marcet, Jane Haldimand. *Conversations on Chemistry: In which the Elements of that Science are Familiarly Explained and Illustrated by Experiments.* New Haven, 1809.

The Silk Museum. www.macclesfieldmuseums.co.uk.

Warner, Frank. *The Silk Industry of the United Kingdom: Its Origin and Development.* London, 1921.

About the Author

Alissa Baxter wrote her first Regency romance during her long university holidays. After travelling the world, she settled down to write her second Regency novel, which was inspired by her time living on a country estate in England. Alissa then published two chick lit novels, The *Truth About Clicking Send and Receive* (previously published as *Send and Receive*) and *The Truth About Cats and Bees* (previously published as *The Blog Affair*).

Many years later, Alissa returned to her favorite era. She writes Regency romances that feature women in trend-setting roles who fall in love with men who embrace their trailblazing ways… at least eventually. Alissa currently lives in Johannesburg with her husband and two sons.

These are my social media details:
Alissa's Instagram page: alissa.baxter.author
Alissa's Facebook group: Alissa's Regency Companions
Alissa's Twitter page: @alissa_baxter
Alissa's Facebook page: facebook.com/alissa.baxter.writer
Alissa's website: alissabaxter.com
Alissa's blog: alissabaxter.blogspot.com